ISTANBUL GATHERING

Roddy O'Connor

Çitlembik Publications 123

This book is for Olga
and our fellow members
of John Freely's
Gençlik Kulübü

Entre morir y no morir
Me decidí por la guitarra.

Neruda

Author's Note

Chapter Six of this work describes a play entitled *Anatolia*, by a fictitious playwright named Enver Yakut. My description is based entirely upon a very real play entitled *Ben Anadolu*, by a very real Turkish playwright named Güngör Dilmen. The play has been performed with great success in the original Turkish and in English translation under the title *I, Anatolia*. The English translation, by Talat S. Halman, was published in 1991 by the Turkish Ministry of Culture, Drama Series/46. My two quotations from the play are from pages viii and 64, respectively, of that edition. The biographical information attributed to Enver Yakut is entirely fictitious and has no intended relation whatsoever to the life of Güngör Dilmen.

Contents

1 Malone	13
2 Erden	47
3 Yakup	80
4 Sylvia	107
5 Malone	142
6 Nicolette	165
7 Marco	193
8 Boncuk	225
9 Malone	254
Pronunciation Guide	271

1

MALONE

i

You're home again, old stranger, he thought, you're home again.

For how else express the exhilarating rush he felt as he stepped from the bejeweled and aromatic corridor of the Egyptian Spice Bazaar and into the sunshine blazing along the esplanade in front of the Yeni Cami and over the Galata Bridge, the ferry landing at Eminönü and the lower reaches of the Golden Horn, the distant Asian shore of the Bosphorus lost in a fiery glare. Oh, to be in Istanbul, he thought, now that April's here, for as sure as it was April, here he was, as if by the act of willing it, and the twenty long years dividing him from this city and his youth had vanished at a stroke and he had found himself again as if completed in this vibrancy of life. Let there be light, yes, but let there be mists also and darkness and fire and filth and the clashing and thrashing of bitter harmonies and the occasional hot stink, for balance, and no fewer than those hundreds of pigeons cooing and dumping on the steps of the Yeni Cami, the New Mosque, new in 1663, he thought, built, burnt, neglected, and built again over a span of half a century and seen again now as never before, in double exposure, and from one of whose twin minarets the *müezzin* would shortly loft his call. For as he stood stock-still in his meditation, he supposed there should be nothing missing here, real or anticipated, the memory lingering of his passage through the Spice Bazaar, of incense and olives, thyme, roses, saffron and pepper—red, yellow, black, green—and of aromatic candle wax dripping into a copper dish, the flame reflected bobbing and dodging among the facets of a thousand crystalline decanters, the vaulted ceiling dark with millennial soot which, of a season, would ooze black droplets to fall into the hat brims and baskets of the wayfarers below and lay a patina of slime upon the cobblestones, a world that would aspire to be a world for all seasons, out of all seasons, symmetrical, contained; and yet the soot oozed and the slime, and the heat would grow unbearable in July and the wind in January would whistle and carve through the length of the bazaar, extinguishing the candles, the aromas, and the lights and gather all up into nothing at all. Nothing at all. And the blind wayfarer would stagger forth into the gray gloom of a January afternoon, unhinged, till memory recall what once had been, what would surely be again, of another golden April afternoon, perhaps this very day.

And so you're home again, he thought, as he stepped into the sunshine blazing along the esplanade and the lower reaches of the Golden Horn, where I belong as assuredly as Borges found his deepest self expressed in the rising and writhing arabesques of "certain guitar arpeggios," and Stendhal, returning forlorn to Grenoble from Milan, saw his reverie of the lost beloved slowly, achingly, become material in the undulating contour of a distant hill. For, it being shortly after noon and the traffic along the shore road and across the bridge somewhat diminished, he had a relatively unobstructed view of the Golden Horn and the lower Bosphorus beyond Sarayburnu, where a single ferryboat, now turning into the main current, stood momentarily stock-still, as if bewitched, the smoke from its stack standing straight up in the motionless air, with a slight lateral dispersion at the top that reminded him somewhat, but enough, of the bird's-beak pommel of an antique walking stick that had belonged to his father-in-law, or ex-father-in-law—twice ex-, because Sylvia was no longer his wife and the old man was dead—a walking stick that had come down to him from Cajun ancestors who had made piles of money sailing around the Caribbean—at what trade was never specified—though life in those far-off days in New Orleans had held dangers for everybody, and there was nothing shameful to be concluded from the fact that one carried a cane concealing a tempered steel blade some eighteen inches long. He remembered that the blade had a broad flat top so that, if thrust through a sheet of paper, for example—the old man had kept the blade wonderfully sharp and had loved, as he said, to show off its wonders to small boys, among whom he numbered his son-in-law—the blade left, upon withdrawal, a neat incision in the form of a T, Saint Anthony's cross. This also gave the blade great strength and rigidity and made it easy to withdraw from its victim, especially if twisted, much like the short sword of those old Roman Legionnaires.

But into what grim detail was his mind leading him now? he wondered, as he noticed that the steamer, having regained headway, was advancing crabwise across the current towards Üsküdar on the Asian side, still invisible in the glare. So the mnemonic token had been dispersed as just moments before, in the bazaar, among the smells and the candles, he had heard, in the distance—what was it?—a sound that had seemed for a moment to mean more to him than what?—a prelude certainly to this feeling of wholeness and of joy, a music as from the distant past, perhaps not his alone, weaving him into a present where all things seemed to be connected—though he knew that they could not—a being alive as in a trance, illuminatedly, to all this. And he perceived advancing from the horizon of his reverie a figure that was really the form of that sound, or music, again, and with a sudden return to consciousness he recognized the sound for what it was, for what it must have been as he had heard it in the Spice Bazaar—a radio broadcast from Ankara, perhaps, or Konya or Izmir, no two cities in the country keeping the same time—the early afternoon call to prayer. The call was coming now from one of the twin minarets of the Yeni Cami. The singer, however tinily rendered by the antique, cracked loudspeaker, had a splendid tenor voice, and the stunning clear eruption of the opening call—Allaaaaahhhhhu Akbar!—had sent the great flock of pigeons below rocketing and billowing into flight, as if launched by an explosion, as he now became aware of having heard something very like a cannon shot or an explosion in a hollow drum or from the bowels of one of those ancient communal taxis, ponderous old GMCs, still rolling after all these years; and as his eye traversed the line of traffic before the bridge, he noticed numbers of pedestrians running to the upstream railing, where others could be seen bent far over from the waist as if vomiting into the water below. Something seemed to be happening under the near end of the bridge. He could just make out a rising whisp of smoke, but that could be from one of the many open charcoal grills set up, as he remembered, by the fishermen to cook and sell the strange samples of aquatic life they drew from that mephitic stream.

But what was this to him or he to it? For he had other fish to fry, ha, ha. With hours to kill before he met Sylvia and Frank and the others at Boncuk, he knew where he was going next, under the bridge across from that quaint scene of vomit and smoke, to the second beer stall on the left for a snack and a brew, where he could sit on a stool and, leaning one elbow on a makeshift countertop or barrelhead, gaze out to sea and imagine himself on that diminishing ferry bound crabwise for Üsküdar, or, better yet, for the Princes' Islands and Büyükada, the Prinkipo of the

Byzantines, where he would join the pilgrimage to the church and monastery of Haghia Yorgi, old Saint George, and he would drink all afternoon at the taverna around back overlooking the sea two hundred meters down with Sylvia, when she was still his wife, and Frank, before she began playing around with him, and Erden and Minna and Charlie and Enrique and John and Dolores and Tony and Eileen and Gülen and Tony and Emin and Magali and Hilmar and Mete and Kevin and B. A. and Umay and Jim and Carla and who else? And Marco—of course—and Aliye and Peter and Rose and Neil and Mimi and David and Mine and Keith and Joanne and Bruce and Kate and Aydın and Jan and Rufus and Fruzsina and Rocky and Sylvianne and Yakup and Mimi and Willa and Faruk and Verda and Mike and Cathy and Bob and Gwen and Lafitte himself and Brendan and Dimitri and Elena and Ernst and Nina and Sam and Claude and Maurice and Eddie and Mac and old Joe Fiedler himself, and lord only knows who else, by George, the whole gang. They would sit at a single long table under the trellised arbor out back and pass the *rakı* and trays of *meze* till they tired the sun with talking, as the poet said, and by other means, but he'd have to rethink how they could have come there all at once, because some had never set foot in Turkey and others were dead, and dead forever, wasn't that the rule?

With his mind thus pleasantly occupied, he made his way across the esplanade and through the traffic, somehow, and down the wrought iron stair to the boardwalk under the bridge and along to the second beer stall on the left, which was the phrase one used though there was nothing on the right but a handrail and the water below; and here was the bar, just as he remembered or imagined it, with the same tall stools for drinking at the makeshift counter or from the tops of several barrelheads, two of which were placed outside along the rail, and there was just one client at the far end of the counter and the *patron*, who might almost be the same as twenty years ago, with his knitted woolen *hacı şapkası*, the Muslim pilgrim's cap, the requisite thick mustaches and three or four days' stubble, the frayed and fading but stylish shirt, standing, or rather leaning, one shoulder to the wall, thick forearms crossed, taciturn, his mind perhaps a blank.

Merhaba, patron.

Merhaba, hoş geldiniz, hello to you too and you are most welcome in my humble stall, or something. Perhaps not so blank.

And how are you today, *patron*? he asked. You are well, are you not?

Oh, well, very well, thank you, uncle, and yourself?

Oh, *bomba gibi*, he answered, and he was almost as surprised as the *patron* to hear the phrase, which, learned years ago from a Turkish colleague, seemed to rise unbidden from long disuse, at once spontaneous and pertinent, certainly more comical than sinister, though it took the *patron* a moment's consideration before he hit the counter and laughed—the other client jumped at the concussion—"like a bomb." That's rich, the *patron* said, or something. Like a bomb, he said, in the best of health, as if rehearsing the meaning to himself, full of piss and vinegar, or something, ready to go off at any minute. And you did, said the *patron* slapping the counter again for sheer joy—the client jumped—you did, and now you're ready to do it again. The *patron* must have said something like that, though the meaning wasn't perfectly clear, and he regretted, as so often in the past, the inadequacy of his Turkish, grown more inadequate over the years, and he apologized to the *patron* and said his Turkish was small but that he was very happy to be back in Turkey where he had lived and worked as a teacher many years ago, and the *patron* waved his hand and said that his Turkish was wonderful and that any foreigner who could make a joke in Turkish was really one of them and that the joke about the bomb was really rich, or something, and showed not only that he was a profound philosopher and knew what the world was coming to, but that in spite of this profound and necessarily depressing knowledge he was still full of piss and vinegar, or something, and ready to laugh out loud at the world as he, the *patron*, had demonstrated that he was too and that he wanted to shake the hand of his uncle, or brother, the foreigner, and offer him a drink—which rather confirmed the impression that the *patron* was halfway blotto himself—and, wiping his palm quickly on his thigh, he extended his hand and introduced himself as Mustafa—for how could it be otherwise?—Mustafa Terzioğlu, and he pointed to a wooden plank nailed up at the back of the stall where you could still make out a series of faded red letters composing the name: Terzioğlu. My father was a tailor, he explained, a man who made shirts and suits for the new generation of westernized Turks and who had made two shirts and a three-piece suit—two and three, he smiled, holding up fingers—for Mustafa Kemal, the Gazi himself, in memory of which event he had named his son Mustafa, and he was named Terzioğlu because *oğlu* meant son of and *terzi* meant tailor, so that his name meant "tailor's son," explaining it all as if to a child or an idiot; and what is your name? he asked, pouring out a half-glass of *rakı* and extending his hand to be shaken a second time.

Well, there's plenty in this man's name, he thought, unless he's making it up. But nobody makes up a story like that, and the client, who had occasionally looked their way, he noticed, seemed unimpressed, a friend, perhaps, who had heard the story a hundred times and whose face expressed a kind of weary assent. So what's my name? Andre, he said, Andre Malone. And he could tell by the expression on the *patron*'s face that he hadn't understood, and why should he? He looked somehow downcast, as if he'd expected him to have a Turkish name.

This is difficult name, said Mustafa Terzioğlu. You will write it down.

He turned and got a slip of paper and a stubby pencil from the shelf in back of him and put them in front of his customer, who printed his name out carefully and turned the slip of paper towards the *patron* and, pointing to each syllable, right to left, pronounced slowly, Andre Malone. The *patron*'s face brightened as he studied the name. We have a Christian church by that name on the other side, he said, on İstiklal Caddesi, and as he spoke he pushed the piece of paper down the bar to the silent client. He's deaf, he said, but he can read.

What? said Malone, but the *patron* was carefully pouring water into the half-filled glass of *rakı*. He then did the same for himself and, raising the glass, toasted to honor, *şerefe*, and then again to the deaf client, *şerefe*, for the client had somehow been served a glass of *rakı* too, and the client raised his glass and said, Şerefe, and the *patron* said, He's deaf but he can talk. And he went on to say that his deaf friend had lost his hearing in the war—what war?—but that he had certainly known when the bomb went off, because he was very sensitive and he had felt the concussion, and the deaf man raised his glass and said Şerefe, and the *patron* said, He's deaf, but he can drink, and he laughed and slapped the bar again and the deaf man jumped.

Malone finished his drink, because it seemed to be expected that they drink quickly, and he offered to buy another round, but said that he would have a beer this time, because he had a long way to go, and a plate of grilled sardines. The *patron* drew him a glass of beer and said he should sit outside while he went for the sardines—he'd just climb down to the landing on the other side of the bridge—because he would be much more comfortable in the sunshine, it being such a fine spring day.

So now he sat with his half-finished beer, gazing out over the water to where the steamer had disappeared crabwise into the haze, and he watched a second steamer now leaving the landing at Eminönü—Whoop! whoop! said the whistle, and whoop! whoop! whoop!—and the steamer drew slowly past Sepetçiler Köşkü, the Pavilion of the Basket Weavers, now housing, he remembered, the International Press Club, for what had the honorable craft of weaving come to? And he remembered a spring day twenty and some-odd years ago standing at the stern rail of that very steamer, surely, as it took him and Sylvia and Frank and Erden, perhaps—there was a fourth—out to the Princes' Islands, and that was the day they had seen the storks, a million storks or more, flying north out of Egypt and Ethiopia, out of Jordan and Israel and Libya, to gather for the crossing over Cyprus and Crete and western Anatolia, to be compressed finally into one enormous flight for the narrow passage over the Sea of Marmara and Istanbul, to fan out again, north mirroring south, across Russia and Central Asia and Europe to the west.

Malone wondered if Sylvia had been happy during these years living with Frank, whose company would have been less radically shabby than his own, and he remembered a Saturday afternoon about two years after their marriage when they had come up from New Jersey to New York to visit her father. He had just successfully defended his doctoral thesis and Sylvia's father had been plying him with drink, "in honor of this occasion as of all others," and he had started calling the old man Lafitte—either the pirate or the wine, for he was a vigorous and amusing old tiger—and Lafitte had started calling him Baloney Maloney and the two of them had been collapsing in laughter all over the place when Sylvia went suddenly white, calling them the two most irresponsible and disreputable men she'd ever met. Gone today and gone tomorrow, said Lafitte, and it was then he had realized that Lafitte was as blotto as he was and that Lafitte had realized something too, it seemed, because he had looked suddenly sheepish in the face of Sylvia's evident emotion. He had consulted then with his friend B. Maloney and it was decided that they had been unkind and that at least some portion of Sylvia's ill humor had been caused by her having felt left out. So the two of them had resorted to soda water for the next few, and Lafitte had turned his attention to his daughter, plying her with drink until she had caught up, which, in those days and sometimes even afterwards, she did, and they knew her humor had been restored when she said that where he, Andre, was all Irish and half French, Lafitte was all French and half Irish and that that was why they got along so well together.

And it was true that they got along. Lafitte had been like a father to him, or an older brother, but a good deal older and very fatherly through all the fun. After the separation, when he'd returned from Turkey, and the divorce that followed, he and Lafitte had continued on the best of terms, going out to dinner whenever he got to New York and playing pool in the bars along Third Avenue. He almost never mentioned his daughter, and when he did it was almost apologetically. He said he quite understood a man's being attracted to Sylvia because she was so obviously beautiful—was that the phrase?—but that he knew also that she was a bit of a square if not a prude, though he couldn't be sure about that. It was not entirely her fault, her mother having died when she was only six, growing up with maids as she had done and going away to posh schools. He supposed she hadn't had the warmest upbringing. He loved Sylvia, of course; she was his daughter, and he loved her both for herself and for what survived in her of his wife. She resembled her mother to an astonishing degree. From the physical standpoint, at least, she could have been a clone. So he was happy enough to see Sylvia now and again, but not too often nor for very long at a time. They had laughed then, and the serious moment had passed, but their friendship had been the richer for this kind of understanding, and when the old man died he had felt a loss greater even than the loss of his wife.

And, he thought with a smile, some gain. For hadn't Lafitte made possible his return to Istanbul? During the old man's last weeks in the hospital, Malone had visited him every weekend. He was getting the best care possible, of course, and if he seemed a little punchy from the drugs, they both agreed that this was his normal state anyway, but more fully expressed, and that it should in no way call into question his being "in full possession of his faculties." Andre had witnessed brief visits from business associates and lawyers, during which time the old man had played it superbly straight, relaxing only when they were alone again into a punchiness which then assumed the guise of one of their old-time Saturday nights, and they had laughed together in spite of themselves. But the drugs were real enough. The old man's state was very serious, and he had died on a Monday, fewer than twenty-four hours after a visit during which he had seemed very much himself. Andre received the call that night in Boston from a lawyer who said that they had met in the hospital, though Andre didn't remember him. All the arrangements had been made. The old man was to be cremated at the hospital and buried in Dedham, with no ceremony, next to his wife. Oh yes, they had lived in Boston in the early days, and Malone realized that he knew next to nothing of the old man's past. The lawyer was also instructed to inform Mr. Malone that he was the recipient of a gift of five hundred thousand dollars in the form of negotiable securities, upon which no estate taxes would be paid, which would not appear in the will, and about which therefore the deceased's sole heir, his daughter, a Mrs. Sylvia Corrigan, presently living in Istanbul, need know nothing at all. It was clear to Malone from the lawyer's phrasing that the old man had told him what he needed to know and no more.

After the call, Malone had smiled in spite of himself. It was, so to speak, vintage Lafitte. And he, Malone, was now a man of means, the means to fly to the ends of the earth, if he wanted, and the means to stay there. He would live in Cuernavaca in a villa on a hill, with a shaded terrace and a hammock and a pool, and he would write in the mornings and exercise and have a nap in the afternoons, and in the evenings he'd go into town and sit in a cafe by the *zocalo* and drink cold beer and listen to the mariachis. Or he would go back to Paris and rent a studio on the Isle Saint-Louis, next door to old Joe Fiedler himself, and work in the National Library—his card was still good—and take courses in mime from Jacques Lecoq and eat steak and fries and green salad and Brie and drink bottles of Nuits-Saint-Georges and Gigondas and Saint-Amour forever to the strains of distant accordion music floating over the Seine. Or he would go to Sarawak in the footsteps of the great James Brooke and every year visit by small steamer—whoop! whoop!—a new site he had dreamed of from the novels of Joseph Conrad: Banka and the Seven Isles, Samarang and Celebes, and up the Berau River to Tandjong Redeb, unchanged since the days of Almayer and Tom Lingard, the *Rajah Laut*, great "Lord of the Sea." For this would be his life in the world of Conrad, Maugham, Gauguin, and Stevenson, of purest possible romance.

Sardalya, said the voice. It was Mustafa Terzioğlu, home from the sea—ha, ha—with the plate of grilled sardines and another beer, for he knew the wishes of his friend Andre, whom he wished to inform also that there had been no bomb. What, no bomb? And it was a good thing too, for bombing could be a very bad thing for business, for tourists, though he would not have thought of that himself, being such a very small businessman, who never saw tourists anyway here under the bridge, this being a thoroughly disreputable place and no place for a reputable tourist to be, not even a journalist, the only exception being those who spoke such perfect Turkish as his brother Antoine—who?—who would be reputable anywhere, but that was the story the fish sellers were telling on the other side. Even the police had come, no sirens, no horns, nothing. Secretly they had come, and what had they found? Nothing. What they had found was a bundle of fireworks forgotten since the end of Ramadan, or maybe intended for the next? But who could know such things? Such things were in the hands of God. They had also found a small gas canister, with the top blown off, but when it had exploded no one could say. But there was certainly no bomb, no sort of situation, that people mean to hint at when they say there was a bomb. The only thing certain was that all things are in God's hands and that there were more fish in the sea and more sardines where these came from and plenty of beer, thanks be to God; and anyway, he'd been told, the police were looking for a Greek.

Surely nothing could be more straightforward. There was no bomb; they are looking for a Greek. They will most certainly find a Greek, and when they do, there will have been a bomb. The true danger will not have been revealed until it was past. Now truth and tranquility have been reconciled and all is for the best in this best of all possible worlds. And who is to say it isn't so? Who is to say what the one and indivisible truth is or will be and what the method of attaining it? Who indeed? And he was pleased to allow his eye and mind to wander again over the scene before him, romantic enough, the blaze of light along the water, Sepetçiler Köşkü and Sarayburnu, behind which the steamer had disappeared on its way to the islands, the gardens of the Saray above the point, the rising spread of Topkapı Palace on the slope of this first hill of New Rome, the center of the world, crowned at its summit by the dome and minarets of Haghia Sophia, irrefutable. Haghia Sophia. Not a plumb column nor a straight line anywhere, not a true curve anywhere, yet there she stands. The seat of her dome neither circle nor true ellipse, no two of the great limestone building blocks exactly the same, each hewn to the irregularities of its predecessor, yet there she stands, irrefutable. Today, as she was some fifteen hundred years ago, today as she was twenty years ago, but his view of her was then from the stern rail of the steamer heading for the islands—was Sylvia feeling slightly sick?—and the great mass of her dome—Haghia Sophia's, not Sylvia's—seemed to drop down slightly as the distance increased—but surely the distance wasn't that great—and her contours to become softened—Haghia Sophia's, not Sylvia's—and, finally, all but effaced in the brilliance lying over the surface of the sea.

As to where they were going, he had no clear idea. To the

largest of the Princes' Islands, Büyükada, the Prinkipo of the Byzantines, and to the top of the island's highest hill, two hundred meters up, to the church and monastery of Saint George; but he had never been there before and the words alone meant little. They would walk, it seems, and there would be Judas trees in a profusion of bloom, for the islands lived in a microclimate ten degrees warmer than Istanbul. And they had indeed walked through the town and south through the countryside, where the road began to climb, when, quite without warning, on either side of a sharply rising, stone-strewn avenue, rows of bushes appeared, shoulder-high, backed by the exploding blossoms, lilac and blood, of Judas trees. And the bushes themselves seemed alive with the fluttering, struggling wings of thousands of pure white butterflies, impaled. It was along this avenue—he could remember Erden explaining it, for of course it had been Erden who made up the fourth—that earlier in the day the pilgrims had climbed steeply, painfully—for many of them were old—to Haghia Yorgi, stopping periodically to rest and to knot to the branches of the bushes small strips of paper or cloth as votive offerings. But he couldn't rid himself of the impression, which no subsequent experience or explanation could dispel, that he had seen butterflies, and they seemed still to dance before him as he stepped from the heat and glare of the stone-strewn avenue into the cool, dark interior of the church.

It was like stepping down, so much so that his first step inwards, on what was in fact a perfectly level surface, caused him to stumble. His head swam slightly and his vision danced, tiny pinpricks of white light, the residue of butterflies, until Erden struck a match and lit a votive taper for each of them. They were to descend two flights underground to the *ayazma*, or sacred spring, to which a shepherd had been guided, according to legend, by the sound of bells. The shepherd had dug in the earth until he came to the spring, beside which he also found a holy icon of Saint George. As portrayed in the icon, the saint's horse wore around his neck a string of bells, and it was the ringing of these bells that had guided the shepherd to that spot. The church and monastery were therefore dedicated to Haghia Yorgi Coudounas, Saint George of the Bells, and, as the simple shepherd had become in the instant of his discovery both eloquent and wise, it was afterwards believed that the waters of the spring had a curative effect, like the music of bells, upon diseases of the mind.

But surely the violent slaying of the dragon could not be just another form of the gently curative power of music or bathing. And the icon to which Erden had led them in the church upstairs—the work of a nineteenth-century monk—was, as Malone had seen it, of a particularly violent rendering. In its subject matter, it was perfectly conventional. The saint, in full armor, is seated on a rearing horse, his torso leaning forward to give weight to the lance plunging into the dragon's chest. The saint's visor is down and he has, as it were, no face. By contrast, the dragon is shown writhing in a disturbingly expressive attitude, the head thrown back convulsively, one arm stretched flat on the ground, palm down, the other rising as if it might attempt to grasp and repel the lance. Malone remembered thinking that the artist's sympathies seemed to be on the side of the dragon and recalling Goya's *Third of May*, in which a squad of Napoleonic riflemen, faceless and identical, the machinery of the modern state, shoot into a defenseless crowd, one of whom, in a white shirt, arms thrown out and chest exposed, embodies their collective fate. As a social allegory, the legend of Saint George Coudounas would seem to be asserting the existence of a dangerous underclass, with which, however, the creator of this particular icon seemed in sympathy. As a psycho-allegory, it would seem to illustrate the repression of all mental processes other than those leading to doctrinal orthodoxy. If true, this interpretation would lend a yet more sinister meaning to the iron rings which were affixed to the masonry of the floor and walls of the room that occupied the level between the *ayazma* and the chapel, a transitional room, as it were, from which the mad—or the impenitent—were taken to bathe in the holy well. Malone remembered standing for a moment at the water's edge and waiting for the others to start back up the stairs so that he might verify, alone, his impression that the water in the well was not entirely still. He had raised his taper overhead for maximum light and dropped a bit of white paper which had fluttered for a moment before coming to rest on the surface, where it was snatched and devoured in a rolling turbulence that caused him to shudder in revulsion. Eels, he thought. The bathing pool is full of eels. Malone had looked up, then, as the little procession of candle flames reached the top of the winding stairs, and he could feel now the panic he had felt then at the absurd but chilling certainty that he was going to be shut in.

Mustafa, he called. *Lütfen, başka bir bira alabilir mıyım?* May I have another beer, please?

Good old Mustafa! thought Malone. Always there when you need him, or almost. He had climbed the stairs up out of the well as fast as he could, and as he stepped once again into the open air—he didn't stumble—he felt greatly relieved. He took a deep breath and noticed that, off to his right, Erden and Frank were just disappearing around the corner of the monastery. Sylvia, however, had stopped and turned, apparently waiting for him to catch up.

Slow poke, she shouted. Lunch.

She had waited. That was nice. It had been a long morning, and Malone realized that he was ravenous.

They had been seated under a latticed arbor in the garden of the taverna behind the church, a few meters only from the great cliff that drops some two hundred meters almost straight into the sea. The bottle of *rakı* had been opened, and the *meze* were on the table. They had eaten a bit of everything that day, *meze* cold and hot and some meat and a bit of fish: hummus and *patlıcan* (three or four of the thirty-seven recipes the Turks have for eggplant); *cacık* (yogurt with cucumber and garlic and mint); and white cheese and olives and *acılı ezme* (the Turkish hot salsa); and the *yaprak dolması* that the Turks call *yalancı* (fake) because the vine leaves are stuffed not with meat but with rice and black currants and pine nuts and mint (delicious); and deep-fried *kabak* (squash) with scallions and dill and served with grated cheese and cayenne pepper; and the meatballs in sauce called *terbiyeli*, with onion, lemon, and thyme; and some diced and grilled calf's liver served with chopped raw onions; a platter of the delicious and inevitable *sardalya*, lightly breaded with basil and grilled; and finally a taste of the fish of springtime, the noble *kalkan* himself, so ugly in the market, warts and all, so refined and savory on a bed of parsley of a sunlit April afternoon. Could we have eaten all that? Malone wondered. Could we possibly have eaten all that?

And what had they been talking about? Erden had talked about a trip he had taken recently to Kayseri and Avanos, in Cappadocia, where he had a friend who owned a textile shop. The friend also had a shop in Paris, on the Isle Saint-Louis, which had elicited a start from Malone, though he hadn't explained, and Frank had talked about "King Midas' Feast," as he called it, the results of a recent analysis of some culinary remains found in the Midas Tomb at Gordion, which showed that they had eaten a spiced lamb and lentil stew and had been drinking barley beer and honey mead and two fermentations of grapes, one a wine, the other much more powerful, like *rakı*, perhaps.

I'll drink to that, said Malone.

As will I, verily, said Erden. And Frank had done the honors and Malone had thought the time might be ripe for him to talk about the icon and the eels, maybe a little less about the eels, and

Napoleon and the dragon and the *Third of May*, when Sylvia had surprised them by suddenly rising from her chair and exclaiming as she pointed out to sea, Oh, look!

They had all turned to look in the direction indicated, south and slightly east, where they could just make out, coming slowly but steadily at them, what appeared to be an undulating line, like a living thread of silk, advancing into visibility out of the distant glare, at an elevation of thirty feet or so above the water, until the line seemed to break into smaller sections and finally into differentiated parts, rhythmically advancing. It was the storks. You could see them clearly now, their great wings cleaving the air, as they advanced in a continuous undulating line that extended as far as the eye could see, thousands upon thousands of migrating storks, funneling through the narrow passage over Istanbul. The leader appeared now almost under them, over a hundred meters down, and there he seemed to suspend his efforts, each wing extended from his body in a graceful arch, and glide into a rising turn. Stork after stork followed into the rising column of air whose motion was made visible in the spiraling line of birds. And still they came, the spiral rising now to the level of the cliff edge, and now another hundred meters and another two, until the leader, perhaps no longer the same bird, sensing that the upper limit of the spiral had been reached at about five hundred meters above the sea, emerged at its summit in an even glide to the north, to Istanbul, to Russia, to who knew where. And still the line of storks came on, the undulating line emerging from the distance and skimming over the water, the rhythmical approach, the entry and rising through the thermal spiral, the gliding exit at its summit towards the north.

The little group stood at the cliff's edge, motionless, amazed. The spiraling motion of the great white birds was a study in power and grace. It seemed to Malone a symbol, not of any durable absolute, but of a momentary reconciliation of intent and accident, of harmony and freedom, of progress and return. It was, of course, inherently none of these things, and what, he thought, if Sylvia hadn't noticed, or if we hadn't come to the islands that day, nor anybody else? The storks would surely have come, as surely as the world turns and the stars, but their passage, unobserved, would have meant nothing at all.

ii

The glare had softened on the water now, and the Asian shore and Üsküdar and the twin hills of Big and Little Çamlıca beyond were clearly visible. Visible also in the nearer distance was the island rock of Kız Kulesi, the Maiden's Tower, one of whose upper windows glowed with reflected sunlight, as if recalling its service as a lighthouse in times gone by. Malone stood up for a moment to stretch. He flexed his shoulders and arched his back, then stepped over to the chest-high rail and looked down at the lead-gray water swirling out from under the bridge. Through the length of his body he could feel the rhythmical drumming of the automobile traffic as it passed over the expansion joints in the bridge above. He listened absentmindedly, looking down at the water, where he could see a series of small whirlpools form at either side of a stanchion just beneath where he stood. One after another they appeared, each turning in a graceful eddy until swallowed up again in the general flow downstream. The little drama began to acquire, for him, a moral dimension, for how else might he explain the feeling of mixed pleasure and anxiety which came over him, much like the premonitory excitement he had felt in his earlier passage through the Spice Bazaar. He was reminded of watching whirlpools slide away behind his skiff as he rowed on the Merrimack River north of Boston during the time he taught at Essex College, and of another time, much earlier—he couldn't have been more than ten or eleven—when he had learned to paddle a canoe on a lake in Maine. But intimate as these memories were, they seemed to have nothing to do with the emotion he had felt just moments before. The emotion seemed somehow significant, though he couldn't have said why. It troubled him unaccountably, as having its source in an experience both various and painful, and somehow linked to the present, though he couldn't have said how. Leaning his chest and forearms against the rail, Malone could feel more insistently the beat of the traffic moving over the bridge. What was it? Could he hear a voice? It might almost have been the voice of a woman—Sylvia's perhaps—speaking his name, but drawing out the second syllable in a long moan, like the foghorn of a distant ship, and he could feel the engines drumming in the bowels of a great ocean liner as they watched the wake slide away into the mist astern. It was an image out of their crossing in the old *Vulcania* almost twenty-five years ago. But the memory faded, and Malone looked down again, a little dazed, at the lead-gray water flowing under the bridge. There, at either side of the stanchion, a new pair of eddies formed, drawing his gaze inwards as each spun through its graceful course downstream. The emotion reappeared, wavered and intensified, becoming finally intelligible as the wild look on Sylvia's face towards the conclusion of a night's carouse in Beyoğlu, her beauty enhanced by the disordered mood she had caught from the drinking and the music and the dance, for their evening had begun with the Mevlevi Dervishes.

Erden had taken them to a ceremonial performance of the *sema* in the oldest surviving dervish monastery in the city, having been founded in that eventful year of 1492. They had reached the monastery by descending the precipitous slope of Galip Dede Caddesi, a slope which he would soon be climbing to Beyoğlu from the Galata side of the bridge, a slope they had often descended to the Taverna Boheme for wild nights spent in the company of assorted other friends in addition to Frank and Erden, notably Dimitri and Elena Papas and the painter Marco Fontane.

Marco had been with them at the *sema* also, having made a special point of wanting to go. Yes, there had been five of them, and Malone remembered the circular dancing floor of the monastery and the polished marquetry surface that seemed to move like water in the flickering candlelight. They had become aware then of the rhythmical soft beating of fingers and palms on drums, when there seemed to glide through the penumbra the shapes of the dancers. More candles were brought in as the drums were joined by flutes and the strumming of the long-necked *saz*. The dancers stood still for some minutes, listening, eyes closed, each in a long white gown with wide sleeves and a flowing skirt. Then slowly the dancers began to move, each man spinning upon himself as he circled around the floor, like a solitary waltzer, sleeves and skirts flaring out, one arm lifted with the palm up, the other harmoniously continuing the same line downward on the other side of the body, the palm turned towards the floor. The cadence of the dance increased for a while and then subsided, resolving itself into a seemingly endless trance, onwards and onwards, and around and around, until the trance deepens into ecstasy and the soul and body fuse, heaven and earth linked through the microcosmic harmony achieved by each dancer, while the whirling motion of the troop in unison imitates and invokes the music of the spheres.

The mystical significance of the *sema* had been explained to them after the ceremony by a Mevlevi master visiting from the home monastery in Konya. The master explained that the founder of their order, Mevlana Celaleddin Rumi, had been known, at the beginning of his ministry, to dance on the occasion of his hearing the humblest of rhythms, the hoofbeats of a passing horse, for example, the reiterated song of a bird, housewives beating laundry over the rocks in a stream, the hammer strokes of a coppersmith molding a casserole. The rhythms of all life were sacred to Mevlana, as they are sacred to the embracing egalitarianism of Islam; and all things living had their rhythms, some faster, some slower, some audible, some not. And as all life illustrates rhythm, so all rhythm contains life, be it the rhythm of the tides or the circling moon—between which, seven hundred years ago, Mevlana had seen the true relation—the seasons, the menstrual cycle in women—than which no rhythm is more holy—the planets passing, and the stars. God, therefore, is everywhere, but man, in his imperfection, must strive for an awareness of this Presence in himself and everywhere. Meditation and study—scientific study, which leads to a vision of the beauty of all things—have this awareness as their end, but it is an intellectual and preparatory awareness only, for only in the annihilation of the ego-centered consciousness can full awareness and oneness with creation and the creator be achieved. All should now understand the essence of what the *sema* is, a technique that contains its end within itself, in which all the components of creation are brought into their true relation, which is not a relation of cause and effect but a relation of harmonious simultaneity.

It was a heady brew indeed, and when Erden suggested that they recover over a drink at the Boheme down the street, down they went. The slope seemed to Malone to drop at a very dangerous angle, and the darkness contributing to their sense of disorientation, he and Sylvia proceeded hanging on to each other and by small steps. Frank was just explaining over his shoulder that the street actually changed its name about halfway down, becoming the Yüksek Kaldırım where it flattened out before reaching the square at the north end of the Galata Bridge, when the figure of Marco, leading their small procession, dropped out of sight to the left. It was a stairway, with three iron handrails for safety, one in the middle, and at the bottom of which some twenty feet of landing led to another stair. On the landing, they stepped into a pocket of yellow light that fell from a single streetlamp and from the taverna window where, in art deco script, was lettered out the Turkish spelling of BOEM. The length of the window was traversed by a brass rod, from which hung the folds of a plain muslin curtain and above which could be seen the side-cocked head and hunched left shoulder of a violinist, the only musician standing up.

Inside, the room glowed smoky and aromatic, a mix of cigarettes and *rakı* and grilling meat and fish, and the clatter of silverware and conversation mixed with the music: violin, piano, accordion, and guitar. It was about ten o'clock, the evening was in full swing, and it looked as though they might not find places to sit, when a great bear-like shape of a man rose from the head of a long table near the bandstand and gestured them over. The bear-like man found the initial spontaneity of his gesture rewarded when he recognized Frank Corrigan, his colleague at the College, and, sure enough, the painter Marco Fontane, whom he admired as much as he had ever admired anybody, living or dead, and that was not just the *rakı* talking. And they have brought with them a man whom I don't know, he thought, and a woman who is without any doubt and certainly the most beautiful woman in the world. The bear-like man could hardly contain himself. He had been born to love this woman and she him, and rushing at Sylvia theatrically, but with bulk, he said, I am Dimitri and you, you are, he paused, delicious! But you are all of you delicious and you must join us for we have been deserted by half our company—gesturing at the empty seats—three couples of beautiful young people, so beautiful, who rose to dance between the tables last night—oh yes, we have been here all week—and danced, and danced, and danced right out the door. So beautiful, and they are gone, and we are bereft, and where do such beautiful young people go so early in the evening do you think?—with a forlorn look at Sylvia—and they have left me with the bill, he laughed, pounding the table with his bear-like paw, and the platters jumped.

The bear-like man had gathered Frank and then Marco into his embrace, clapping them soundly on the back, and he had taken Malone's hand and clapped him also soundly on the back, without the embrace, and returning delicately to Sylvia, but with bulk, he had suggested that the two groups mix and, taking her in one hand and Marco in the other, he went back to his place at the head of the table and seated them, with a resultant small commotion, Sylvia at his right hand, Marco to his left. She would remember afterwards, would Sylvia, that she had at first felt isolated and even a little annoyed. Her husband and Frank were at the other end of the table, and Erden seemed to have simply disappeared. She didn't really know Marco—it was no comfort to have been told he was some kind of mad genius—and as for these other two women and the men, especially this Dimitri, she'd never set eyes on them before. She was in alien company in an alien land; but having put it so dramatically, or melodramatically, she began to feel better at once. In fact, she supposed it was one of those times when she should have a few drinks, and she remembered her father coaxing her—what kind of a father was that, you say?—to loosen up.

So she's been captured by this bear, ha, ha, and Maloney was in another world, ho, ho, and maybe she knew from the lessons of her gypsy mother how to get a ring in his nose, not Baloney's, of course, but this bear's. And she remembered a photo of her mother taken in Barcelona years and years ago dancing with a rose between her teeth, and that was the woman she had always wanted to be and this minute had become, and she felt suddenly quite tender towards her dear boy Andy Malohohone, away down there in his other world, and leaning forward slightly to get a look at him, she raised her glass in his direction, though he had just turned his head to look at the orchestra, and she smiled a slightly cockeyed smile that said, I love you tenderly and I shall remember you always. Now what kind of a line was that? she thought. She had moved into a role surely, the beautiful gypsy dancer who was her mother or some actress in she couldn't quite remember what romantic film, and maybe it was dangerous, but it was fun, and turning towards the bear she put her bewitching and magnetic hand upon his arm and she leaned towards him and he looked into her eyes and then into her dress and saw there—was it possible?—the most beautifully formed breast he had ever seen in his life, and he looked again into her eyes, which seemed to have dimmed with emotion, and he was struck dumb.

What could he have been saying to produce such an apparently amorous effect? You'd think he had been saying something deep and moving about life and love, but he had only been talking about sociology, and not even very seriously about that. He was a sociologist, so why not? The essence of sociology lay, he had explained, in the effort to establish norms. But as there were no real human beings who actually realized the norms, nobody could be described as normal. Everybody is slightly cracked, by definition, and some are very cracked, which is a state of affairs which our colleagues the psychologists and psychiatrists are in a good position to profit by. Isn't that right, Marco?

Don't let those guys get their hooks in you, said Marco. Electrode city.

And Sylvia thought, Did he say that?

Of course, sociology has uses other than feeding the shrinks—that's a vile expression, feeding the shrinks—even if some of its uses are negative. What I mean is that sociology is based on the analysis of what people do and what they say. Now one of the ways in which you can observe and analyze what people say is to provoke them into saying something, which is what you do when you conduct a poll. But in Turkey, you can't conduct polls because you can't believe anything anybody tells you. The polls conducted prior to the last elections, for example, were scandalously wrong. The polls were not conducted by Turkish sociologists, who would have known better, but by the press and some private pollsters who, as it happens, were Americans. Americans always suppose that American patterns of behavior and human nature in general are the same thing, as if there were, strictly speaking, any such thing as human nature, but that's another story. The polls were wrong, because if you ask a Turk for his opinion—ask him, he's all around you—he will lie. He will lie because he doesn't trust you and who gave you the right to ask him these questions in the first place? Inside he's saying, get outta my face, or he's saying I'm gonna blow you bastards up and burn you bloody down; but outside he says to you that his vote is for the Fatherland and all things are in the hands of God. He will lie to you because he doesn't trust you and he doesn't trust you because he thinks you might be from the secret police, even if he couldn't prove there is such a thing. And the more innocent your question, the more he will think he is being fooled. Ask him what his favorite vegetable is and he will say eggplant, because this is what he has been told Turks should say and he will say it to disappear in the fiction of the norm. And he does. The Turk is the real invisible man. Do you know this book, *Invisible Man*? Who needs another drink? Marco, pour the lady another drink. Marco, pour yourself another drink. Do you think I need one too? Okay, pour me a drink. But I have lost my train of thought. Oh yes, the Turk is your real invisible man and this is what I meant by a negative virtue in sociology. We have learned something through the failure of one of its traditional tools. But the Turk's conduct is not invisible. So scientific sociology in Turkey must restrict itself to an analysis of what Turks do, to the visible. Now Marco here knows all about the visible. Marco is a painter, you know. She knew. And a very great painter, certainly the greatest in Turkey and maybe the greatest in the entire world. And his whole life has been given to an analysis of the visible, just like me, isn't that right Marco?

No, no, no, no, no, said the voice, as if in pain, and Sylvia couldn't tell if he had been hurt by Dimitri's banter or was responding to a flow of painful meditation entirely within himself.

Dear friend, said Dimitri with a hand on Marco's shoulder, you know I think the very world of your work and I know you are not an analyst. I was kidding you. You are a maker. You are a builder, a great synthesizer of the visual experience, each canvas a monument to your will and skill, the ever-expanding corpus of your work an illustration greater yet ...

Stop, said Marco, now that you've got my attention, I wish you would relinquish it. In a word, I wish you would shut up. Who is this man, he thought, to make jokes about my work? Some things you joke about to keep your sanity. Electrode city, yes, to keep your distance and your sanity. Yes, he thought, this joking is distance, but your work, your real work, is something you do not want to be distant from. In your work, distance is death. What you want to be with your work is thoroughly inside and at one with it, fused with it, your hand, your eye, your mind. It is as the dervish master said, as it has been known also to the Zen masters. In your work and for the artist distance is death and madness. There are only two poles—what is this man Dimitri now saying about poles?—work or madness, madness or work, never again, he thought. No, no, no, no, no. If only this man would shut the hell up.

I think I had better shut up, said Dimitri, and he felt Sylvia's hand upon his arm, and as she leaned forward her dress fell open and he could see that she was naked underneath, and he looked into her eyes—moist, dreamy—and what he saw, or thought he saw, was sex.

Malone had noticed that no sooner had they come through the door than Erden had disappeared. They were halfway through the meal and suddenly here he was again. He'd been to see his old friend Yakup Toledano, who was sitting with his wife at a table in the back of the room. Yakup—Erden pronounced it Yacoop—was an antique dealer and something of a business partner, who kept a shop in the courtyard of that wonderful old building across from the Swedish Embassy. Did Malone know the place? Malone did. Frank had taken them there, Sylvia and himself, a couple of weeks ago, and they had bought a samovar.

On the subject of samovars, said Erden, I learned just now that the old fox speaks Russian along with everything else. He knows everybody in the orchestra and he's been trying to get them to play "Moscow Nights," but they're apparently making a joke of not playing it. They are all Russians. The elderly woman at the piano is a countess. The three men—the angular violinist, the guitarist with the woeful countenance, the accordion player with the dark glasses, who was indeed blind—had been in the civil war, and they all had frightful stories to tell of their various escapes, but, as Yakup liked to say, they never told them. Yakup had met them in a business way—so many had had things to sell—but they were friends now after all these years. They were wonderful musicians, full of warmth, and they played Greek and Russian and European songs and they knew the Turkish sentimental favorites as well.

    Malone had turned to look at them, just as Sylvia, from the other end of the table, turned to lift her glass in his direction. But as he looked at the musicians, his memory of "Moscow Nights" resolved itself into an image of Yul Brenner in *The Brothers Karamazov* playing the guitar and singing with the gypsies in a basement cabaret, his left foot on a stool, left elbow resting on his thigh to help support the neck of the guitar, the fierce, oriental cast to his features, the wide lips and deep melodious voice. The musicians on the dais had paused briefly to confer and were smiling now as the angular violinist lifted his bow and, with a nod to the table at the back of the room, intoned the sweeping and melancholy strains of "Moscow Nights." Malone looked down the table now towards Sylvia, with whom he had seen the movie at least twice, he remembered, remembering also that he loved her, but she had turned towards Dimitri and was gazing up at him, her hand on his arm, immobilized, as in a photograph, or one of those eighteenth-century engravings which the moralizing artist would have entitled, *Don't*. But here now was Marco shouting something at Dimitri over the sound of the music and

Dimitri turning away from Sylvia and shouting back: not Poles, Russians—not a Pole in the house, he said, laughing and thumping the table and, as he did so, Sylvia jumped in surprise and in pain also, because she had been kicked under the table very hard.

What's that old stud Dimitri up to anyway? thought Frank. As if I didn't know. There isn't a man in the room who wouldn't want to get into that woman's pants. She's beautiful all right, but maybe she's too obviously beautiful. Look at me and see how beautiful I am. Am I not just the sweetest thing? She needed to be kicked, maybe, but maybe that element was lost on Dimitri, who would be blinded by all that blond shimmer and shine. There was something else to her, of course, because she liked to play the game she was playing now with the old stud, and he had more than once thought she had been playing it with him. What makes some women like that? The husband? The need to be reassured of their attractiveness? Hot pants? Damn, he muttered, knowing exactly what had happened at the other end of the table and that somebody should intervene quickly because Dimitri would be too slow in reacting and that Dimitri's wife has just kicked Sylvia.

Malone remembered Frank reacting as if his movements had been choreographed. He had stood up quickly and taken him, Malone, by the arm and swept him to the other end of the table and reintroduced him to Dimitri, who had risen with some puzzlement at first to shake his hand, and he had swept Sylvia from her chair to replace her with Malone, by which time Dimitri had understood and said, with a bow, we meet again, and Dimitri had introduced him to a Turkish gentleman with a flower in his buttonhole and to his wife, Dimitri's, who was sitting next to Marco and to Marco, who said how do you do as if he'd never seen him before. He wondered for a moment how drunk Marco could be, but he had difficulty withdrawing his attention from Dimitri's wife, whom he was now seeing for the first time, a woman in her forties, surely, and who looked it, but to whom age had brought something fabulous. He had never seen that kind of beauty before, and she was smiling at him still as Dimitri went on about Russians and Poles and the fact that the musicians were all Russians every one and his friends forever, although he was himself only a Greek, and Malone thought that Sylvia lacked what this woman had and wondered if she might not acquire it with age, though he knew it wasn't time that did it but life, and he wondered about Sylvia's life, their life, when he heard Dimitri saying that his wife had once said of him that he was only half Greek and all Turkish and that he knew he was impossible and that he wasn't the only one in the room who knew just how impossible he was, looking now wistfully at his wife. And a skilled charmer, thought Malone.

She had turned her smile upon her husband, for a moment, before returning it to Malone. It was a smile at once sweet and self-confident. If I were a woman, he thought, this is the woman I'd want to be. And if I were this woman, what would I be thinking? I'd be angry with my husband, most likely, but not too angry, because he's done this before and even acted upon it and been unfaithful, but so had she and this was the life they had together, a sad life sometimes and lived at the edge of nervous collapse, but then they would recover and love each other first desperately and then more calmly and both times were wonderful, though the calm seemed to lead inevitably to a renewed need for excitement, and the round would start all over again. So this was their life—she didn't see how it could change as long as they were healthy—and it was a life that ran through all the colors of the spectrum and was always new and she dearly loved her old bear with whom she would lay herself down tonight, she thought, for they had had that again for some months now, and grasp that delicious bulk for all she was worth and his body would inhabit her and it would be as if the two of them were together tumbling in her womb to the dark rhythms of a dance they would create and it would be like giving birth to a pleasure that was as terrible as pain. And Malone was stunned and a little flushed at the course his thoughts had taken, wondering where they had come from and how many of them might be true, either factually, or as representative of a real mood or state of affairs. And he wondered whose mood or state of affairs they might turn out to be, and he imagined that the sexual fantasy might well have been Sylvia's and that maybe this woman had come to the same conclusion, living in Sylvia's thoughts, and that that was why she had kicked her.

Elena Papas, she said, leaning across the table and putting her hand on his arm and, through the sounds of the music, intoning again the name Elena Papas, for I am Dimitri's wife and I am sorry if I make mistake but I am Greek woman and Dimitri is Greek man and sometimes we go off in wrong directions. Boom, she said, boom, so that's what she meant by going off, and she might even have thumped the table had Dimitri not raised his glass between them and said *Yassou* and *Şerefe* and *Şerefe* and *Yassou* and they drank to each other and to everybody else to the strains now of music by the great Hadjidakis, and Dimitri rose from the table waving a wine-stained napkin in his raised right hand and took Marco's right hand in his left as Elena grabbed Marco's other hand and Malone's as she went by and Malone grabbed the hand of the man with the flowering buttonhole who grabbed the next until the whole table was following Dimitri in a serpentine course between the tables around the room and around the room again and finally right out the door from where, as they circled, Sylvia could see over the curtain rod the violinist turn to look at them, expressionless, and then not at everybody but at her, and she thought his features looked not expressionless but full of longing as the music stopped and Frank still held her hand, but she was lost now in a dream of making love not to Malone or even Frank, but to Dimitri, a man she had met tonight for the first time.

iii

In his slow climb along the Yüksek Kaldırım and up Galip Dede Caddesi from the Galata Bridge, Malone had now arrived at the top of the flight of stairs leading down to the Boem. He had been told that many things had changed in Istanbul, that the Boem had been closed, the orchestra dispersed, wild nights now few and far between. But, curious to see what might remain, he went down to the landing where they had danced that night. The painted lettering of the restaurant's name had flaked and worn to a filigree, illegible but for those who knew. The brass rail across the window was still there and the curtain hanging from its rings, but the window glass was gray and Malone could just make out, with his forehead against the cold surface and his hands cupped around his eyes, what appeared to be packing cases stacked against the walls. The space was probably being used as a depot by one of the shops on the street above. Malone stood for a moment remembering that night again, when the party had broken up right where he was standing now, and he remembered that Marco, instead of going back up to the street with them, had said goodnight and turned away and walked to the other end of the landing and dropped into the darkness down the next flight of stairs.

I did something like that, he thought, but I've come back, and he walked back up the flight of stairs and what remained of Galip Dede Caddesi, past the dervish monastery, the underground tram station at Tünel, and across İstiklal. Perhaps he knew where he was going without knowing it. There was certainly nothing hesitant in his demeanor, nothing of the tourist, and the passersby took no more notice of him than of each other. Nor did they take any notice when he stepped up very close to a shop window to peer in, for was there not another man, most unusual, this one, doing the same thing? Malone was certainly unremarkable as compared to this man, very tall, gaunt to the point of emaciation, wearing a long, black overcoat and a wide-brimmed, black hat. The man's pose was equally remarkable as he bent forward angularly from the waist and very low to peer at some object on display. It was a sextant, an object wonderful in the precision of its manufacture, complex and compact, maintained in the highest state of polish and efficiency, an object described on an identifying label as having been centrally important to navigation for over two centuries. Lying next to it was a fully extended marine telescope and a ship's log lying open at a page dated 14 November 1887, though the entry beneath was faded and illegible. Malone then noticed that these objects were lying on a spread-out map of the Malay Archipelago. Conrad, he thought, Joseph Conrad, realizing that he had thought of Conrad now for the second time today, and sure enough someone had traced a light green line from Singapore through the Carimata Strait to Benjarmassim and the Isle of Pulo Laut, to Dongola on the western coast of Celebes, across the Makassar Strait to Borneo and up the Berau River to Tandjong Redeb, where Conrad had met the man who was to be his model for the hero of *Almayer's Folly* and *An Outcast of the Islands*. Conrad had made this very trip between Singapore and Tandjong Redeb repeatedly, Malone remembered, during the summer and fall of 1887 when he was mate of the steamship *Vidar*, and he turned excitedly to speak to the angular man in black, but he was gone.

Malone, now standing back a pace from the window, saw that the whole display was devoted to the works of Conrad, with editions of *Almayer's Folly* in most of the world's languages. Standing behind the map, framed under glass, which had made it at first difficult to see, was a portion of an admiralty navigation chart, number 1263, for the year 1887, showing the Makassar Strait at its upper end, the Sambaliung Peninsula, the Tidung Estuary, and the Pantai and Berau Rivers leading up to Tandjong Redeb. Finally, Malone saw what he realized must have been intended, by its positioning, to be the dominant piece in the display, though the play of late afternoon light upon the windowpane made it difficult to see. Suspended from the ceiling and angled slightly downward to meet the viewer's upturned gaze was "an enlargement of the only surviving photograph, badly damaged," of one Charles Olmeijer, the original of Conrad's Almayer. It looked more like a photograph of a ghost. The image had neither foreground nor background, but a surface of light filigree, as of the leaves of a great tree, with patches of light showing through from an indefinite beyond. But neither in front of nor behind these leaves, but dwelling, as it were, within them, was the face of a young man. The young man's shoulders were also visible, and Malone could make out his costume as consisting of a jacket, perhaps with piping on the lapels, a white shirt, and a small, black bow tie with its ends tucked under the shirt collar. A lot of light showed through the young man's jacket, portions of his chin and forehead were blank, and something seemed to be amiss with his left eye, giving to the face an expression at once exultant and perverse, and with a shock, Malone realized that the image bore a striking resemblance to the Carjat portrait of the French poet Arthur Rimbaud. Marco! thought Malone. Poor crazy Marco, who had been a scholar and a writer in an earlier life and who had once known more about Arthur Rimbaud than anybody else in the world, perhaps, when his life had blown up in his face, his house burned to the ground, a thousand pages of typescript gone; and an image presented itself, as Erden Sakarya had described it to him years ago, of Marco's old wooden house in Ortaköy, metamorphosed into a single, devouring flame that imploded with a rush of sparks, leaving nothing at all, and of Marco turning and walking away from his house and from the whole of his past life as if it had never been or was all that could ever be.

2

ERDEN

i

Erden Sakarya looked up from his work at the sound of the late afternoon call to prayer and leaned back with a sigh of satisfaction. Absorbed as he had been in the meticulous demands of his accounts, he had not noticed the passage of time and the approach of this most delicious moment of the day. It was not that he was a religious man, though born and raised in the Muslim faith, but he would never have applied so frivolous a word as delicious to the experience of prayer. Such an application might even be said to qualify as sacrilegious and—who knows?—might bring bad luck. No. What provided this feeling of profound satisfaction was, as he liked to pretend to himself, the knowledge that he had accomplished yet another good day's work. It was also, however, that hour of the day, recurring once a day each day, that released him from his vow not to smoke.

He had tried on many occasions to quit entirely. In fact, he could identify himself without bitterness with the fellow in the old joke who knew that quitting was easy because he had done it a thousand times. He had also tried to ease off the habit by smoking only pipes or cigars, but he discovered that, as a cigarette smoker, he inhaled everything, he made a mess of cigars, which stank anyway, and he smoked pipes with such ferocity that they got too hot to hold. So he had hit upon the scheme of daytime abstinence which, regulated as it was by the rhythm of the first three calls to prayer—the first just before sunrise, when he would have to stop if he were still alive, as he liked to say, the second just past noon to give him fortitude, the third right now—provided him with an objective discipline which brought him also into harmonious relation, however worldly and eccentric, with Islam and the rhythms of his countrymen.

He therefore took particular pleasure in prolonging and savoring this moment of release, and instead of lighting up immediately—though neither would he permit himself ever to smoke inside the shop—he leaned back in his chair with his hands clasped behind his neck, as if he hadn't a care in the world, and suggested casually to Mehmet, his young assistant, that they might begin to think of closing up. He would himself just step out the door for a moment to see if the press of business had begun to wane; and it is here we pick him up again, a controlled and happy man in a beige gabardine suit, spotless light blue madras cotton shirt, and regimental necktie, lighting up his first smoke of the day.

Erden liked order and comfort, and he liked style. In his dress and manner and in the accents of his speech when he spoke English, he had adopted Britannic ways. He believed—and as a student of languages he could cite you chapter and verse—that Americans spoke a degraded form of the language and that, from his vantage point—he saw them arrive in successive waves—they seemed to degrade it further every year. He believed also that their manner of dress was generally appalling and they were deficient in what he liked to think of as—the phrase may have been original with him—a certain "poise of pose" before their fellow men (and women). What he meant by this was a respect for the niceties, the refinements, the subtleties even, of civilized life, and the recognition that one had a responsibility for upholding them. That his theory had a theatrical dimension to it he was the first to admit, claiming further that civilized life was, like the theater, a form of art and should be conducted as such. Nor would you get anywhere by pointing out, with whatever aim to deflate, that he sounded very like a Turkish version of Oscar Wilde, for he would reply, with the utmost pleasantness and urbanity, and, if the time were right, a whisp of smoke about his lips, "My dear fellow, you have found me out."

And with all that, Erden Sakarya was the grandest of companions. In spite of the foregoing, he was utterly without pretension and there was nothing in him of the snob. He did not pretend to be English. He simply thought that Englishmen dressed better and spoke the English language better than anybody else. And he would follow or lead you anywhere: a hitherto unexplored Roman cistern, a gypsy camp, a fishermen's taverna, a strictly illegal scramble around the top of the scaffolding in Haghia Sophia some forty meters above the floor, the pastry shop at the Pera Palace Hotel, or on a spur of the moment dash across the country to his house on the Aegean coast. No, he was neither a fake Englishman nor a snob, but simply the unusual mixture that he was.

He was born and had spent his boyhood in Thracian Greece, in the Turkish quarter of the town of Komotini, where he still had relatives. In the late thirties, his father had brought the family to Istanbul, where he had adopted the name Sakarya. Like many Turks before the Republic, he had had no family name, being known only by his first name and place of origin or by his first name and his trade or a trade traditional in the family. In Komotini, his father had been known variously as Dokumacı Mehmet, because his family had worked traditionally as weavers, or as Nişli Mehmet, because his grandfather had immigrated to Komotini from Nish in Yugoslavia, the very town, they liked to remember, that had seen the birth of Constantine the Great, founder of the imperial capital of Constantinopolis-Istanbul. But like many immigrants to Turkey in the early days of the

Republic, Erden's father wanted to play down the cosmopolitan aspects of his background and find a name with a patriotic ring. So he chose the name Sakarya, which was the name of an important river in the Anatolian heartland and the site of a battle and early great victory of Mustafa Kemal in the struggle for national independence.

So Erden's origins, far from being lofty or pretentious, were rather humble and a bit crazy, and he made no effort to conceal them. He was proud of his father's heritage as an artisan and of his achievement in having founded a lucrative export trade in Turkish rugs. Like himself, his father had grown up speaking Turkish and Greek, and he had added French and English as he was setting up business in Istanbul. His father had traveled widely in Turkey and across the Turkic nations of Asia as far as China, and he had begun taking his son with him, school permitting, from the time the boy was twelve. It was also in the company of his father that Erden first saw Paris and London, and everything having to do with his father and his father's family and his own early experiences was wrapped in an aura of romance.

So there he stands, composed, elegant, very erect, almost military in his bearing, his gaze lost in the much diminished crowd of passersby, savoring the thought-brightening and blessed rush of nicotine. His shop is situated near the center of the Grand Bazaar in the select and envied locale known as the Bedesten, for its being devoted exclusively to the sale of the highest quality wares: finely crafted gold and silver, fine crystal and glassware, fine prints, antiques and oddities—there is a shop devoted entirely to marine memorabilia: charts, gyroscopes, sextants, and the like—the finest Kütahya ceramic work, or, as in the case of Sakarya, handwoven Turkish rugs. The shop is situated at the intersection of two street-corridors near the north entrance to the Bedesten. The shop's main door is cut into the corner, leaving a triangular step outside, and it is on this slightly elevated platform that Erden stands.

The room behind him, spacious for its location—the rent is high—is piled from floor to ceiling along two sides with folded rugs, several hundred immediately at hand, and he can identify for you the type, weave, size, color, design, age, condition, provenance, and price of every one. He has followed his father's lead in specializing in the weaves known as *kilim, cicim, zili,* and *sumak.* He can sell you all wool, all cotton, wool and cotton mixed, or silk. He will show you indigenous Turkish rugs from Sivas, Ortaköy, Şarkışla, Bitlis, Ahlat, Hereke, Konya, Manisa, Antalya, Deniztepe, Serik, Kayseri, Isparta, Gedikli, Artvin, Bergama, Milas, Maden, Kars, and more, and from towns and regions beyond the national borders too numerous to name. Erden lives in a professional world of great breadth and complexity—geographical, technical, esthetic, historical—and he has an encyclopedic command of it. But he harbors an eccentricity; he will not sell carpets. He will sell no textile where the weave is secondary, as with carpets, where indeed the weave is nothing but a base and passive surface to which an independent design can be knotted at will. Design should grow from within the limitations, as well as the advantages, of technique. This is the true and traditional discipline of textile art, and if the truth were told, Erden's first love is the *kilim,* where the variously colored threads of warp and weft are themselves the source, the only source, of visual design, where absolutely nothing is added on, for the added on is always and by definition the superfluous. It should come as no surprise, therefore, to find that Erden's esthetic sense favors the geometrical and, though he recognizes in the work of his friend Marco Fontane, for example, a virtuoso command of color, he finds the emotional chaos repugnant.

One might well find in Erden's attitude the beginning and end of a philosophy of life, although, by the effect of what we might call a consequent irony, he has little patience for philosophical speculation as such, especially of the airy sort his friend Frank Corrigan sometimes indulges in. He prefers to call his position not a philosophy but a cultivated attitude, for he is capable of spontaneous and visceral responses which reveal themselves as being logically coherent only if interpreted indulgently. He had recently decided, for example, to supplement his daily diet with the morning ingestion of a vitamin pill. He went to the pharmacy near his house in Kandilli, bought the vitamins, stuffed them in his carrying case, and boarded the ferry that would take him to Eminönü and work. Only upon arriving at the Bazaar did he remove the vitamins from the little brown bag and open the screw top of the opaque plastic container, a cylindrical object with a label describing at length the virtues of the pills inside. Upon opening the container, he encountered a wad of cotton which, as he drew it out, seemed to go on forever. It was, proportionally speaking, the biggest wad of packing cotton he had ever seen in his life, and his fever had already begun to rise when, peering into the bottle, he saw that it was almost empty. The subterfuge of modern packaging technique enraged him, and he had capped the bottle and thrown it violently into the corner waste bucket, when he noticed the look of surprise and near-panic on Mehmet's face. He wondered, suddenly, what he must look like from Mehmet's point of view, and burst out laughing, which did little to recompose Mehmet. All things in moderation, Mehmet, even moderation itself, he said, with a twinkle in his clear blue eye.

But I'm wasting time, he thought to himself as he dropped the butt of his cigarette through the grille of the drain at his foot. He returned to his desk, asked Mehmet if he wouldn't mind closing up, and, taking a brown paper package the size of a book from his desk drawer, dropped it into his carrying case. He left the shop and the Bedesten, passed in front of the shop of his friend Bedros Acemyan with a wave of the hand—he couldn't stop—walked up the street and past the main teahouse, through the curving tunnel of Fesciler Caddesi, and out of the Bazaar. He then crossed the street separating the Bazaar from the precincts of Beyazıt Mosque and the *sahaflar*, the secondhand booksellers, an area he would cross with a determined effort of the will, because he loved to browse. The *sahaflar* enclosure was for him a magical place, its sun and shade, its smells, the quiet that always seems to accompany books like the sound of falling water; it was a dream museum. But he would not weaken; he had an errand to perform.

It was an errand he was looking forward to, and he had soon left the enclosure of the *sahaflar* for the open esplanade behind the mosque. The book that he carried was one of two copies that had been given him earlier that afternoon in the shop of his friend Yakup Toledano, one copy for himself and one for the extraordinary man standing right there surrounded by his books and leaning against the vast trunk of a millennial sycamore. The children of the quarter, who were his impromptu pupils and his friends, called this man Çınar Baba, Father Sycamore, for this was where he had been standing for as long as any of them could remember. For them he might well resemble the tree, tall and of unusual breadth of chest, with a shaggy, unkempt head of hair, and a full beard. And the children loved him. He was kindly, and funny, and tolerant, and he always had time to spare. He would listen to them as long as they had something to say, and sometimes longer. He was a masterful teller of tales, which he often pretended to them were true, and he used also to recite to them verses from the Koran or from the great Turkish poets or of his own. He was himself the author of some thirty books of poetry and tales, which he had printed at his own expense, and which he sold right here under his tree. It's true they were not very thick books, but his natural audience, the simple people, young and old, who passed by him every day, were not very fond of thick books anyway. He was one of the last of the *meydan şairleri*, wandering minstrels in a tradition that disappeared into the night of time, and he had come to roost, as it were, beneath this noble tree. He had signed his early books Ekin Yoldaş, his real name, then just Yoldaş, because it had the virtue of signifying "a companion along the road," but when he heard the name the children had given him, he knew that his fate had been revealed, and all subsequent editions of his books had been signed Çınar Baba.

Çınar Baba was at that moment talking to a boy of perhaps twelve years, a boy whom Erden knew. He had met him last summer, a fiercely hot day in August. He had left his shop in Mehmet's care to spend an hour in the little open-air teahouse that shared in the shade of the poet's sycamore. He had been quietly drinking his tea when this very same small boy had asked him if he wanted a shine, for this is how he earned his living. Upon questioning, the boy told Erden that he and his small brother were orphans and, in the summer, lived in the street. Erden suspected that this was just the usual line to curry sympathy and a large tip, but his curiosity was aroused when the boy said he spoke English and French. Erden tested him, and it turned out to be perfectly true. When asked how he had managed, the boy said he owed everything to Çınar Baba. Erden, again suspicious, pointed out that Çınar Baba spoke not a word of either English or French, but the boy responded with great dignity that Çınar Baba had "opened his mind to the world." The rest was easy, he said. He borrowed books from the apprentices in the Bazaar, and he shined as many French and English shoes as he could get his hands on, said he. See for yourself, the boy went on, your shoes are now so beautiful you can't tell them apart. Erden had to admit he'd never heard that one before, and, back in his shop that very same fiercely hot August afternoon, he had had an idea. Mehmet, his young apprentice, was now eighteen. He had taken him out buying in the countryside, and he had begun to teach him how to keep the books. If Mehmet were to follow the usual routine, he would some day soon think about moving on, to a bigger shop, perhaps, or of going into partnership or out on his own. He would need to find a replacement, and maybe this boy was the one.

Erden Bey!—it was the boy greeting him—Hello, Sir—his English had funny quirks like that—we have a problem you can help with us—and like that. He knew that it would soon be Saint George's Day—he called him Yorgi Baba—because he had been looking at a Greek calendar, but he remembered reading in an English book that it was an important day for the English too. This might be useful information for somebody who might be shining English shoes. Erden had no trouble explaining about patron saints as the Turks have saints for everything. There are patron saints of alleyways and ashcans, of the one-eyed and the marooned at sea, of hermits and crowds and virgins and prostitutes, of moods and the weather and cisterns and vegetation and machinery and of haters and lovers and malcontents. No, the boy had no difficulty understanding that Haghia Yorgi was a *gazi*, a defender of the faith—though he would have to refer to him as Saint George to be properly understood by the English—and he went off, delighted, to put his new knowledge to use.

The book that Erden carried from Yakup's shop in Beyoğlu had been entrusted to him for delivery by a mutual friend of theirs, Faruk Selvi, a man well known and respected in certain circles around town. He was a practicing journalist, a poet, and a translator into Turkish of some of the more arcane examples of modernist literature in English. He had translated much of Yeats, some Eliot, was forever publishing, *seriatim*, sections of *Finnegans Wake*, but he had now undertaken to render into Turkish a writer surely as dedicated to his art as any of the foregoing, as he thought, but as surely more accessible, Joseph Conrad, the Pole turned Englishman, master mariner and novelist, and he had decided to begin with *Almayer's Folly*, Conrad's own beginning. Over the years Faruk had also undertaken the translation of some of the best of modern Turkish poetry into English, poetry of a much more populist and communicative turn, and his researches into the work of living Turkish poets had brought him to Beyazıt Square and Çınar Baba. He and Çınar Baba had now published half a dozen bilingual editions that could be found displayed under the sycamore. He had also published an article in the *Turkish Daily News*, with a photograph of the poet "loafing" under his tree and a developed comparison between the life and work of Çınar Baba and that of the arch-loafer himself, Walt Whitman. The article was of the sort that people cut out and save for its picturesqueness and for its insider's knowledge of the "real" Istanbul, and there was hardly an English-speaking household in town, these days, that had not at least one bilingual edition of Çınar Baba.

The translations were, in Erden's opinion, as in that of many others, very good. But the comparison with Walt Whitman, if somewhat forced—or so it seemed to Erden—brought into focus an aspect of Faruk's personality of which he, Erden, had only recently become aware. Faruk had always been an aesthete, both in his literary tastes and his public behavior, but there seemed to have crept into his life, in recent years, a hint of something slovenly, something long hidden, perhaps, that was beginning to invade his personality in flashes that would surprise his friends, momentarily, only to be passed off as a fleeting indisposition of Faruk's or a mistaken impression of their own. But his wife had told him that from time to time Faruk would disappear for several days at a stretch, to return with a look in his eye that she didn't want to question.

These thoughts had occupied his mind intermittently since being asked by Faruk, in front of Yakup's shop, if he wouldn't mind delivering a copy of *Almayer's Folly* to Beyazıt Square. Faruk explained that he wanted Yoldaş—he couldn't bring himself to refer to the man by his persona—to receive the book today, if possible, this being publication day and his having promised it. He would have gone himself, he should have gone himself, would have been on his way, in fact, but for this chance meeting with Erden, who would save his life by delivering the book in his stead. On this note, Faruk had bolted, saying that he had urgent business at the paper and that the first bottle of *rakı* tonight was on him, because they were all meeting tonight at Boncuk, right? Wasn't it tonight? It was, and Erden and Yakup had stared after his retreating figure, rather perplexed at the mood of their friend.

Erden had shortly thereafter taken his leave. He had walked quickly along İstiklal Caddesi, hardly noticing the familiar sights, until he came to Tünel and the bookshop where his friend's new publication was on display. He had himself provided the sextant and the telescope, on loan from his neighbor in the Bedesten. Faruk had provided the photograph of Olmeijer, enlarged from a photograph he'd found in somebody's book on Conrad. Yakup had found the ship's log, lord knows where. He had meant to ask him about its authenticity. He'd try to remember to ask him tonight. He thought he might walk down Galip Dede and the Yüksek Kaldırım, but decided to take the underground tram instead and missed all but the last trailing notes of the early afternoon call to prayer. He crossed the Galata Bridge and noticed that there seemed to be some commotion under the far end, but he passed on, paying no attention—such things were commonplace—walked on through the Egyptian Spice Bazaar and up the hill behind, through the seeming miles of cheap modern clothing, imitation leather jackets, Chinese sneakers, Javanese baseball caps, and finally, blessedly, through streets named for tradesmen—hammer-makers, wicker-makers, and weavers—to his destination at the back of his shop, among his beautiful rugs, to his desk and his accounts.

Yes, there was something about his friend Faruk that bothered him, but he mustn't let it bother him too much or for too long. This was discretion, this was wisdom and the better part, and if there were in it a touch of self-centeredness, that couldn't be helped. We are imperfect creatures in an imperfect world, and we must simply go about our business as best we can. Cheerfulness, that was the thing, and here was that great bear, Yoldaş—he couldn't call him Çınar Baba either—exuding warmth and humor and conversation and poetry and selling his books. There were two musicians with him today, one with a double drum between his knees and the other plucking a long-necked *saz*, and they continued to play as Erden and Yoldaş exchanged greetings and Erden explained about Yorgi Baba to the shoeshine boy.

When the boy was gone, Erden took the book from his case and gave it to Yoldaş and explained why Faruk had not come himself, but that he had wanted his friend to have the book today, its publication day, and he told him about the exhibit and where it was, across from Tünel, in case Yoldaş got up to that part of town. Yoldaş opened the package, carefully removing the brown wrapping paper and spreading it out on his stool with the flat of his hand. He then turned the book over, hefted it, and opened it to the title page where his friend's name appeared as translator. He then picked up one of his own books, and with the broadest smile possible, pointed out to Erden where Faruk's name appeared beneath his own. Oh, I know, I know, said Erden, Conrad and Çınar Baba, but Yoldaş wasn't listening. Again he hefted the Conrad, this time doubtfully. I don't think many people read so heavy a book, he said, fanning himself with his own. The reaction was genuine enough, but Erden thought that the accompanying smile was not without unpleasantness. He said his farewells to Yoldaş, then, and as he crossed Beyazıt Square, the *saz* player under the tree began to sing. He had a beautiful voice, and Erden paused to imagine how pleasant it would be to sit in the shade of that millennial tree, sipping tea and listening forever to such music and the tales and poems of Çınar Baba, so expressive of traditional scenes and ways; but the thought occurred to him that their being translated might have already brought a change in the poet that had engendered in him something arrogant and base.

ii

Erden's course now took him around the Beyazıt fire tower and into the Street of the Sea Corals, continuing through its name-change to the Hammer-makers, from there retracing his steps of earlier that afternoon down to the Spice Bazaar, which he circumvented, however, to cross the bird and flower market, staying in the open air. He looked forward, as he always did, to his leisurely trip home on the ferry. On the landing, he bought a copy of the evening paper, *Akşam*, and a copy of the *Turkish Daily News*, went on board, and found a seat on the open, upper deck in the stern. From where he sat, with the Galata Bridge at his back, he could look across the Golden Horn to the docks at Karaköy and Tophane, the site of the old Ottoman cannon foundry, where for centuries had been manufactured the finest cannons in the world, for the finest cannoneers, and his thoughts went back to a memory that had crossed his mind fleetingly earlier in the day, of the dervish monastery on Galip Dede Caddesi and of the cemetery where Galip Dede himself, the poet and mystic, is buried in close proximity to the celebrated and disreputable Bonneval Pasha, the renegade French nobleman who had once been commander of the Ottoman artillery. The story went that the Count Bonneval, fighting the Austrians in Italy in the armies of Louis XIV, had received a reprimand from one of the King's new bourgeois bureaucrats in Paris to the effect that his accounts showed a gross over-expenditure for champagne. This was but another illustration of the King's efforts to humiliate and subjugate the old aristocracy—he would soon have them wearing rubber swords at court—and it was the last straw for Bonneval, who promptly went over to the Austrians, whom he left because of a similar failure to recognize his merits and offered his services to the army of the Ottoman Sultan in Belgrade. He had converted to Islam, adopted a new identity as Kumbaracı (Cannoneer) Osman Ahmet, and finished his days wealthy and esteemed in Istanbul.

Strange, thought Erden, but he was now thinking not so much of Bonneval Pasha as of the fact that he owed his knowledge of the French side of the story to the American, Andre Malone, who was returning to Istanbul after so many years and whom they would see at dinner tonight. He remembered wondering why Malone should know anything at all about Bonneval, and had asked him. It appeared that there was a literary connection, and that Malone was something of a specialist. Malone told him that Bonneval had been married in France and that, during his youthful campaigns and lengthy stays away from home, his wife had written him a series of letters, many of them equal in literary merit to the letters of Madame de Sévigné. Bonneval had kept these letters and then abandoned them with some other valuables addressed to his wife from Austria, his last post before disappearing. When Bonneval had later resurfaced in Istanbul, he was described by a member of the French legation, who had known him earlier in France, as a man not so much changed, in spite of the new clothes, as one who had become more fully what his nature and career had intended him to be, a man with a great talent for war and no restraint.

Erden's thoughts were interrupted by the sound of the gangway being drawn up and the slightly dizzying sensation of being cut loose as the steamer slid from the quay and into the stream. As the bow had not yet begun to swing, he still had a fine view straight across to Üsküdar. As the sun began to drop in the western sky behind him over the ancient city that was his life, his town, his mood softened with the softening pink tones that the light now threw along the surface of the water towards the Asian shore. It was a feeling not unlike the onset of sleep, yet more like sadness, but before he could turn his thoughts inward to examine these effects, he noticed that a shaft of the declining light had settled on an upper window of the Maiden's Tower, causing it to blaze. The sight caused him to feel a sudden twinge, as at seeing a signal of distress. He imagined for a minute that the sight of the tower must have recalled the silly legend of the princess imprisoned there, but the legend was very silly and the twinge was real, and the distress, he realized, was his own. Now why had he suddenly felt that way? And at so insignificant a sight? Nor was the feeling of distress acute enough to be unsettling. Or was it? Perhaps he had been made aware of the passage of time, seeing Faruk again and changes in Faruk, or thinking of this man Malone, whom he had not known very well, but who brought back memories of what he had been, of what they all had been, was it twenty years ago? He had not changed, surely. He had drunk at the fountain of youth. No, he must have changed. It must be there, the change, mining him imperceptibly from the inside, perhaps, like Dorian Grey. And what had he accomplished, what had he become? The steamer had now moved fully into the stream, and Erden saw, from this changed angle of vision, that the light in the tower had gone out. And he realized, now that it was gone, that the light had seemed to beckon him towards his own distress, like fire, like the fascination of a radical leap into death or the unknown, and, perhaps as an act of self-preservation, of an instinctive recoil from the abyss, his mind evoked the scenic and consolatory picture of his itinerary home, with stops at Üsküdar, Kuzguncuk, Ortaköy, Bebek, and Kandilli.

The trip was unerringly the same, swift coming down, slow going home. Why should he not be a happy man? he thought, lighting up a cigarette and flipping the match up for the wind to carry over the starboard rail. Yakup had said he should marry, find a good woman to take care of him. That's what Yakup had done. Meryem was a good woman indeed, had given him two children, kept his house. But she was a good deal younger than he was, had been a dancer and kept herself in shape still by working out. Wouldn't it be natural for such a woman to have regrets? He admired and liked Meryem, but he wondered if she or her type would safely answer to Yakup's formula of "a good woman to take care of him." He doubted it. And he didn't think that that was what he wanted anyway. He took very good care of himself, thank you. And he had his Minna, who was at least as young as Meryem and who also kept herself in shape, thank you very much, but he was just as happy that she lived in Bebek and not with him and he knew he would never ask her to marry him. Nor did he think she'd accept if he did. She had better sense. She knew him for what he was, a confirmed bachelor—like Marco, he thought suddenly, and there it was again, that feeling of distress, if more acute this time, for Marco was beyond help, poor Marco, working all day at his crazy paintings and drinking until he couldn't paint anymore and going out to drink all night and wearing that crazy long black overcoat that fell to his ankles and that he wore in all seasons so people wouldn't see the sorry state of his clothes and which made him sweat like a wrestler when the weather began to warm up, and stink, oh God, did crazy Marco stink, till some kind soul got hold of him and took him to the public baths and gave his clothes to the quick laundry while Marco was being soaked and scrubbed and scraped and soaked again. They probably had to pay the attendants triple time, thought Erden, and he laughed out loud. Yes, when you went over the story that way, and that was surely the way to go over it, it had its comic side. And even Marco, all shaved and polished and buffed, would laugh at himself. No, there was no such thing as a hopeless case; so he hoped, did Erden, that someone would have got hold of Marco recently, because he was supposed to come to the dinner tonight, and you couldn't very well have him stinking up the place.

In spite of it all, he liked and even admired Marco, liked him with a brotherly affection, admired him for being so wholeheartedly something he, Erden, could never be. And what was that? A crazy fool! No, that was a dodge, a convenient misrepresentation to hide behind. Marco was the real thing, body and soul, a whole life consumed by his need to paint, an addiction overwhelming as a curse, and yet surely the one thing that had saved him since the destruction of his former life—his literary work, his wife, his child. It was a tale from which the healthy mind averted its gaze, as Erden knew, and yet its simple horror held a fascination. The brilliant young critic—praised for his early work by Lukacs, Bachelard, Auerbach—with a thousand pages of typescript unraveling the mystery of the French poet Arthur Rimbaud, at work on the finishing touches late at night in the old wooden house in Ortaköy, his wife and their baby asleep upstairs. He is smoking and, because he is smoking—the memory will haunt him forever—he doesn't smell the smoke. In fact he is unaware that his house is on fire until he feels the heat. He jumps from his chair, rushes to the door, and opens it upon a sheet of flame. He runs to climb the stair, and the stair collapses under him. From this point on, his mind is blank, a terrible and haunting blank. The image of the sheet of flame is succeeded by an image of a sheet of flame, but this one, seen from the street, is the stupendous torch his whole house has become. Never again. Never again. Erden had to wrench himself back from the image of the burning house. How must it be for Marco? he thought. It certainly does no good to dwell upon such things. Better to occupy the mind elsewhere. Better to paint. Better to adopt a philosophic attitude, cultivate a style, wear well-cut suits and madras cotton shirts and regimental ties, and cultivate one's garden in Kandilli. Better to have a smoke.

 The image was gone. Erden leaned back and stretched his legs straight out in front of him. He sighed and stood up and, buttoning the middle button of his jacket without thinking, walked over to the rail. The steamer had called at Üsküdar and was now making up the Asian shore of the Bosphorus for the landing at Kuzguncuk. The wind coming down the Bosphorus now from the Black Sea blew small whitecaps on the surface of the water, and as he looked across to the lights now coming on here and there in Beşiktaş and Ortaköy, he thought he smelled oysters as so often, smelling oysters, he thought of the sea. Kuzguncuk was where Yakup lived, with Meryem and their two children. Yakup told him he must build a house. Build a house, he had told him, build a house so you'll have some place decent to put that good woman you're going to marry to take care of you. He had a perfectly good apartment in Kandilli, but Yakup, having inherited some land and a fine old house in Kuzguncuk, had a somewhat more grandiose idea of how a man should be installed and, as there were no more fine old houses to be had—all of them now either treasured by their longtime owners or utterly dilapidated or long ago burned down—you had, according to Yakup, to build your own. Design it yourself, he said, and you'll learn something. You know the way you can tell something about a person by the way he lives—the furniture, the paintings he likes, his clothes—so how much more personal would be a house you had designed yourself. Erden remembered replying that, if Yakup's theory were drawn out to its logical conclusion, his house would open his privacy to public view, a glass house, no house at all. No, no, said Yakup, the house I mean is inside. The outside is a wall, a mask. But I'm not theorizing, Yakup had said, I do not theorize. All theories contradict themselves, as you have just shown. I do not theorize and I do not contradict myself and you know that I am right. Build a house for that good woman. Build it for yourself. It'll give you something to do, something to occupy your mind. You imagine yourself a very busy man who has much to occupy his mind. But you do not. You imagine you do, but all you really do is ride the ferry up and down the Bosphorus and smoke.

And they had laughed together at that, and Yakup was right in a way he might not have suspected. Erden did have a great feeling for places, places in which he felt comfortable, or anxious, or excited, or afraid, places that seemed to harbor lives of their own, deep, very old, mysterious, just out of reach, and the more fascinating for just that. Yakup Toledano's shop was one such place. He liked his own shop in the Bedesten, a much better place for business, but this was not an affair of business. There was something magical about Yakup's shop. It was to this spot, according to legend, that the son of the last Emperor of Trebizond had come to live after the fall of his empire to the Ottomans in 1461. The Prince had converted to Islam, for whose tenets he had long had a strong affinity, and he had been installed in splendor on this spot by Mehmet the Conqueror himself. But it was finally thought that he could not be trusted, and he was murdered here. His palace had long since disappeared, and the building that now stood in its place was falling apart and all but deserted, save for Yakup's shop and a flower merchant installed in the rear of the central courtyard, and two small apartments at either end of the fourth story in front.

The building was still an impressive structure. Under the Ottoman Empire and until the removal of the capital of Turkey to Ankara under the Republic, the building had housed the Russian Embassy. It had been built to impress and impose, and it must have done so in its glory days. It formed an almost perfect square, measuring about forty meters on each exterior side and about thirty along each side of the interior court. It was four stories high and, on the side facing the street, the first two stories were pierced by an arch wide enough to allow for the passage of carriages. The two huge panel doors that permitted this archway to be closed had long since disappeared, but a much smaller door, originally set into the right-hand panel for pedestrians, had survived. It stood at the rear of Yakup Toledano's shop, partially shielding a small wing where Yakup had his desk and kept his books. The door acted as a screen only. It didn't reach the ceiling nor the opposite wall, and you could pass around it easily to the office behind. It was beautifully carved and was pierced, at about eye level, by a small, barred window that could be opened and closed from the inside with a hinged shutter. The face of Yakup Toledano would sometimes appear at this window if he happened to be in his office when somebody came into the shop.

Erden remembered a summer evening not many years ago

when he and Yakup were standing in the courtyard in front of the shop. He would miss his usual ferry home, but he wasn't expected and there was no rush. The evening was beautiful—clear and warm—and he had the additional satisfaction of lighting up, because he wouldn't smoke in Yakup's shop any more than in his own. He had come over earlier that afternoon to see Yakup because he was his friend, in the first instance—the two men had been friends since their days as undergraduates at the American College in Bebek—and also because, though the two were not business partners, they enjoyed helping each other out. Each regularly recommended the other's shop and handed out the other's business card. They also lent each other merchandise which they displayed in their windows, paying each other small commissions on sales.

One would have thought that, with the better situation of Erden's shop and its greater exposure to public view, the advantage would be all on Yakup's side. But Yakup's business, though hidden away, had attracted a large and loyal following. His word was trusted absolutely, for both his honesty and his expertise. He was a member of an old and far-flung commercial aristocracy that could trace its history back to the expulsion from Spain in 1492. One branch of the family had accompanied the general exodus to Morocco, establishing themselves at Fez and, later, in Essaouira. From Essaouira, they had begun trading with the British, particularly with manufacturers in Manchester, to which place a nineteenth-century ancestor had emigrated with a *compagnon* named Disraeli, father of the future prime minister. Another branch of the family had fled to Holland. Some of these had moved on to Venice and from Venice into Venetian possessions in the eastern Mediterranean, where they had encountered relatives who had come directly from Spain many years before to Istanbul. Yakup had commercial contacts, then, all of them either directly with, or through, members of his own family, in Beirut, Alexandria, Venice, Genoa, Paris, Amsterdam, London,

Casablanca, Marrakech, and, since the war and 1948, in New York and Jerusalem. And it was through Yakup that Erden had established contacts in Paris and New York, and his exports to those two cities accounted for up to fifty percent of his annual income, depending upon the year.

So the arrangement had not been all to Yakup's advantage, and, contrary to appearances, it may have been the other way around. But Yakup does very well, very well, and he loves what he does and the way things are, including a somewhat imbalanced commercial arrangement with his friend; and he too has heard, as it would appear Erden has heard, to judge from the look on his face and his holding his breath so as not to make a sound, unless this is just the way he inhales the first drag on his smoke, the muted tones of an expertly played and nearby piano. Erden supposed, at first, that it must be a recording, but the pianist faltered for an instant and began again. He turned towards Yakup and was about to question him, but Yakup simply lifted a finger towards the glimmering illumination of a curtained fourth-story window behind which, evidently, somebody was practicing. The Countess, he said. What Countess? The pianist from the old Boem.

The Countess Nadia Drubetskaya had been born in Saint Petersburg somewhere around 1910, and her story was that of thousands. With the Revolution and the ensuing Civil War, in which her father had been killed, she and her mother had spent several rootless years, fleeing from one city to another until forced to emigrate. They did so in a steamer which brought them from Rostov across the Black Sea to Istanbul. The Russian community, very large at first, began to dwindle as many thought they could build a better life in Athens or Paris. But the new Turkish Republic was hospitable, and a nucleus stayed. They had quickly learned the languages of the city, Turkish and Greek, and most already spoke French and German as well as their native

Russian. The men drove taxis or went into commerce or taught fencing or gymnastics in the schools. The women too went into commerce or taught dance. Everybody opened restaurants and taught painting or the piano or the violin. Nadia's mother taught piano and dance and she doted upon her daughter. She had a dream of Nadia becoming a great pianist. Nadia had talent and energy. She was, in addition, very pretty, both as a girl and a young woman, and she was everybody's darling. She was a little spoiled, so that when the opportunity to marry and become the Countess Drubetskaya presented itself, she said yes. She loved the idea of being a countess. She thought she loved the Count, but she did not, and when the real thing came along in the unlikely form of an angular violinist, she didn't know what to do. She met her lover secretly. He loved her and, for him, that was enough. She loved him, but their love on the sly was not enough, and she didn't know what to do. She would kill herself. She would kill her lover first and then herself. She would kill the Count. But none of this was necessary. The Count found out and demanded a divorce. He played the outraged husband and got his divorce and had moved to Paris before you could turn around.

    The Count gone, the field was clear, and Nadia married the violinist and legally became Madame Nikolai Krinsky and his pianist. They started playing together at the Boem. Then they added the blind accordionist, Vladimir Popov, and finally the guitarist, who called himself Pavel Kirzanov, though there were those who said that couldn't be his real name. Kirzanov was an excellent musician, well educated, to judge by his speech and his knowledge of literature, and the best of *compagnons*; but he was evasive on the subject of his past. As for Nadia, she had found herself. Her mother was dead, her old life was gone, and her new life suited her; but she still allowed others to refer to her, for professional reasons, as the Countess Drubetskaya.

    This was the woman, then, whose piano could be heard, of a clear, warm summer evening in the courtyard in front of Yakup's shop. She had come to see Yakup shortly after her second marriage to sell some jewelry, and as Yakup had been doing business with the Russian community for years, he knew who she was. He could tell she was embarrassed. Ah Madame, he said to her, you do me a great service. I have been looking to acquire stones of such quality and cut for several months now. I have a client already waiting, in New York, he added, thinking to himself that the Countess need not worry about how such transactions actually worked. She need only receive her money, which she would, and trust that the jewels would not reappear in Istanbul society, which they would not.

Yakup was to see the Countess frequently thereafter, as he began to frequent the Boem with Mimi, sometimes bringing Erden, who had introduced the American and his wife, Sylvia, who had been first Malone and then Corrigan, and that character Dimitri, who was a colleague of Frank Corrigan's at the American College. But when her husband died and the great times at the Boem began to wane, the Countess wondered again what she would do. She still had a few jewels left, a couple of valuable icons, a wonderful old samovar, and a dozen or so other trinkets she could sell, but she loved these old possessions, and as long as her fingers and her brain were nimble, which they were, she would work. No, the trouble was not financial. The trouble was that she couldn't stand living in the old apartment, she said. Krinsky's ghost was everywhere. It's not that she minded thinking about Krinsky. In the afternoons and early evenings she would sit at her piano for hours and think of him and of their lives together and be only intermittently aware of what she was playing, though she used to think with a smile that whatever she played while thinking of Krinsky she would play extremely well. It wasn't these sessions that she couldn't stand, it was the sudden surprises. She would turn from her stove in the kitchen, for example, to reach for a certain object in a certain spot, and, as if conjured by the configuration of this gesture in accord with the configuration of this room, there he would be, tall and angular, his features drawn, his mouth open as if he wanted to speak and then no, only as if he were dead. And he would be gone. Or she would be just gathering up her purse and basket in the little hallway to go out shopping, thinking of butter and bread and onions and squash and a spiced sausage, perhaps, one of those wonderful *sucuk*, and a bottle of wine against the chill in the air, and she would hear the floor creak behind her and without turning she would know that he was there and he would, as he had so often done, drop her cloak onto her shoulders and the cold would run through her bones for very fear.

Call me a superstitious old fool, if you like, she had said to Yakup, but I must move. They were sitting in Yakup's office at the rear of the shop. He had supposed she might be in financial difficulty again, but the conversation had taken a quite different turn. She had heard that there might be rooms to let in this old building. She had been told so by her friend Roxelane Bishkek, whom she had known forever and whom she had been to visit a million times right up there, she said, gesturing towards the invisible southeast corner of the building where Madame Bishkek lived, and who had said she should talk to Yakup because Yakup collected the rent. Our little fiction, thought Yakup, because what he collected every month was only her small share of the building's electricity and water bills, budgeted by Yakup to result in the same charge every month throughout the year. Madame Bishkek was right, though, about there being another livable apartment in the building. It was on the fourth floor also, in the southwest corner, with the rooms laid out exactly as in Madame Bishkek's apartment, but reversed. The Countess had moved in over the course of the following week, her upright piano being the last thing to come. They had brought it in through one of her front windows, hoisted by a winch and pulley set up on the roof. The piano had been roughly handled, and the Countess had to get a tuner in, but by the end of the following week she and the apartment were ready for the housewarming party she had planned in order to get her new life, as she had put it, off to a festive start. She had a new job playing four evenings a week in the Cafe de Pera, and the neighborhood of her old friends Roxelane and Yakup gave her a renewed sense of optimism and security.

And I too was to be her friend, thought Erden, remembering the frequency with which the four of them had subsequently taken tea together, sometimes in one or another of the ladies' rooms, Fridays always with Madame Bishkek, often in Yakup's shop, and remembering also the unusual arrangement that Yakup had with Madame Bishkek and in which the Countess and he, Erden, would also participate. Erden had no idea how long Madame Bishkek had been living there, but Yakup told him that one day she had come to him with a painting that had been given to her by an admirer. It seems that she had grown tired of the painting, as she had grown tired of the admirer, and wanted to get rid of it. Yakup said that he would be happy to try and sell it for her, but that surely the blank space on her wall would be unsightly and a reminder. So he proposed that she go home with another painting chosen by herself from the stock he had in reserve in the back room. He was delighted to have Madame Bishkek, as later the Countess, get some pleasure and use out of objects that would otherwise languish in the dark. He liked to tell them they were really his partners, because the arrangement gave him the space he needed to enlarge his inventory. In addition, Madame Bishkek had an unusual circle of friends, almost exclusively men, loyal to her since the days of her youth, a nucleus of whom used to turn up every Thursday between the hours of five and seven, when the lady was officially "at home." Among them were writers and journalists, theatrical people of various sorts—actors, designers—a professor here, a politician there, and a banker whom she would remember always for having said to her one morning: I know I should be thinking about money, but I'm not. The banker was openly admiring of the lady's taste and of a wonderful silver samovar in particular. The lady explained to him, without embarrassment, that the samovar was on loan and that he could surely have it if he wanted it. He had only to talk to Yakup. Yakup had later made the sale and the lady her commission. They had both laughed heartily at the unexpected turn their arrangement had taken, Madame Bishkek remarking: I still love them all dearly, and they still pay. Rumor had it that when she was sixteen she had been the friend of Mustafa Kemal, become Atatürk by then, during one of his visits to Istanbul, and that it was he who had first called her Roxelane. Madame Bishkek remembered these things and they nourished her moments of solitude, but her temperament was too buoyant for nostalgia. Her memories were a source of amusement for her, and her friendship was a tonic for the Countess. So the arrangement—they never referred to it otherwise—was extended to include the Countess and to Erden, who was only too happy to lend the ladies rugs—*kilim* or the flashier *cicim*—knowing that even the ladies' foreign visitors knew the custom of the country and left their shoes at the door.

The two ladies had indeed known each other for a number of years—if not exactly forever—but their new proximity deepened their friendship to the point where they reacted to the world like sisters, knowing each other's thoughts and opinions in advance and, more often than not, sharing them. They argued, of course, but the subject of their disagreement was almost always to decide who between them had been the first to come up with some idea. Madame Bishkek always claimed to be the one who had first thought that the Countess should give a party. It was certainly she who decided that the party should take place on a Friday and that it should start at her place. Between six and eight, she would serve drinks and *meze*—cheese dips and hummus, *börek*, pistachios, snow almonds and the like. A huge goulash they could prepare the day before. The salad also could be prepared in advance, needing only to be mixed. The only thing requiring last-minute attention would be the pilaf. The whole party would then troop down the hall for dinner at the Countess's on the stroke of eight. The effect of opening the door upon Nadia's new apartment was calculatedly theatrical. Erden, carrying a case of wine, was among the first to come into a closed-off and darkened entrance hall. The hall was allowed almost to fill and the guests to begin asking themselves what was going on, when a broad set of double doors opened upon a room which compared favorably, in its effect, to a combination of the Egyptian Spice Bazaar and the Bedesten. There was no electric light, but aromatic candles everywhere and half a dozen antique oil lamps. Polished silver, copper, and brass on the walls and furniture threw the light with bewildering effect. The room was rectangular in shape and from the ceiling in the approximate center of either end there hung two mobiles which the ladies had constructed of light wire and wings of folded aluminum foil, which fluttered and turned like so many bright butterflies, imparting to the illumination a dizzying effect of motion, as if the room had been set afloat.

The reaction of the guests, already giddy from their two hours down the hall, was that of schoolchildren let loose, and the dinner got off to a riotous start. They toasted the ladies together and separately. They toasted the goulash, they toasted the pilaf, they toasted the *rakı* and the wine. They toasted the mobile and then the mobile, and the spangles and the angles and the bangles, and each other by title: la Comtesse Largesse and the Rose of Bishkek, Yacoop's Troops, and the Malone Ranger, and Erden's Merry Men, and He-Tree Dimitri, and Frank's Pranks, and Faruk's Spooks, and Marco's Moult Magic Marks, though Marco hadn't shown up, and the Malone Eagle, and Miss Malonely Hearts, and Frank Stank, and so on while they danced and talked of other things, and Rank Frank's Pranks Stank and, as had to be, Baloney Maloney, and Marco Sharko, though he hadn't shown up, and so on while they danced and talked of other things, and a lady of distinguished bearing who had accompanied Faruk rose unsteadily to inform the company at large that when she was a little girl at school she had been lifted up and kissed by the great Atatürk, and Roxelane Bishkek lifted her glass in the ensuing silence and said, "Me too," and shrieked with laugher so violently that she would have fallen off her chair if Erden hadn't caught her, and the conversation resumed and at last the Countess went to the piano and took up the opening strains of "Moscow Nights" and, as they were all remembering the old days at the Boem and had paused to listen, there was a knock at the door. The Countess stopped playing. She felt a chill. Nobody said a word. What must the person outside the door imagine had brought the party to a sudden halt? The Countess knew. The person didn't knock again, and the Countess knew she must go to the door. She rose and walked to the door and opened it, and there he was, the tall, angular figure, and she couldn't help herself, she screamed. She screamed and the figure in the hallway, aghast, turned and fled and Erden put his arm around her, holding her up, and he took a step forward into the hall and shouted after the retreating figure: Marco! We've been waiting for you. Marco! Come back!

iii

The steamer had now left the quay at Kuzguncuk and was making its way crabwise across the Bosphorus to Ortaköy. At the port rail, Erden now found himself partially sheltered from the Black Sea wind that seemed to be freshening. He managed to light his cigarette on the second try, however, and letting the wind carry the dead match from his hand, he remembered that Marco's brief appearance had put an end to their evening and his mind returned to the moment when, in front of Yakup's shop, he had heard the piano music start and stop and start again. Yakup had walked him across the courtyard and out onto İstiklal Caddesi that evening, talking all the while of his arrangement with Madame Bishkek and the Countess and suggesting that he join them, which Erden said he would, and of the expressive and personal relations that people maintain with beautiful objects, and he returned to his old theme of Erden building a house and he suddenly brought them both up short with the inspired suggestion that Erden build a summer house, a weekend house, on that little island Erden had spoken about—what was it called?—Cunda, that was it, just off the Aegean coast above Ayvalık.

That was it, all right. Cunda. Erden couldn't afterwards get the idea out of his mind. His father had first taken him there years ago scouting for rugs among the nomad Yörük living in the mountainous regions of the Troad and as far south as Bergama. He remembered his father one time telling him that they were now going to visit a magical place. His father, for all his practical business sense, had these sudden outbursts of pure enthusiasm and it was this quality in his father that Erden found he most liked to recall. They were going to Ayvalık, or not exactly Ayvalık, but his son should know that at the conclusion of the War of Independence, there occurred that exchange of populations, Turkish and Greek, that had brought them to Turkey from Komotini. The Greeks of Ayvalık and the surrounding area as far as Edremit were shipped off to mainland Greece, and as they had outnumbered the Turks in the region by something like two hundred to one, there was a great deal of land and whole villages left absolutely untended and empty. This situation couldn't be permitted to last, because the area was enormously rich in olive trees, thousands upon thousands of hectares of the finest olive trees in the world. The region also had a long and irregular coastline, and another source of wealth had been from fishing. So what had happened, and Erden's father had permitted himself to observe that it was one of the few intelligent applications of the resettlement plan, was that Turkish olive growers had been brought in from Thrace and more olive growers and fishermen from the islands of Mytilene and Crete. The place they were going to, the island of Cunda just north of Ayvalık, had been resettled by fishermen from Rethymnon, many of whom still spoke Greek, just as they did.

Erden had not been back to Cunda since his father's death, but he remembered the village and the island well and he had spoken of it to Yakup. All right, he thought, I'll go back and have a look. He had gone back, and back again. He rented a little room over a restaurant run by an escapee from the hustle of Istanbul. The room was simplicity itself and just to his taste, a plain board floor with a faded small *kilim*, a marine chart of the bay and islands on the wall, a wooden writing table and a straight-backed chair, and a balcony overlooking the restaurant terrace and the fishing port. The food downstairs was excellent. The village market was always well supplied, and the village population—the few merchants, the fishermen, and their families—seemed to have been formed of an ideal fusion of the best qualities of the two races, the quick wit of the Greeks, the warmheartedness of the Turks. Had he made it all up? Was this not paradise? No he hadn't and yes it was, and it was in such a mood that, on his third visit, Erden went to see the mayor to find out if there were still an unoccupied house in the village or if somebody might be willing to sell him one. It seemed there was a house that had never been occupied—not since the Greeks had left—because of the ruinous condition in which it had been found. It would have to be torn down and completely rebuilt. The floors and the very walls were caving in. It's my fate, thought Erden. Yakup told me to build, so I will build.

The ruin was beautifully located at the top of the village at the end of a narrow curving street lined on either side by well-kept, whitewashed houses. Its situation would later remind Yakup very much of his own in Kuzguncuk. Erden's plan was to rebuild in such a way that his house would conform to the dimensions and style of its predecessor and so also of its neighbors and the village at large. The interior, however, would be of his own design:

one floor to be a single, high-ceilinged, open room for living, dining, and cooking, two more floors each with two bedrooms and a bath, and a terrace on the roof from which you looked out over the tiled roofs of the village and the port, and from which, at night, you could see the lights of Ayvalık across the bay. It took a year to build the house, with visits averaging twice a month for Erden to coordinate the work and keep it going. His first guest had been Minna, he remembered, not so very long ago, and then Yakup and Mimi, and Frank and Sylvia, and then everybody all at once for a memorable weekend, and Sylvia had said she thought she could live in Cunda forever. Erden liked having guests and it was exciting being there with Minna, and when they were alone they would make love all over the place and on the roof terrace on warm nights under the stars. But the extra excitement with Minna came because she would always be only a guest, because he also liked being there alone.

So that was it, thought Erden, I should have been a monk, not a Christian monk of course with their crazy vows of chastity, but a Muslim monk, a dervish. The only trouble with that plan is that I don't believe in God. Can you imagine God grabbing for his notepad and thinking, I must write all this down—Ahmet wants a skateboard and little Heidi wants never to get breast cancer and the Dalai Lama wants the atom bomb and Mr. Momboto has finally remembered to thank me for the rain and blah, blah, blah. It's patently absurd. So what synthesized the first amino acids? Lightning. And where did the lightning come from? Or the big bang? An infinite regress is what Frank Corrigan called that and an illustration of the madness hiding within the concept of causality, which is nothing more than a creature of Western scientific rationalism and no absolute and Whoop, Whoop, Whoop, said the whistle as the steamer approached the landing at Ortaköy, and Whoop again and Erden noticed that a crowd had already gathered on the deck below to disembark, pressing forward at the rail and even where there was no rail, and two sailors appeared and ordered them to step back, which they pretended to make an effort to do, but as soon as the steamer was within a meter of the quay some of the younger men began to leap ashore, followed by the older men and the pregnant women and the halt, the lame, and the blind, or so was the effect, so that by the time the two sailors had wrestled the gangplank into place, it was useful only to a young couple with a baby who came aboard. Chaos, he thought with a touch of anger, some day the whole mob will spill into the water and be crushed. No system, no discipline.

No, he thought, I must have my monkish little room, my monkish little life, if that's what it is, and I will treasure my friendship with Yakup and his family and their world and keep my Minna for as long as I can, and he caught himself looking down with interest at the young couple that had just come aboard. They were obviously of humble means and may well have been carrying all their worldly goods in the single scuffed and ancient suitcase that the young man had set down at his feet. The young woman held the baby to her breast in the hollow of a shawl wound over one shoulder and around her back. The young man held her and the baby tightly to him, for the steamer was swinging now towards Kandilli and once again exposing the port side to the Black Sea wind, but they did not move to shelter because the young man was waving goodbye to a fast-receding figure on the quay. Erden turned to see who that person might be, an old man, evidently, hunched and immobile and now almost indistinguishable in the surrounding dark. He was perhaps the young man's father, and perhaps they would never see each other again.

Erden drew on his cigarette, then, and turned away, wondering at this small drama of his own imagining, and he was struck by the resemblance of the young family on the deck below to a poster illustration of Heroic Young Turkey that the propagandists in Ankara had been peddling for years, a young family just like this one, facing the future, and the wind, with resolute confidence. His recollection of the poster appealed to something in him that would have liked to remain detached and cynical, but as his eye fell again on the scuffed old leather suitcase at the young man's feet and the deplorable condition of his shoes, the little drama renewed itself in his imagining. Where were they going? Had the young man failed in the city and were they going back to some lonely village on the Anatolian steppe? And what of the old father left standing on the quay? What will he do? He'll dry his tears and forget about the whole thing, he thought, like somebody else I have in mind, and go home to his flat for a quick look at the evening papers, which he's been too preoccupied thus far to do, and a quick shower, maybe, before driving over to İstinye to get Minna and take her out to a festive dinner with the gang at Boncuk.

3
YAKUP

i

Yakup stood for a moment looking across the courtyard at the now empty archway through which his two friends had disappeared, and he imagined Erden making his way along İstiklal Caddesi towards Tünel and the bookshop and stopping for a look at the window display. He had meant to tell him where he'd found the ship's log. It was quite a story. He'd try to remember to tell him tonight.

Faruk had been fretting over this opening like an expectant mother. The *Almayer's Folly* was, as he had said, the first of his translations that might actually sell.

Whatever you might think about Faruk—his bouts of arrogance, his moody unpredictability—you had to admit he was a worker. He had his weekly column in the *Daily News*, in addition to his regular work as a reporter and a member of the editorial staff, and yet he managed to find time to turn out these translations, none of them easy. The Yeats had been not only difficult to translate but had required a lot of careful footnoting, historical and political. The publisher had required, for example, that Faruk supply a lengthy explanation as to why the publication, in Turkey, of poems containing references to "Byzantium" was not an insult to the national honor. Then there had been Joyce's *Ulysses*, published in two volumes of seven hundred pages each to accommodate the notes, and now the Conrad, with an introduction but no footnotes, which was certainly one reason why this might be the first book actually to sell.

As a faithful subscriber to the *Daily News*, Yakup had firsthand knowledge of Faruk's work as a journalist, and he admired it. But he had read none of Faruk's book-length works, and the favorable opinion he had of his friend's abilities as a translator was based upon his reading of a few poems in one of the bilingual chapbooks published by Çınar Baba. Although Yakup read fiction from time to time, especially on Mimi's recommendation, admired Shakespeare unreservedly, and owned copies of the Bible in English, Turkish, French, German, Latin, Russian, Ladino, Hebrew, and Greek, his principal intellectual interests lay in enriching his already encyclopedic knowledge of antiques and in the closely related field of history. He had a fondness for the study of history that was altogether personal. There were threads running through his life and family history which, if followed back, led to surprising finds.

There was, for example, on a small side table in his living room in Kuzguncuk, a framed, yellowing photograph of his grandfather and grandmother standing under an enormous olive tree among the ruins of Gortine on the south shore of the island of Crete. The year was 1898, and they were on their honeymoon. They had been married in Rethymnon, where both their families had been established since the Turks had chased the Venetians out of that city in 1645. Both families had originally come to Crete from Istanbul, and the Toledanos traced their history back to 1492, when Sultan Beyazıt extended the hospitality of the Ottoman Empire to the Jews expelled by Their Most Catholic Majesties from Spain. His grandmother was a Nasi and a direct descendent of that celebrated Joseph Nasi who had been appointed Lord of Tiberias in Palestine by Sultan

Süleyman in 1561 and Duke of Naxos in 1566 by Sultan Selim II, also known as Selim the Sot, after whose death, a short eight years later from drink, Joseph Nasi's influence had waned. Nasi had retired soon after to his beloved country house, the Villa Belvedere, which had stood somewhere on the very hill where Yakup now sat, perhaps occupying this very spot. It pleased Yakup to think it might be so, and he thought again of the photograph of that young couple and of that ancient olive tree, which his father told him had been believed by the Greeks to be older than any of the ruined buildings on the site of Gortine, which would have made the tree well over two thousand years old. He doubted it was true, but there was a romantic fatalism in the story that appealed to him, as such stories appealed also to his friend Erden, and he wondered quite seriously what might be the age of the olive tree growing right here in the middle of his courtyard. He had heard of millennial olive trees. Their age had been determined scientifically. The trunk of the tree under which he was now sitting measured a good four meters across at the base and had been almost certainly here in Joseph Nasi's day. Strange that the idea had never occurred to him before, that it had been waiting to be stirred up by his recollection of a yellowing photograph that stood in a simple silver frame on a table in the living room in Kuzguncuk. We are a proud people, he thought, and we have a right to be. We carry our histories with us, histories that link us to near and distant relatives in the four corners of the earth and to the near and distant past. And the history that we are rooted in is not the history of families only, of Nasis and Toledanos, but of the nations and empires and cultures and religions of the West, and we have been builders of that history.

When you learn European history as the history of your own family, it becomes palpable. He remembered sitting with his father one evening in the living room in Kuzguncuk and his father picking up the old photograph and, with it, the thread of the story, as if there had not been a break of several weeks: Of course, as you probably know, his father had said, Joseph Nasi was a Christian. A Christian? How was that possible and how could he possibly know? But his father was a man of infinite tact, and an explanation was sure to follow. Oh yes, he was from a family of *conversos*, which is to say that he was of those Jews who put on the trappings of Catholicism rather than be exiled or killed. Unlike the Toledanos, who had accompanied the Moors in their long retreat south and left Spain with them at the fall of Grenada, the Nasis had stayed behind, and like thousands and thousands of other Jews in the same predicament, they had accepted conversion. Publicly they were Catholics, but privately they remained Jews and continued to practice Judaism secretly, and one of the driving forces behind the Inquisition was to find them out. Joseph Nasi decided to escape, first to Antwerp, then to Istanbul, where he was finally able to declare himself openly a Jew. It must have been a very moving time for him, a time of great release and the first real freedom he had known. Turkey had never persecuted the Jews. Turkey may be the only country in the world that has never persecuted the Jews, and was the first country in the world to recognize the new state of Israel in 1948. Yakup remembered listening to his father and feeling suddenly proud to be a Turk, prouder than he had ever been listening to one of those insipid history lectures at school. Perhaps he could give a talk on Joseph Nasi to the class and end the story just as his father had done, so that the old slogans of *hürriyet* and *istiklal*, freedom and independence, would mean something. But he knew that for his Turkish classmates he was not a real Turk, but a Jew, and he decided to keep Joseph Nasi for himself. He was a Jew and he was proud of it, but he thought of himself as a Turk as well, as completely and sincerely as he had felt that rush of pride just moments ago, and Yakup now, leaning against his millennial tree, remembered the anguish he had felt as a boy thinking how unfair it was that he should be two people instead of one, like everybody else.

Yakup rose then from where he had been seated against the olive tree and stood still for a moment arching his stiffened back. He clasped his hands behind and walked meditatively and without seeing it towards the old gateway leading from the courtyard out to İstiklal Caddesi. I'm getting old, he thought, stiff in the back and portly in front. Set in my ways, the children grown and about to leave the nest, married for over twenty years to a woman fifteen years my junior. Now what? And it rather amazed him that the answer to this potentially troublesome question should appear in the person of old Joseph Nasi sitting in the garden of his beloved Villa Belvedere. He sits in the shade of a spreading olive tree. At an angle to his right, two rows of blossoming Judas trees define an avenue leading to the rear of the villa and a terrace where two women are conversing over tea, one of whom must be his wife, though at this distance he can't quite make the figures out. He is wearing a loose-sleeved caftan and a turban and he is smoking a light mixture of hashish in a water pipe. To his left and below, for this is the view for which the villa is named, the lower reaches of the Bosphorus are spread out. A graceful sloop with a billowing lateen sail has emerged from the Golden Horn and is making for the Asian shore, heeling over and advancing smartly under the impulse of a freshening Black Sea wind. The light over the water and the hill has softened to a diaphanous pink. A beautiful spring day is drawing to a close. A book of Spanish poetry lies open on his lap. His meditations are elsewhere, but we shall never know what they are, because they are interrupted by the arrival of a man in European costume, looking very much like a sixteenth-century Erden, who says to him: My Lord, today is Celebration Day and you are expected to dine this evening with Faruk and Marco and Malone. Damn, thought Yakup. He'd much rather go home to Kuzguncuk and to Mimi and the children and the fine old house that he loved almost as much as he might have loved this ideal Villa Belvedere.

So Andre Malone was back in Istanbul. How long has it been? Fifteen years? Twenty years? A long time, anyway. He remembered Malone from their first meeting because he spoke such good French, which was unusual for an American, or whatever he was. Sylvia had said he was half French, but what she had actually said was that he was all Irish and half French, which might have been true enough in one sense but not in the other, so where were you? He remembered that they had bought a samovar, a quite beautiful old Russian samovar that had been sold to him by the guitarist who called himself Pavel Kirzanov, but who may not have been Pavel Kirzanov because Pavel Kirzanov was a character in a novel by Ivan Turgenev. And they had had evenings out together more than once in Zambak Street with the gypsies and the Grand Cafe de Pera and the Çiçek Pasajı and Boncuk, like tonight, and the bar at the Pera Palace and at the good old Boem in its heyday.

He remembered one night when he had gone to the Boem early with Mimi and he had wondered, on entering, who had reserved the long table by the orchestra and Dimitri had arrived a short time later with a large group and the table was his. There had been two or three very pretty young women in the party, but they had left early with their young men and he could tell even from where he was seated at the back of the room that Dimitri had gone into a funk. He knew Dimitri and was sure that he had hoped to preside over an extended feast, but what do you do when half of your party just has a nibble here and a sip there and then gets up and leaves the evening in ruins? If you're lucky—and Yakup remembered being fascinated as by the events of a play—your funk is dispelled and your good humor restored by the miraculous arrival of Frank's Pranks and Erden's Merry Men and Magic Marco and the Malone Ranger and your energies rekindled by the glimmer and shine of Sylvia, completely effacing your loss. What loss? Oh, he knew Dimitri and he saw him gather Sylvia up and he saw Marco follow them to the end of the table to embrace Elena, who perhaps alone among them would remember Marco's wife.

And all that seems so very long ago, thought Yakup, walking slowly in the courtyard still. That had been a time in their lives when Mimi was still new to Turkey and to Istanbul and she had needed diversions and, while she was still learning the language, the company of her compatriots. That time had passed, however, and the party fever had seemed to cool, and he and Mimi had settled down to a less agitated routine that apparently suited them both. Malone's return now seemed to require a celebration, which he could understand without being terribly pleased. Yakup paused for a moment to arch his now much loosened back again, hands clasped behind, and his gaze rose to the corner of the building where the Countess lived and he thought also of Madame Bishkek. They can't go on so very much longer, he thought. They had become so inseparable in his mind that it seemed impossible that one should die without the other, and yet it surely would be so. The Countess was probably the older, but not by very much, and Madame Bishkek hadn't exactly spared herself. The wonder of it was that they both looked so good, and with a smile he thought to himself, when I'm as old as they are, I'll be dead.

But Mimi will not change at all, and he realized that it was impossible for him to imagine Mimi grown old, indeed impossible for him to imagine her as other than she was the first time he had seen her in the middle of a potato field on the Dror kibbutz about ten miles west of Jerusalem. In those days, he had been half in love with Silvana Mangano, the Italian actress whom he had admired with her skirts tucked up and water to her knees in *Bitter Rice*. The other half of him laughed along with the Italian press at the domesticated, pasta-loving woman who was known to gain as much as fifty pounds between films. But on that day in Dror, as he looked out across the potato field—not the most romantic setting in the world—there suddenly she was, the Silvana

Mangano of *Bitter Rice*, her skirts pulled back between her legs and tucked up under her belt at the small of her back, thighs of marble like the goddess herself, and when she stooped he held his breath, though he couldn't have told you exactly what he'd seen, if anything at all. At one point she had stood and stretched her back and seen him looking at her, and she had laughed at him and waved. She was obviously at ease with herself and her surroundings and happy to be alive on this glorious fall day, harvesting potatoes for the revolutionary new Jewish state. She seemed to him a perfect symbol of modern Israeli womanhood and she had surprised him that evening in the kibbutz dining room when she said she was American. As it turned out there were other young Americans there, as there were all over Israel, along with Jews from all over the world, so that what had at first surprised him seemed fitting after all. Her name was Meryem, but she had always been called Mimi. She was young and tan and graceful and full of health. She wore her long, dark hair twisted into a knot at the back of her head. She had gray-green eyes that smiled as her full lips parted and smiled and flashed at you that perfect set of American teeth. He didn't think he'd ever seen teeth like that, and he laughed at her, knowing that she couldn't know why. And she had laughed back and he had laughed again and the two of them had laughed together for the wrong reasons, but they weren't the wrong reasons after all. He hadn't felt so buoyantly giddy in years, and the thought occurred to him that if she touched him he would disappear. She later told him that all during that first week she had felt so moved that she thought at any moment she might cry.

  He couldn't imagine what he had done to be so lucky. He had come to Israel on a business trip, not entirely routine, but a business trip nevertheless. A London Toledano had written to him a year before saying that he was going to emigrate and that they would be in touch. He had managed within a few weeks of his arrival in Jerusalem to locate and buy a building in the old city, within the walls, and had since built up a respectable inventory of new and antique jewelry and copperware. He had written to Yakup, inviting him down. They might work out some very interesting exchanges between Jerusalem and Istanbul, and Yakup could visit the new country. The idea of visiting Israel had been maturing in Yakup's mind since his reception of the first letter. He could visit this reincarnation of the Jewish homeland. He would live briefly with his relative in the holy city of Jerusalem, whose walls were the work of the Ottoman Sultan Süleyman, the patron of his ancestor Nasi. He would visit a kibbutz, this new experiment in communal farming, and he would rent a car and drive up to Tiberias where Nasi, as governor, had established a community for Jewish refugees from Europe almost four hundred years ago. So there would be plenty to see and do, with all the requisite pilgrimages, and he would not be bored and there would certainly be some commercial advantage to be gained, and all this had been expected, but Mimi had been the perfect surprise, and Mimi had changed his life. He had thought he might never marry, and now his fate had presented itself in the form of this exquisite young woman standing alone in the middle of a potato field and then later right next to him on a hillside in Tiberias. Like her, he had felt suddenly that he might cry, as the idea of a life together with her began to formulate itself in his mind. He knew she would love Istanbul and the house in Kuzguncuk and his family and friends. And they would make new friends and have children, oh yes, they would make love and have children and make love and it was as if he were making love to her already and he gasped and turned to her and caught her in his arms and said, Marry me, you must marry me, and she had said, I will. And they held each other and they kissed and then they kissed again and for a long time and he could feel the whole length of her body against his and he knew he was going to have that difficulty in walking gracefully which will occur to men under such circumstances and she said, Oh my, and then she said, Do you think we should be married very soon? and they had laughed like crazy. They were crazy still, and he could hardly believe his luck.

ii

Yakup looked up from his meditative stroll around the courtyard, as if surprised to find himself there. In the old times of the Byzantines, this had been open countryside, and probably the first building on the spot had been the villa of the Prince of Trebizond, razed after his murder by the Sultan in 1462. The site had then been chosen a century later by Joseph Nasi for his Villa Belvedere. Now here he was, Yakup Toledano, strolling around on the same hilltop, surrounded by the noise and bustle of a modern metropolis and by the sagging and all but uninhabited remains of an old building, the Russian Embassy in the days of the Empire, and as he looked up towards the sky overhead, as Joseph Nasi must have looked up four hundred years ago, the diaphanous pink began to recede westward before the thickening approach of the night, and Yakup felt descend upon him a mood of longing and loss and, walking slowly back to his shop, he gave his thoughts over to an effort to understand its source.

From the moment he had proposed marriage to Mimi, he had known with perfect certainty that he must return to his real home in Istanbul. With perfect clarity he had visualized the two of them at home in the house in Kuzguncuk, with their children, building a new life upon the old. And it was the essence of his connectedness with the old life and culture, a culture that he could not imagine himself without, that seemingly now, for the first time, he was trying consciously to understand. The power of his first love for Mimi had blinded him then to the fact that he had found life in the new state of Israel repugnant to his sensibility. It was all so young, so militant, so forward-looking and progressive, so—materialistic; he couldn't find a better word. And nobody had seemed more militant than some members of the ultra-Orthodox religious community he had spoken to in Jerusalem. Their religion no longer seemed to be of a piece with their general culture, which celebrated power, material progress, and war. Their religion was compartmentalized and directed towards the afterlife, where perhaps, according to a rationalist philosophy, it properly belonged. But the irony was that he, Yakup, not at all a religious man and caring nothing for the afterlife, was pained to see the role of religion so reduced. For Yakup, religious ceremonial was integral to Jewish cultural life, as was also, he now realized, a profound and irremediable sense of exile and longing. Since the disastrous failure of the Jewish revolt and the dispersion of the Jews over the face of the Western world, the one hope had been summed up in the slogan "Next year in Jerusalem." So for almost two millennia the Jew had been suspended between the two emotions of pain for Jerusalem lost and aspiration towards a Jerusalem to be one day regained. It was a dynamic equilibrium suspended between two ideals that mirrored each other across the millennia, the one a creation of the historical imagination, the other a spiritual utopia whose dwelling was in an ever-receding horizon of time. And Yakup supposed, indeed he was quite sure, that you didn't have to be a Jew to feel this way, but, he added to himself with a smile, it helped.

So that was it. On a very pragmatic level, once you gave a Jew his homeland back and thus stripped him of the attributes that formed his sensibility, he wasn't a Jew anymore. The Israeli would ask you, quite correctly, what did you expect? A country without mortgages or garbage collectors or cancer or what? But by asking you, quite correctly, such obvious questions, he would show you also that he is perfectly incapable of grasping the idea that Israel should be no country at all. He remembered asking in Tiberias to see the grave of the great twelfth-century Jewish philosopher Maimonides—born in Cordoba, buried in Tiberias—and receiving only blank stares. Mimi, bless her heart, understood all this perfectly well. Mimi would even tell him what the book might be that Joseph Nasi has been reading under the olive tree and what his thoughts, as the sloop turns sharply into the wind, luffs, and heels over onto the starboard tack. Perhaps she will tell me it is the work of one of his contemporaries, thought Yakup, Fray Luis de Leon, the *converso* poet, his translation of "The Song of Solomon" or Psalms:

> By the rivers of Babylon, there we sat down,
> Yea we wept when we remembered Zion.
> Upon the poplars in the midst of her
> We hung our harps,
> For how could we sing the Lord's song
> In a foreign land?
> If I forget thee, O Jerusalem,
> Let my right hand wither,
> If I set not Jerusalem above my highest joy!

Yakup rehearsed the familiar words in his mind, at once sad and consolatory, and he realized as he sat again at his desk in the rear of the shop that the afternoon had grown quite dark. He leaned forward and pulled the beaded cord of his lamp, and there was the green rectangle of his writing blotter, the renewed weight of the desk and walls, the ceiling, his own weight upon the chair beneath him, weight and weight again in all its implacable material reality, which was for him no reality at all. The strangeness of the visible world around him was, momentarily, the strangeness of death. The objects seemed utterly alien to each other and to himself, and it took a moment before his mind, as if returning from another world, was able to reconstitute and reimpose upon them their various roles and their familiarity. Never before had he been so clearly conscious of activating the intellectual equipment by means of which he was able to chart his course through an otherwise alien world. Either his mood or this realization made him feel slightly dizzy, as if he had forgotten to eat lunch—had he forgotten to eat lunch?—or as if the mixture of hashish in the water pipe had not been so weak as he had thought, and he imagined a conversation between his material and his spectral selves, the former, accusatory: My friend, beware, you are living in a dream; and the latter, with an urbane and resigned simplicity uncannily reminiscent of his friend Erden: My dear fellow, you have found me out.

Feeling now quite pleased with himself, and to be, as it were, in such good company, Yakup rose from his desk and crossed the front room and turned the sign in the display window around from *açık* to *kapalı*, open to closed. He was about to close the door in preparation for locking a few things up in the safe, but he decided to step outside for a moment to breathe the air that had sweetened with the coming of evening and he heard, then, the familiar and welcome music of the call to prayer. He had no recollection of having heard the afternoon call, but the daytime noises were usually enough to muffle it in this part of town. He stood for a moment, breathing the air and listening to that plaintive music, which he loved. He looked around the worn old courtyard and upwards to where small lights had gone on in the apartments of the Countess and Madame Bishkek. The *müezzin* finished his song and Yakup, looking at his watch and remembering his date with Mimi at the Pera Palace and their dinner with Malone, thought to himself, Everything is going to be all right. He went back inside the shop and removed a display of antique jewelry to the safe in the back room, switched off the lights, and locked the door. He crossed the courtyard and the arched tunnel of the carriage gateway and turned left on İstiklal Caddesi. Everything is going to be all right, he thought, at least we can keep on hoping so.

In anticipation of his meeting with Mimi, he had been reminded of his son İshak, who was nineteen and in his second year of studying economics at the American College and whom they were expecting to see tonight. İshak had taken a room for himself near the College in Etiler to avoid the commute from Kuzguncuk and, though they saw him almost every weekend and had perfect trust in his standards and integrity, they worried. Yakup especially worried about İshak's politics, not because he had any politics of his own, but because he was afraid of İshak getting himself into trouble. Most of İshak's professors had been trained abroad and, though Turks themselves, saw Turkey through the eyes of the European left. He had met some of them through Frank Corrigan, and they seemed to him a doctrinaire and arrogant lot. They talked of nothing but their own superior understanding of the world, which they represented in exclusively economic terms, knew next to nothing about history or art, and were conspicuously absent from the protests they inspired and where their disciples among the students were sent forth to have their heads bashed in by the police. İshak could talk as much as he wanted. In fact, Yakup enjoyed their weekend battles, and he was happy to see that İshak, though certainly animated by all the enthusiasm of his youth, was capable of listening. They agreed on many things: social justice, equality before the law, safeguards for the environment. They disagreed, sometimes heatedly, on the importance of the cultural context. But let them disagree. Let İshak disagree. Let İshak grow angry and arrogant and doctrinaire, which he had never done, but if he ever did, let him do so in Kuzguncuk, and let him not go out to get his head bashed in by the police.

He understands, thought Yakup. He's a good boy and he'll be careful for our sakes if not for his own. It would be unmanly for him to be careful for his own sake, wouldn't it? Aren't we a silly lot, with our machismo and the other roles we play? But what would we be otherwise? Nothing at all. With no roles to play we would be nothing but brute beasts living off muck. And so instead of being a brute beast living off muck, I have become that paradigm of the cultured human being, an antique dealer. That paradigm of the cultured human being? inquired the voice, And who else are you trying to kid? You're right. I might be overstating the case, but my work has given me a certain perspective on things. I know something about history and something about art, and I learn a little more each day. And when I walk down the avenue like this, I know something about most of the things I see, and I know lots of people and talk to them and I read the newspapers and I know what's going on, and there is always something going on in this city, even among one's nearest friends.

Yakup loved this moment of the evening, when the avenue's businesses were closing down and most of the shoppers had gone home, a moment of unsullied anticipation before the cinema and dinner crowds made their appearances, the moment for a quiet stroll before meeting someone for a drink at the Pera Palace. Yakup checked his watch and decided he had time to see what was going on at Marco Fontane's retrospective exhibit at Galatasaray. It seemed that, after all these years of working in obscurity, their old friend Marco had been taken up by the Arts Foundation of Şimşek Realty, and they had offered him a lavishly laid-on retrospective exhibit entitled *Marco Fontane: Twenty-five Years of Art.* Handsome invitations had been sent out to people with money who were known to be interested in buying works of art, either as an investment (by far the largest number), or for reasons of social snobbery (only a slightly less numerous group and largely overlapping with the first), or because they were genuinely interested and knowledgeable and had been invited to give the affair a proper tone. There would have to be somebody in the room who would actually look at the paintings and not just the price and who might be counted upon to make the appropriate remarks, framed—ha, ha—in the appropriate vocabulary. Marco's friends fell almost exclusively into the latter category, and each had received an invitation addressed and signed by Marco himself, with a brief injunction saying: Don't go.

Marco had for years been known around town as a mad genius, and his drawings and prints (certainly) and paintings (less so) had been judged sufficiently decorative to allow for purchase and display. Except for a nucleus of personal favorites that Marco held back, everything he had ever produced had either been given away or sold, though Marco knew nothing of the art market and there was little difference between selling and giving away. One thing Marco did care about, however, was knowing where his works had gone, and he kept a complete record showing the title (with a brief description), price (if any), and owner of each. So much was common knowledge. But as Marco had later told his friends, he had been visited about three months ago by the head of the Arts Foundation of Şimşek Realty, a distinguished gentleman in a three-piece suit who had already bought, on his own account, as many as a dozen works. That day in Marco's studio, the distinguished gentleman had asked, Now, how are we going to gather these paintings and prints together for the show? I have a list, said Marco. Of course you do, said the distinguished gentleman, Why didn't I think of that? and off he went. Back in his office, he was able quickly to confirm his suspicion that nobody had paid Marco close to what his paintings were worth, and he now knew who these people were. He had then sent out about fifty letters announcing the Foundation's plan to hold a retrospective and suggesting that as many works as possible be offered for sale. As head of the Arts Foundation, he would be happy to offer his expertise on questions of price. Nor was he so naive as to imagine that Marco would not get wind of the strongly mercenary quality of the enterprise, and he had proposed to Marco that a dozen or so new paintings be shown and offered for sale at prices sure to dazzle the artist out of any qualms he might entertain. Finally, all the expenses of the affair—the use of its gallery, the formal invitations, and a suitable advertising campaign—would be borne by the Arts Foundation.

It was a clever scheme. It had all the appearances of a genuine cultural event, and it was a genuine cultural event in many respects, so how could anybody object to a few people, including the honored artist himself, making some money? It will be seen that although Marco's participation was not essential, it was nice, or would have been. When Marco finally understood that he had been taken in, he felt not only anger, but humiliation, and the combination produced rage. Faruk Selvi had been one of those who had been early invited to contribute to and even help organize the show. Faruk had told Erden, and Erden had told Marco. The terrible part, for Marco, was that he had to admit that he had indeed been dazzled, first by the apparent honor and then by the prices proposed. But when he saw the full shape of the plan, he recognized the extent to which he had been played for a fool. His anger was only increased by the fact, which he admitted to Erden, that he was still dazzled. Erden tried to help. He saw both sides. The Arts Foundation should have explained everything to Marco from the outset. In fact, had they done so, everything would have gone smoothly. It was the element of surprise, the explanation after the fact, that made the plan appear to be a calculated subterfuge. But perhaps it was not that at all, and perhaps the head of the Foundation, in his genuine enthusiasm for the idea in its most honorable guises—honor for Marco and a few good prices at last—had simply forgotten to go into details. And what were those details?

For twenty years now, a fairly small number of people has recognized your work as that of a great painter.

Marco grimaced and waved the idea aside.

Right, said Erden. What is a great painter anyway? Who knows what a great painter is? Who decides and on the basis of what? Or a great painting. Why is this a great painting? Erden asked, pointing.

Marco opened his mouth as if to speak.

Rhetorical question, Marco, because the question now is not whether the painting is great, but how much it is worth. And by this we mean one thing: money. We can simplify the problem. Some great paintings, or paintings thought to be great, have sold for next to nothing, while some inferior work has sold for a great deal. Conclusion: the monetary value of a work is separable from its artistic value, whatever that may be, and the monetary value is nothing more nor less than what somebody is willing to pay. This may or may not be ethically coherent, but it is a fact.

Erden only half believed what he was saying. He thought it his duty to try to reason with Marco, to get him to see another side of the question, but he had begun to observe the progress of his own thinking with some amusement, wondering how far it might go. He had realized, then, at the point of "ethical coherence," that he had probably made a mistake, in the sense that "ethical coherence" was something in which he actually believed and which might well defeat his own intention. He had noticed, moreover, that Marco had seemed to be only half listening until he had reached that very point.

No, no, no, no, no, said Marco. Murder is a fact, but I don't have to condone it. I shall withdraw my paintings—it was for Marco as if they were already being shown, although they had not left his studio—I shall have nothing more to do with this show. I won't even go to the opening, and—the idea then occurred to him—I shall instruct all of our friends to stay away.

"Instruct" was pretty good. There was that in Marco which, when aroused, might say, "Let there be light" and wonder that the light did not appear. It was in such a mood that he had sent out the special invitations scrawled over with the imperative "Don't go!"

Yakup carried one of these invitations now in his pocket as he advanced up İstiklal Caddesi, nearing Galatasaray, when he became aware of a vibration moving in the cobblestones under his feet and a roaring in his ears and a blindingly bright light coming at him down the avenue from the direction of Taksim Square. It was the southbound trolley and, as he had unthinkingly permitted himself to wander onto the tracks in the middle of the way, he had to step rapidly aside. The occurrence was sufficiently rare. The avenue had for some years now been closed to all but pedestrian traffic, except for some commercial deliveries and emergencies, but where was he now? Yes, he half remembered passing Markiz and the new Russian Consulate and there was the church of Saint Antoine up ahead on the right, which meant that he was coming up to the alley on the left leading to the old Russian restaurant Regence and, just a few steps farther along the avenue, to Şimşek Realty at Galatasaray. He didn't have much time now before his appointment with Mimi, but the temptation to have a look at the forbidden reception was irresistible. He therefore picked up the pace a bit, passed in front of Saint Antoine and the alley, with a quick look left at the warm and welcoming windows of Regence, and was just about to cross the street when he felt a vibration underfoot and heard the warning roar again, this time from behind.

He stopped and turned to wait for the northbound trolley to pass, and as he did so, he thought he saw Dimitri Papas directly across the street, walking, like him, towards Galatasaray. His first thought was the obvious one that Dimitri had succumbed, like him, to the temptation of sneaking a look at the opening of Marco's show, if only from the outside, like pauper children in a holiday season, when he realized that Dimitri was being followed, at close quarters, by a young woman, perhaps a very pretty young woman, of a gypsy aspect, to judge by her clothes, carrying an infant in a shawl wrapped around her back and holding by the hand a second child who, with his other hand, clung tight to Dimitri's trouser leg. The pauper children in the flesh, he thought, and can this really be Dimitri? Yakup took another few steps up the avenue to keep pace. He hoped he might be able to keep an eye on them through the windows of the trolley as it passed, but the evening crowds having begun to gather, the trolley was full, with a mass of people standing in the aisle. His view was cut off, and, when the trolley had passed, Dimitri had disappeared. There was an alleyway and a commercial arcade into which he might have turned, and a couple of doorways, but the experience had as much in it of a hallucination as it did of the cinema cliché, and Yakup thought he had better keep his wits about him or end up walking into a wall. If Dimitri comes in with a new family tonight, he thought, I'll know I didn't dream them up.

Yakup had now arrived at a point from which he had a clear view of the Arts Foundation Gallery across the street, and he stopped for a look. There were so many guests that they had apparently been forced in significant numbers out into the street. He decided not to cross, therefore, for fear of being recognized and questioned about the absences. Everybody seemed to be having a marvelous time, drinking and smoking and talking and gesticulating with an animation more typical of two in the morning, but liberal supplies of champagne and *rakı* on a spring evening can have a wonderful effect. The opening seemed to be a great success, and he wondered what Marco might have to say at dinner tonight.

iii

The Pera Palace, where Yakup was to meet Mimi, is situated on what is now called Meşrutiyet Caddesi, or Constitution Avenue, which some of the local wags have suggested was named not for the national constitution but for the robust physical constitution of the founder of the Republic, Mustafa Kemal, latterly known as Atatürk, who spent many an exemplary evening at the Pera Palace, in the bar and in the suite of rooms upstairs that were his domain on visits to Istanbul. Yakup had first been shown these rooms by Madame Bishkek, who had first seen them herself when she was sixteen. During a brief period, the rooms had been known as The Atatürk Suite and were open to the public, with memorabilia on display and a member of the hotel staff to explain them with anecdotal commentary, in the best of taste, illustrating the legendary robustness of the great man. With the passage of time, however, the opinion slowly formed in the official mind that such tales were inappropriate, probably apocryphal, and a discredit to the solemnity of the State. Yes, Atatürk had stayed at the Pera Palace, but only once or twice and on urgent state business. There was no such thing as "The Atatürk Suite" and there never had been, except in certain degraded imaginations. Atatürk had been a man of luminous intelligence and iron will, requiring neither *rakı* nor dancing girls, and he had died not of overindulgence but of the crushing responsibilities of office. Certain degenerate historians might cite records and documents, cite witnesses, but documents and records can be the work of forgers, and who are these witnesses? Extremist enemies of the good order of the State or nonentities trying to make themselves important. But such witnesses and historians reveal the subversive and insidious nature of their thinking when they claim to know the truth; for everybody knows that historical truth is ultimately unknowable. That point once conceded, as it must be, the only possible version of the past becomes that one which is most useful for the purposes of today. This is what is meant by healthy and progressive utilitarianism, and we have begun to sound like Erden trying to convince poor Marco that there is no such thing as dishonesty and that the charitable thing to do is give everybody the benefit of the doubt and to take your money and shut up.

With his mind thus pleasantly occupied, Yakup had covered the distance between Galatasaray and the Pera Palace, greeted the doorman and the concierge, and made his way along the carpeted hallway to the bar. He stopped for a moment to look around the room for Mimi, and there she was seated in a back corner, by a high window overlooking the street. She saw him enter and he could see her smile and she never took her eyes off him as he crossed the room.

Hello, my love, he said.

Hello yourself.

He bent to kiss her and he took her hand and sat down. Have you had a drink?

Just this tea, she said, with a nod towards the pewter teapot on the little table.

Terrible stuff, tea.

I know, she said. Why would anyone drink tea?

Daft, he said. Will you have some more? We haven't got much time, but I think I'll have a *rakı*.

All right, I'll have a *rakı* too. To show I'm only half daft.

Half daft is good, he said. I like the sound of half daft. I'd like to be half daft myself.

Have no fear, said Mimi, and they laughed and the waiter looked over and when the two *rakı*s came Yakup said he would pour. The waiter had brought two crystal goblets half full of the clear, slightly viscous liquid, two splits of water, and an ice bucket with tongs. Yakup took Mimi's glass and, tipping it slightly, poured the water so that it ran slowly down the inside of the glass, forming white swirls as it mixed with the *rakı*. When all the *rakı* had become a milky cloud, Yakup stopped. Ice? he asked ritually. No ice. He then repeated the operation on his own glass. Ice? he asked himself. No ice. They looked at each other and clinked glasses—*Şerefe!*—and drank a swallow and said ahhhhhhh, and their evening together had begun.

It was now completely dark outside, and drinking inside like this, in the warmth and comfort of the bar of the Pera Palace, it felt more like winter than spring. But that it should be the one and feel like the other seemed perfectly consonant with this crazy day, a day on which everything was happening at once: Faruk's display at the bookstore, Marco's opening, and now this dinner which was both an anti-opening and a welcome back for Malone. They had an evening before them, but Yakup felt like sitting, in this instant, perfectly still, as if charmed into a moment of pure anticipation with the conscious ability to savor it. It was a moment composed of all these things: the events of the day, his memories, the evening to come, this city, this hotel and bar, the *rakı* and the season—or the seasons—and, enveloping them all, their life and lives together, his and Mimi's. It was extraordinary. At privileged times like this, the accumulated weight of the years just seemed to fall away, and he felt not young exactly—it wasn't exactly that—but disembodied; and if he were feeling again the buoyancy of youth, perhaps this was only because he had had more time to feel this way when he was young. Perhaps this is what binds youth to age, he thought, the gift comes back again, and I am getting it back. But how much richer the moment is now, he thought. When he was young, what did he know? Whereas now, his dreams were so much more thoroughly—what would be the word?—furnished. That was it, and why not? I'm in the furniture business! And if the experience and the furnishing were unremarkable, what did that matter? It was of the very tissue of his life, and where, if followed, might the thread lead? Where might it not? Take a book, for example. Never mind what's in the book, which might take you to the throne of Kublai Khan or into the life of microorganisms. Where might the mind not travel into the scene behind the author in his photo on the back of the dust jacket? Or simply the leather binding of a seventeenth-century book that might therefore contain the very text that so inspired Joseph Nasi's meditations on that spring afternoon in the garden of the Villa Belvedere so long ago.

I was thinking of old Joseph Nasi today, he said.

Ah, said Mimi, and Yakup could tell that this was not surprising news.

I was thinking about the years after his return from Palestine, when he exerted such great influence over the Sultan. He hated the Venetians, you know, and opposed Venetian policy wherever he could. They say it was largely because of Nasi that Selim undertook the conquest of Cyprus, though he couldn't have been very happy with what happened to Bragadino.

What happened to Bragadino? Mimi asked.

You don't want to know.

I do now.

Bragadino was the Venetian commander and they had him flayed.

Flayed?

They skinned him alive.

You didn't tell me that. You didn't tell me because it didn't happen, isn't that right?

Absolutely. And I'd hate to think of old Nasi after his retirement from public life blaming himself and brooding and waking up in the middle of the night with the sweats.

Well, said Mimi, you have certainly had an inspiring day communing with your ancestor.

I'm sorry, said Yakup. I was sitting here feeling very happy and self-satisfied and minding my own business when I remembered all that. It must be terrible to be haunted. Nasi must have been haunted. He must have known what happened. Everybody did. The Turkish commander had what was left of Bragadino sewn back together and inflated and displayed from the mast of his ship like a grotesque balloon.

Quite an argument to use against the Venetians, said Mimi, airtight, but she didn't smile, and I suppose they made a present of it so the Venetians would know which way the wind was blowing. Mimi was upset, and it made her feel giddy and cynical in self-defense, and she said, Maybe we could talk about something else, now that we're done reminiscing about the good old days in Istanbul, and have another *rakı* for the road, as we used to say in Brooklyn.

Brooklyn? said Yakup, Now who's reminiscing?

It ain't the same, she said, feeling better. No Venetians, just Sicilians, the most peaceable people in the world, just like children, and the Irish, laughing and fiddling from dawn to dusk, and all of us like sisters and brothers in the garden of bliss; now where's that drink?

It's coming, said Yakup, and it came, the goblets and the splits of water and the bucket of ice. They each took two small cubes of ice this time to soften the edge on the second drink. When Esther graduates from high school, we'll all go to Brooklyn together, said Yakup. İshak can have a look at some graduate schools, if he wants, and we can all sit around in the evenings in the garden of bliss.

It isn't there anymore, said Mimi.

I know, said Yakup, I know. Does it make you sad?

Not in the least, said Mimi, much revived. By the way, I meant to tell you that İshak is taking Esther and Nicolette Corrigan out to the movies tonight, and Esther will spend the night at the Corrigans' in Bebek.

Good plan, said Yakup. So İshak won't be going to any protest rallies. Not that I've heard there would be any, but İshak worries me some.

Me too, said Mimi, but not tonight.

Good for you, said Yakup. Happy thoughts. *Şerefe*, and here's to us, and Yakup felt that the warm atmosphere of this wonderful old bar and the *rakı* and the presence of Mimi and their change of mood had reestablished for him that feeling of anticipatory and dynamic balance which was his spiritual home, an attitude without chronology to which his soul returned as to an image of a graceful sloop, luffing for an instant as her bow swung and her sail snapped and billowed once again and she heeled over sharply onto the starboard tack making for Üsküdar. And the mood produced another image, as of a man seated under a tree, meditating upon some verses just read in a book that lies open on his lap, and another image is now projected in the mind of this meditative reader of a midnight summer sky, the new moon a silver crescent in the east and overhead a million stars, and Yakup realized that he had been transported in imagination to the roof terrace of Erden's house in Cunda. He had urged Erden to find a special spot and to build a special house and now he,

Yakup, had fallen in love with it. Were he and Erden so similar? The answer was yes, of course. Erden was his friend. Damon and Pythias.

Mimi, he said, do you remember the night we spent on the roof terrace in Cunda?

I do, she said. What a beautiful night it was. I can remember thinking that I hadn't seen so many stars since leaving the kibbutz. Mimi paused, thinking of the stars, and she remembered also that, as she looked, a passage from *The Merchant of Venice*, memorized years before in school, had risen unbidden to her lips:

> There's not the smallest orb which thou behold'st
> But in his motion like an angel sings,
> Still quiring to the young-eyed cherubins.
> Such harmony is in immortal souls;
> But, whilst this muddy vesture of decay
> Doth grossly close it in, we cannot hear it.

You quoted those very lines, said Yakup, right there on the roof. Do you remember?

Apparently, said Mimi, and they laughed, and Yakup said, I'm going to tell you a secret, just between us.

What's that?

And you won't tell a soul?

I won't.

I love you.

Is that it?

If that's not enough, I can find more.

It's very nice, but if there's more, I wouldn't mind hearing it.

I'm taking you to Cunda.

Of course you are.

I mean right now, he said. Let's go to Cunda right now, tonight.

Oh, Yakup, we can't, she said.

Erden told me where he keeps an extra set of keys.

We can't.

We can phone Boncuk and ask them to give a message to Erden and he can tell the Corrigans or the kids, if the kids show up.

We can't, she said. You know we can't. I promised Sylvia. She needs as much support as she can get, with Malone coming back after all these years. And there's Marco too, she reminded him. Marco would be hurt if you didn't show up, you and Erden. You're the best friends he's got.

You're right, said Yakup. But you'll come with me to Cunda again some day, won't you?

I will, she said.

And together we shall cast off this—what is it?—this muddy vesture of decay.

You certainly have a way with words, she said. Let's go before we lose the edge.

4

SYLVIA

i

Sylvia Corrigan had been awakened that morning by the predawn call to prayer. The room where she lay occupied a corner of the top story of a spacious, nineteenth-century frame house, perched on the slope of a hill overlooking the Bosphorus. The two windows on the south wall commanded a splendid view over the College road, the pine-forested slope, and the harbor at Bebek. The two windows facing east looked directly across to the Asian shore, where a band of pinkish gray was now lifting above the hills behind Kandilli, the Sweet Waters of Asia, and Anadolu Hisarı. To the north, from these same windows, the view was partially blocked by two tall pines and the south tower of Rumeli Hisarı, the great castle that Mehmet the Conqueror had built in 1452.

Sylvia loved this house and this room. The room was, or so it seemed to her, in the sparse simplicity of its furnishings and in its setting, a thing of beauty and a joy, if not forever, at least for the next while, and she knew that she had only to walk to the bathroom down the hall to discover an unobstructed view to the north. From the bathroom window, she could look out over the castle walls and beyond to where the Bosphorus flowed towards her out of the Black Sea, past Yeniköy and İstinye and Emirgan, and she could see upstream and across the water as far as Beykoz on the Asian shore, easily six kilometers away. She was fully awake now and the temptation to have a look at this privileged moment of the day was strong, as was a certain pressure in her bladder. She listened for a moment to Frank's even breathing, then lifted the covers and eased out of bed. She straightened up and arched her back to stretch for a moment, feeling her breasts lift and her nipples brush against the cloth of her tee shirt, and she walked barefoot across the polished surface of the wide pine board floor and down the hall to the bathroom. No other bathroom in the world like this one, she thought. Brush your teeth with a view, pee with a view, take a shower with a view. Stand in the shower stark naked and look at all this and not be seen. It gave her a crazy thrill, and it was harmless enough. Why not? She would pee and brush her teeth and, early as it was, she'd go for a run. There was plenty of time. She could stretch and run for an hour and still have time to fix breakfast and get Nicolette off to school. She stood again and drew up her underpants in a single supple motion and flushed the twilight and went over to the sink. She pulled her tee shirt off over her head and shook out her hair and then pulled it back with both hands and twisted it into a knot. She held the pose for a moment, elbows back, looking at her breasts, and with her right hand, picked up a hairpin and stuck it down through the top of the knot.

    The young women who run without bras these days are crazy, she thought. She supposed it must make them feel sexy, or something, but what they obviously didn't know was that the violent motion would eventually break the tissue down, and they'd all end up with their breasts hanging down to their knees before they were thirty. She'd tried once running without a bra, but by the time she got home her nipples were raw from rubbing against her shirt. Not a very sexy feeling, thank you very much. With all the exercising she'd done over the years, she'd been careful to protect her breasts, and her body was, she congratulated herself, intact. The face was something else, or the expression of the face. The structure hadn't changed. She hadn't begun to sag. But there was a greater maturity of expression. Couldn't she put it that way? She leaned forward for a closer look. Yes she could and no she couldn't. She had to be honest with herself. She could afford to be honest with herself. There were wrinkles at the corners of the eyes and around the mouth and some lines in the forehead and just the least hint of a vertical line between the eyes, but all these were proof that she had lived, that she had been engaged in the drama and struggles of her times—what drama? she asked herself, what struggles? We may be laying this on a bit thick, she thought; this isn't just any audience you're talking to, this audience knows you pretty well—but, turning now to the full-length mirror behind the bathroom door, she looked and thought to herself, the body is still intact.

She hooked her thumbs inside the elastic waistband of her underpants, bent down, and stepped out of them. Intact, hell, she said out loud, fantastic, and the thought came to her that she hadn't seen her daughter Nicolette in the buff, like this, for quite a while. How could that be? But it was. They hadn't been to the Turkish bath together in two or three years, and Nicolette increasingly had her own life. She'd seen her coming out of the shower once or twice, fleetingly, but not to study her. But what a silly idea that was, wasn't it? And she realized she couldn't imagine herself saying to Nicolette something like: Here, let me have a good look at you. Haven't you grown up to be a big girl? It was absurd. At sixteen she was certainly still very young and a child in some ways, but she remembered her now as she looked in a bikini last summer, and Nicolette was no child anymore in that department. So Nicolette had a fantastic body too, and perhaps the thought had come to her because she had wondered how she, at her age, might still compare, but the fact was that she and Nicolette looked amazingly alike. It couldn't last, of course.

We're all doomed, each in her time. But why think such morbid thoughts? The axe hasn't fallen yet. She even resembles me in the face. We have the same hair, obviously, the same color and length. Nicolette had always wanted to wear her hair long. Did she admire the way her mother looked? Did she want to resemble her mother as much as she could? That was very sweet. But it was more than just the hair. She'd been looking at her old school yearbook yesterday. She hadn't looked at it in years. Was it because Malone was coming back? There was certainly a connection. She had flipped through the pages for pictures of herself until she came upon one, among the candids at the back, that she remembered with a shock. It was a trick picture that she had taken of herself in a mirror with the camera on a time release. In the picture, she sits stiffly on a straight-backed wooden chair, her hands folded in her lap. The apparently innocent camera sits on a table close to her right arm. She gazes directly into the mirror, which is set against an empty wall, as empty as the reflected wall behind her. Her face has the expressionless impenetrability of stone. Sylvia had gazed at the picture as if gazing at a sphinx, until she realized, with a shock, that this was precisely what Nicolette would look like if Nicolette were dead.

Now that was going a bit too far, even a lot too far, but there was some truth in it. It was difficult to imagine the lifeless mask in the picture as belonging, under any other circumstances, to the joyful and animated Nicolette. It was true that if you thought a minute, you might realize that as absent as was the sitter's life, the photographer's irony was everywhere. Was she then the introvert version of her extrovert child? Where Nicolette had grown up happy and guileless and strong, she had become resentful and repressed. But was she to be blamed? There was, after all, a wee bit of difference between growing up in Miss Blossom's all-girls boarding school in New England—exclusive cliques and envious backbiting and conceit—and walking over each morning from home to a coed international school in

Istanbul, Turkey, Europe-Asia-and-the-World. And what about Nicolette's family life? Frank had always talked to her as if she were already grown up. She was sure she could remember him talking to her about the Hittites one time when she was still in her crib. Frank had always talked to her that way, never condescending, using perfectly adult vocabulary, and he talked the same way to the other kids, Nicolette's friends, but it wouldn't be fair to say that Frank didn't know how to talk to children, because the amazing thing was that they listened. At least for a while, but Frank knew when to stop. And as regards their social life, ever since Nicolette had been old enough to sit up in her chair she had gone along with them out to dinner downtown and eaten whatever they ate and listened when things were explained to her and listened also surely to many things she couldn't understand and then did understand so much sooner than she, Sylvia, had ever done or could ever have done, given the circumstances. And the kids these days in conversation alluded easily and without embarrassment to sex and they talked about politics as well as rock stars and, at least here in Istanbul, history and archaeology and poetry as well as fashion and films. All of which had given to young Nicolette's face an expression of open and frank assurance that hers, Sylvia's, had perhaps never had. It seemed to Sylvia that her own emotional maturity had come, in many respects, too late, not until she had married Malone and, later yet, fallen in love with Dimitri; but it seemed to her also that she had learned about loneliness and loss too soon, that they had made her defensive and reclusive, before she had acquired the renewing and compensatory knowledge of life's variety.

But these were the thoughts of yesterday. She would return to them, surely, as they seemed to be telling her something about herself, but for the moment she was principally aware of that powerful opening intake of air and that flexible tension in the thighs and in the small of her back that told her only that she needed to run. Her running clothes lay folded on top of the laundry hamper behind the door: the running bra, the fresh cotton tee shirt (light blue this one), the nylon running shorts (dark red, lined, no need for underwear), and a fresh pair of socks. Her running shoes were downstairs under the bench by the front door in the little entry hall. She would carry the socks and walk barefoot so as not to slip on the polished wood of the stair—she didn't like carpets, anyway, but hated stair runners—and as she opened the bathroom door and stepped into the hall, she was sure she heard Nicolette's bedroom door click shut. That was odd. But then she heard a low, whining sound and a scratch and concluded that it must have been the dog, and she heard him now scratch at the door again and Nicolette whisper his name for him to stop, the merest whisper yet perfectly audible, Fritsky! The old boy must have heard her movements in the bathroom and hall and tried to nose the door open and succeeded only in locking himself in. And Nicolette, bless her heart, had not let him out, because he couldn't be taken along on the run and if he were left loose in the house he would have spent the next hour trying to scratch his way through the front door. Good old Fritsky, she thought, how old was he now? Fourteen in May, she thought, almost fourteen. When they brought him home as a puppy, Nicolette had wanted to call him Frisky. But Frank wasn't having it. He said it would be like having a dog named Fido or Spot, so he had proposed they call him Fritsky. They'd had a good laugh over that, and Frank had no trouble in getting little Nicolette to accept Fritsky as the same thing.

But it wasn't because he was fourteen that he couldn't be taken along on the run. He was still healthy and with a little training he ought still to be able to string a few seven-minute miles together. Years ago she had tried running with him on a leash, but, although he was well trained, the least moment of distraction on his part and she would have to break her stride. But even were his training and obedience to be refined to the point where he could be trusted to run by her side without a leash, there were always other dogs, or the possibility of other dogs or some other unforeseen distraction, which meant that she would worry, that she would have to be always vigilant and thus never able entirely to let herself go, to abandon herself to the rhythms of the run. Running was something you did alone. Not everybody knew that, of course. Not everybody wanted or knew how to listen to themselves alone. Real running was for loners.

The nylon running shorts were like wearing nothing at all. Now, that was sexy. She turned in at the College gate and caught a glimpse of the watchman asleep in the gatehouse, his cap askew and his head down on his folded arms on the desk. Or not quite like wearing nothing at all. More like wearing the breeze, even if there were no breeze. It played around your backside, all a cool caress, and down around your thighs and into your crotch, and she thought to herself, easy does it. Clear of the gatehouse now and the parking lot, she ran slowly up the hill towards the central campus and turned onto the terrace in back of Hamlin Hall and jogged over to the stone wall at the edge of the terrace to stretch. She threw her right foot up on the wall and slowly bent forward over the length of the leg, the fingers of both hands reaching for the toe, breathing evenly and drawing the hamstring muscles out a little more with each slow exhalation. She then rotated her pelvis slightly to the left and bent down along the length of her left leg slowly towards the ground, carefully controlling the pull on the big groin muscle of her right leg. Men can't do this one so well, she thought, and straightened up and repeated the same operation from the other side of her body, her left foot on the wall. There was a slight breeze blowing now and she thought to herself that the breeze felt just as if she were wearing nylon running shorts—ha, ha—and when she finished her stretches, she jogged along the terrace wall to the far end and jogged back, a little faster now, warming up and watching the sun rise over the

Asian hills across the way—was this not the life? the very life?—and she had decided not to run all the way up to Etiler—too busy, even at this hour—nor over to Rumeli Hisarı—too hilly—but to cross the campus and run the stairs behind the Chemistry building and up to the new running track, with its beautiful clay surface and its beautiful view.

As she reached the top of the long climb, Sylvia's heart was pounding and she had begun to feel that constriction in the muscles that comes from a lack of oxygen and the buildup of lactic acid. She continued to run at the same pace, however, allowing her body to recover slowly through the reduced effort of running over level ground. When she reached the track, she turned right, out of long habit, to run the circuit counterclockwise. Still forcing herself to hold the pace, she ran through the first long straightaway and the first turn before her pulse rate slowly began to fall and the flexibility to return to her legs. It had been an effort requiring concentration and toughness of will, but she had been training for years and knew what her body could do. She was running in an even rhythm now, and she estimated her pace as being just over seven minutes to the mile. She might increase it slightly later on, but not now. She looked at her watch. It was twenty past six. She would run until seven and see how she felt. She never counted the laps. That would have been an intolerable distraction, even with the lap counter that some runners used, and quite unnecessary. She knew that at her usual pace she would cover just under six miles in forty minutes, which was all she needed to know. When you ran, you wanted the body to take over for itself and leave the mind free to wander where it would.

Sylvia ran through two or three more circuits—she was no longer sure how many—and was rounding the south end of the track when she began to experience that growing sense of weightless euphoria that runners call the zone. Her old school chum Naomi had first told her about the zone, and it was while training that year with Naomi that she had discovered it for the first time for herself. Running in the zone combined a sense of euphoric weightlessness with perfect lucidity of mind. You could, for example, remember facts and people and events—whole dialogues!—from your reading or your life, that you could never have recovered otherwise, short of hypnosis, perhaps. And it sometimes happened that those people or events, if associated with the act of running, would seem especially immediate, as if participating more fully in the psycho-motor dimension of the mind.

As Sylvia rounded the south end of the track, looking across the Bosphorus to the Asian shore, her eye swept north along the water's edge from Kandilli—she thought for a moment of the view looking back towards the College buildings from the great west window of Erden Sakarya's apartment there—to the beautiful blood-red, wine-red Ostrorog Yalısı, home to the last survivor of an aristocratic and once-powerful Franco-Polish family—cousins, apparently, of the painter Marco Fontane—and farther north to the woods and gardens bordering the "Sweet Waters" of the Göksu and Küçüksu rivers, where they mixed with the great Bosphorus stream; and she was struck, not by the recognition of a resemblance, but by the conviction that she was actually looking at a scene called up from the distant past, at the woods that bordered Williams Creek as it flowed into the Brookfield River below the running track at Miss Blossom's School when she was hardly more than a girl.

ii

Sylvia ran on, oblivious to her unchanging course around the track, conscious only of the emergent intimations of her inner life. She might have been running on any track, anywhere, even as she had run the track by the river during her later years at

Miss Blossom's School, imaging herself with her father in New York, or what living in Paris might be like, or, as was more frequent yet, her friendship with Naomi during that magical spring of her freshman year.

Sylvia had transferred to Miss Blossom's from a Catholic boarding school, run by kindly Dominicans, where she had spent the eight years since her mother's death. Unfortunately, the nuns had no high school, and, though they did have a ninth grade, admission to Miss Blossom's was relatively easier for girls who signed up for a full four years. Her grades at Saint Dom's, as they called it, had not been too brilliant, so her father had decided to play it safe and move Sylvia to Miss Blossom's for the ninth grade. It had been the worst year of her life. At Miss Blossom's there was only one Catholic on the faculty, and there couldn't have been more than two or three other Catholic girls in the whole school. And her feeling of alienation was compounded by the thought that all her old friends were continuing together at Saint Dom's and would be graduating together at the end of the year.

Then, one afternoon in early spring, feeling sorry for herself, she had been walking alone across the lower playing fields towards the river when she noticed a solitary figure running on the track, a girl she had admired at a distance, an eleventh-grader, with remarkable dark, Mediterranean looks, and a reputation for being both brainy and athletic, but who seemed to be always by herself. Sylvia remembered one night that winter—it must have been close to midnight— when she had been awakened by the brightness of the moonlight streaming into her little room on the top floor of Winthrop House. The room had been cold, but she had crept out of bed quietly so as not to disturb her roommate and gone to the window for a look. It had snowed heavily all day, but by evening the sky had cleared and, now, nearing midnight, a full moon had appeared. The brightness of the moonlight on the snow was astonishing and Sylvia thought how wonderful it would be to be outside right in the middle of all that when she saw the girl. She was standing very still in profile to the house and you could see her breath condensing in the sharp air and her clear track through the snow to where she stood. The girl made a gesture that brought her hand to her lips for a moment, and Sylvia had the romantic notion that she was blowing a kiss at the moon when she realized that the girl was smoking. Now that was something. That was a daring thing to do. You walked out in the middle of the night in the freezing cold and stood stock-still under a full moon in the snow. That was romance enough. But to do all that and then smoke, right out in the open for anyone to see, that was to break all the rules and more than romance enough. Had Sylvia been able to analyze her own emotions just then, she might have said to herself, I have fallen in love.

Are you okay? the voice asked, for Sylvia, lost in thought, had halted in her progress towards the river and was standing very still. Do you want to run? Let's run together; and they had set off jogging over to the track, and had circled it together two or three times, and then the girl told her to keep trotting along while she picked up the pace and to keep running until she caught up to her again. Sylvia watched her pull away and decided to count the laps and she was just coming up on her second lap when the girl drew up beside her again. How are you doing? she asked. I'm fine, she answered, and it was true, though she didn't think she had ever run so far before, except in nightmares, and when the girl had lapped her once more and said, This time you try and keep up, she had said Okay and, though she knew the girl hadn't increased the pace as much as before, she felt really good and proud of herself for keeping up, and the girl had asked, Are you about fourteen? and Sylvia had said, I'm just fourteen, and the girl had said, At fourteen years of age a woman's body is a running machine! and she had laughed and upped the pace again and Sylvia had stayed with her until she couldn't any more and the girl had been aware of her strain and slowed down with her and said, That's enough for me.

That had been the beginning of her friendship with Naomi. Naomi had convinced her that she should be a runner. She had the talent for it, and the build, long and strong, and she was obviously a loner. This latter remark had come as something of a surprise. Naomi must have been watching her, as she had watched Naomi. Sylvia had blushed, but it was not because she was embarrassed but because she was pleased. They continued to train together, but while they trained they never talked. They talked afterwards, cooling down, and one day Naomi said, You're a Catholic, aren't you? and Sylvia said she was, and Naomi said, I'm a Jew, and then, That's not the only reason why we're loners, but it helps, and she had added, laughing, but now we can be loners together.

We'll be a paradox, said Sylvia.

No, said Naomi, we'll be a pair-adox, and the joke had come so quickly that it had taken even Naomi by surprise. The two girls had thrown their arms around each other and laughed until they cried. They would be friends forever.

As the weather began to warm up, Sylvia and Naomi used to walk down along the river after working out or on Sunday afternoons, and Naomi had asked her once what she knew about boys. Sylvia didn't know much. With her upbringing, she didn't even know very much about girls. It had been a warm Sunday afternoon in May, and they had brought their suits with them and walked up the river to a place they knew and where they wouldn't be bothered by the camel drivers, which is what Naomi called the other girls at school. It was a place where the river curved sharply and where the water had carved out a pool below the bank, and they had stood together on the bank and held hands and jumped into the pool and when they had reached the shallows below the pool and climbed up the bank and walked back to their towels and clothes, Naomi had surprised her by saying, I'm sorry, we shouldn't have just jumped into the river like that. You should never jump into water without knowing what might be underneath, and rivers change all the time. But we were born lucky, you and I, she said and laughed, and she felt very close to this younger girl who trusted her, and that was when she had asked her what she knew about boys, and she asked her if she had started to bleed, though she knew from the evident signs that it must be so and that she would therefore be starting with something obvious and commonplace that would have nothing scary about it. And Naomi then quite unabashedly and naturally took off her suit and said, "you too," which Sylvia did and Naomi said, You're going to be some good-looking woman in a couple of years. You already are. And they had sat down together on the grass, feeling the warmth of the sun on their shoulders and backs as Naomi gave her a very matter-of-fact description of how the female anatomy functioned, and why, and then they had stretched out on their backs with the sun on their bellies and breasts and with a hand over the eyes for the blinding glare of the sun, and Naomi was now only a voice, which made it easier for Sylvia to listen without embarrassment to Naomi's description of the male anatomy, the two and the one, and what the function of the two was and what happened to the one when he got excited, and where it went, and then what.

Is there anything you don't understand?

No.

Is there anything that sounds too terrible?

No, but I think I like that part about what happens last, and I don't mean babies.

I know what you mean, Naomi said and laughed, and she had taken Sylvia by the hand and said, If you're feeling sexy, this will fix you, and she had risen quickly and pulled Sylvia with her, and One, Two, Three, she cried out, and they had jumped.

That had been the Springtime of Naomi, as Sylvia was afterwards to remember it, because Naomi had not returned to school in the fall. She had gone to spend the summer in Paris with her father, and she had first written to say how much she loved living in France, where she actually felt more at home than in the States, and where her father seemed like a different man, more like a friend, unless that was simply because she wasn't a child anymore and saw him differently, or he saw her differently, or something. It was all very complicated, but whatever it was, it was great, and she had finally written that she was going to stay in Paris forever and go to the Ecole Bilingue, which was a day school and coeducational as well as bilingual, and that she would walk to school along the most beautiful streets and avenues in the world and on the way home after school she would go to the cafe with friends to drink espresso coffee out of little cups and discuss poetry and philosophy and the way of the world. And she wrote that they also had a cross-country team that ran three afternoons a week in the Bois de Boulogne and had meets every Saturday in the fall and a track team in the spring, so she wasn't smoking much with the coffee and philosophy; in fact she wasn't smoking at all. Everybody smokes here, she had written, so I don't. It was pure Naomi. When school started, Sylvia missed her terribly, but she was happy imagining how happy Naomi was, and they wrote fairly regularly, almost once a week. Naomi had a boyfriend, a senior, who had everything. He had a car, and he had two and one, and he made the last thing happen (and she didn't mean babies). There was plenty in Naomi's letters for Sylvia to think about, and it wasn't always easy or possible to write down everything that the letters made her think about but that she might have been able to talk about lying on her back by the river with the sun on her belly and her hand over her eyes, and she wondered if her own letters weren't terribly dull by comparison and she felt that this must be the reason why first one and then another of her letters received no reply.

And then, just before the Thanksgiving break, there, standing at an angle in her postal box, was the familiar blue envelope with the familiar stamp, and she had slipped the letter into her coat pocket and taken it back to her funny and comfortable old room in the attic of Winthrop House to read. Her roommate of last year and everybody else had moved on to a tenth-grade dorm, but she had asked for special permission to stay on in the room, alone, if she agreed to help take care of the new girls and help the senior proctors, and they had said yes. She stood for a moment by the bed, looking out the window at the spot below where Naomi had stood in the snow, and, taking the letter from her pocket and looking at it now closely for the first time, she realized that the handwriting was wrong. It was the same blue envelope that Naomi always used, but the return address identified the sender as Joseph Fiedler, Naomi's father. She looked up from the letter and out the window again, and the late fall afternoon seemed to grow unaccountably dark around her, and she knew, without opening the letter, that Naomi was dead. It was as if she had always known that Naomi was doomed, that there was something in the world that hated such courage and beauty and warmth, and that she would be killed in a moment of their full expression, at high speed in a bright red, two-seater sports car, with the sun flashing and dancing on the windshield and the hood and on the wheat fields of La Beauce that stretched out before them to the horizon, with the great spires of Chartres cathedral just coming into view.

The letter said that nobody knew exactly what had caused the accident. There had been no other car involved. Naomi's boyfriend had been driving and he might have swerved to avoid hitting something in the road, an animal, perhaps. After reading the letter through a second time, Sylvia had lain down on her bed and she had wanted to die. She had wept quietly, and finally she had fallen asleep and she had dreamed that she was with Naomi in Paris and her boyfriend had come along in a little open car, and when Naomi had stepped into the passenger seat, she had followed and stepped into the passenger seat also and slid into Naomi's body, and they had driven like mad into the countryside and, by a river, they had gotten out of the car and, walking towards the river, there had been three of them again until they had lain down in the grass and begun to make love and she was Naomi again and her eyes misted and cleared and misted again and when they cleared she was no longer Naomi but the boy and, as she looked into Naomi's shining face and they held each other and grasped their rapture, whatever it was in the world that hated them was with them there, and they struggled to their feet in their panic and they ran. They ran and they ran and they were running on a long oval track and Naomi ran ahead and Sylvia was afraid and Naomi caught up to her from behind and her fear was gone and Naomi said, They won't bother us in Paris, because we're both French, and they had upped the pace and grown stronger yet and soon they were running up a long flight of steel stairs to a landing and another flight of stairs to the highest landing of all in a tall steel tower from where they could see the river and the whole city of Paris spread out below them as the wind blew in their hair and around their bodies in a long caress, and Naomi grabbed her by the hand and cried out, One, Two, Three, and they jumped.

Oh yes, she had wanted to die, had wished she were already dead, and as, somewhere within the even rhythms of her run around the College track, Sylvia relived her feelings of that afternoon, she realized that her reaction to Naomi's death had not been brave, that there was nothing of Naomi's bravery in her perverted wish. It was to be for the years to come as if her personality had turned against itself, or the worst had gained the upper hand. She still had the better part of three years to get through at Miss Blossom's, and she had better learn how to survive. She retained the knowledge that there was something in the world that had been Naomi's enemy and was hers, that hated the warmth and wildness that were in her, but she would keep that warmth and wildness hidden away. It was a hard lesson for a fifteen-year-old, but it was in fact the line of least resistance, and she had models to follow all around her. To the world she would present a mask of innocent credulity, cool and tame, submissive to the least hint of pressure from the established norms. She would play the game. And there was no reason for the sellout to be complete. Success in athletics and in her studies were things she wanted for herself, but she must survive socially, and she was determined not only to survive, but to prosper. She had long ago stopped going to Sunday mass in town, and there was no need to advertise that she was, or had been, a Catholic. Being of French extraction was all right and was even held to guarantee a certain level of sophistication, acceptable so long as it was never displayed. Over the next three years Sylvia played the game. She ran cross-country in the fall and track in the spring and she studied hard and got excellent grades, and with her blond good looks, she couldn't help being sought after. She had joined this and got elected to that, and before it was over, she was playing the part to such perfection that it had become second nature to her.

Oh, yes it had, had, had, it surely had, had, had, Sylvia chanted inwardly in time to the rhythms of the run, because it was impossible for her, in her present state, to remain serious or gloomy about anything for very long, and the words of the familiar song came back to her, "It's second naaayture to me now," and she smiled at the appropriateness of the next line as it came to her, "like breathing out and breathing in." It was Henry Higgins singing in *My Fair Lady* about becoming accustomed to Eliza's face. Silly enough, she thought, when the person acquiring a second nature was surely Eliza. All Higgins had done was fall in love, where Eliza had put on a new language, among other things. But had she become a different person, really? Or was she only wearing a mask?

Sylvia had learned about the "second nature" during her freshman year at Wellesley in a lecture course on the French Renaissance and Classicism, where it was praised as synonymous with civilization's gradual domestication of "the beast;" but in a seminar on Rousseau, taken in her junior year, she learned from reading the First and Second *Discourses* that civilization was an artifice and a corruption of the original freedom of the natural state. Reviewing these conflicting notions in the light of her own experience, she decided that Rousseau was right. She decided that she had always known Rousseau was right, but she also knew that acting upon that knowledge was another thing. Rousseau had faced the same problem. How can you be yourself, in all the particularities of your own experience, which necessarily render you unique, in a world that demands conformity? The answer was that you either bolted for the woods, as Rousseau had done, or you became accustomed to your own hypocrisy.

She was learning things at Wellesley—Kepler's laws, Marxism, Sanskrit roots, Matisse—but it seemed to her, as regards those things that she cared most about, that she was on a treadmill, going nowhere, that what she learned, instead of leading her out into the world, seemed but a mirror and a confirmation of her own predicament. The very logic of it seemed determinant. What she needed to do was LIVE. She had had enough of books and lectures. What she needed to do was get away, to break out of the mold, and both her ancestry and her training told her that meant FRANCE. She had a record of Yves Montand singing songs of the French Resistance and another of Juliette Greco singing in the smoke-filled cavern-cabaret of Le Tabou (with atmospheric photo on the album jacket), and she knew about Jean-Paul Sartre and Simone de Beauvoir drinking espresso coffee out of little cups and creating existentialism at Saint-Germain-des-Prés, and she knew that going to Paris would put her on the high road to authenticity. When she met Malone, late in her senior year, she thought he might be the man to get her there.

Have another drink, said Malone, with just the look and accent of feigned drunkenness that her father affected sometimes when they were relaxed enough in each other's company to play the game, and she had answered in kind, without missing a beat,

Sure, what am I drinking? And Malone had laughed, delighted by her quickness, because this was certainly the most beautiful girl he had ever seen in his life, and she was fun too.

They were sitting at the end of the bar in Pete's Tavern on Irving Place in New York. They had met for the first time on a double date that afternoon, but they had parted company with the other couple when Malone suggested that they have a look at a recently opened photographic exhibition at the Museum of Modern Art. The other couple had wanted to go to Radio City.

I'd love to see some photographs, said Sylvia, unless they're artsy fashion photographs.

Have no fear, said Malone, a little surprised.

So what are they of? she asked.

You'll see in a minute, said Malone.

They had taken a taxi over to the MoMA and bought their tickets and climbed a flight of stairs, and they were standing in a long gallery which had been modified by the installation of a series of panels placed at right angles to the walls, alternately, so that you progressed through the exhibit in a zigzag pattern.

It'll be like tacking, said Malone.

Sylvia apparently hadn't heard. She was looking intently at a photograph of a metropolitan waterway spanned by an old iron bridge partially supported by pontoons. The point of view showed the bridge receding right to left toward the center of the photograph where it appeared to intersect with the bulk of a domed building from which two gray spires rose into a pink and cloudless sky. Bunched against the wharves almost beneath the image of the domed building were half a dozen ferryboats, one of which was just swinging into the current and about to move out of the picture to the left, downstream. The captain must be just announcing his departure, because a white spout leaps from the steam whistle, and two fishermen leaning at the rail of the walkway under the bridge look up, as a third man, an oarsman who rows standing in a doubled-prowed caïque, turns, arrested in his stroke.

It's like being there, she said.

The caption identified the photograph as being of the Eminönü ferry landing, with the minarets of the Yeni Cami set off against a sunset sky. It was unnecessary to name the third principal component of the photograph, because this first section of the exhibit carried the overall title: "Galata Bridge, Variations on a Theme."

I think we're in Istanbul, said Sylvia.

We are indeed, said Malone. Let me show you something.

On a table just inside the door, free for the taking, were photocopies of a review of the exhibit that had appeared in the previous Sunday's *Times*. The reviewer was full of praise, describing the exhibit as "powerfully evocative" and "offering the distilled essence of contemporary life in an ancient town." The photographer, Selim Şimşek, was a native of Istanbul, it said, where he had been educated at the American College, after which he had gone on to obtain a Master of Fine Arts degree at Yale. The notice said that he was currently resident in France.

I know exactly where he is currently resident, said Malone. I've been in his studio in Montparnasse.

You've been to Paris? Sylvia asked.

I went to school there as a boy, he said.

My God, said Sylvia.

What's wrong?

Nothing, she said. I just envy you.

Malone went on to explain that the previous year he had received a grant to spend six months doing research for his dissertation at the Bibliothèque Nationale. He had stayed in a friend's apartment on the Isle Saint-Louis, and the friend had introduced him to a circle of drinking pals at the Select in Montparnasse. Selim Şimşek had been one of them, and though Selim said that he could never again live permanently anywhere but in Paris, he loved to talk about Istanbul, and when he found that Malone was willing to listen, he talked. He told Malone that although he could never live for very long in Istanbul, neither could he imagine never going back. So he spent a month every summer visiting his family in Ortaköy, and he had been building, over the last few years, a documentary portrait, as he called it, of his native town. Malone realized, upon reading the review in the *Times*, that he had probably already seen some of these photographs when a group from the Select had ended a heroic drinking spree in Selim's studio late one Sunday night; but that, Malone said, is another story.

So the photographer is a friend of yours. It's quite a coincidence.

Kısmet is what they call it, said Malone. Fate.

Malone and Sylvia now began to make their way through the exhibit, each section of which recorded the attributes of a different area of Istanbul. "Galata Bridge" was followed by sections on the Grand Bazaar, Beyoğlu, a gypsy village under the Theodosian Walls, İstiklal Caddesi, Galatasaray and the Çiçek Pasajı, several villages and sites along the Bosphorus (Beylerbeyi, Kuruçeşme, Bebek, Kandilli, Rumeli Hisarı, Beykoz), and an extended concluding section on the ancient city's First Hill—the site of the earliest acropolis and still first in cultural significance—including shots of Topkapı Palace, Haghia Sophia, Sultanahmet, and the Hippodrome. The reviewer was correct in calling attention to a number of motifs which were repeated from section to section and which gave, as he said, a sense of community to the whole. Principal among these were the pervasive references to water: itinerant water-sellers in their colorful Janissary costumes, street-side fountains, and *şadırvan*s (the fountains used for ceremonial ablutions in the courtyards of mosques). There were also constant reminders of Istanbul's geographic situation between two continents and two seas (a variant of the water motif), with periodic glimpses, between buildings or over rooftops, of the Bosphorus, Golden Horn, and Sea of Marmara. The reviewer was finally struck by the reappearance of certain characteristic types: the westernized professional with briefcase and suit, the peasant mother cradling her baby in a shawl, the midday toper, an itinerant dwarf (with donkey) selling lottery tickets, the shopkeeper lounging in his doorway, the street urchin, the camera-clad Japanese, the westernized professional's fashionable wife and child, the evening toper, the fishmonger, the costumed doorman, groups of hip young people going in and out of shops and cinemas, the street accordionist, the holy man (imam or dervish), the contemplative waiter, the dandy, the lost peasant girl, men playing backgammon in a smoke-filled coffee shop, the midnight toper. The reviewer concluded that he had been so caught up in Selim Şimşek's world that he was sure some part of him, perhaps his better part, had actually been to Istanbul.

Isn't that what I said? asked Sylvia, very pleased. Isn't that exactly what I said?

Close enough, said Malone. You said, It's like being there.

It was, she said. It was just like being there.

Maybe you'd like to go back some day and visit the old haunts.

The old haunts, she said, I like the sound of that.

We'll go back together, what do you think?

I think, she said.

Therefore you are, said Malone.

Ha, ha, she said. This is all very true and beautiful, but I thought we were having another drink.

Bartender, said Malone, two more of these please.

These please, said Sylvia. I like these please. It's almost as good as old haunts.

The bartender knew what they were drinking. Margaritas. It was their fourth round.

Maybe we should sit down at a table and get something to eat, said Malone.

Malone had settled the bill at the bar, and they had carried their drinks over to a corner table. She was enjoying herself. She was pretty sloshed, but she knew it, and she was genuinely enjoying herself. She liked listening to Malone. She liked Malone. He had been places and done things and she found it easy listening to his talk. She remembered he had told her a little about Pete's, the tavern they were in—so she would know that they weren't just anywhere—and some of the great names associated with the place: O. Henry, the short story writer (they had a display case with a signed first edition of *The Voice of the City*, 1908); Christy Mathewson, who won thirty-seven games on the mound for the New York Giants in that same year of 1908; and John L. Sullivan, before he had sworn off the booze, "The Great John L." himself, the "still and forever undefeated bare-knuckles champeen of the world."

Malone had told her afterwards that he had fallen in love with her that very night at Pete's, but that he had been afraid to say so for fear of sounding like a moron, and she remembered telling Malone that the same thing had happened to her, but that she hadn't been aware of it until he had begun sounding like a moron. They'd had a good laugh over that, but it was true enough for her. She had been waiting for Malone to come out of himself, to stop weaving a web of words and just let himself go. She knew now that she had expected too much from her marriage and expatriation—she had looked upon the two as one—and too much from Malone. Malone was to have carried her off to a wild and woolly world, away from the repressions and constraints that she had so thoroughly interiorized, and so save her from herself. He had indeed carried her off, in the literal sense, but the release, his or hers, had never occurred, and their marriage had never sparked the explosion that she had dreamed about.

Explosion was the word all right, and the spark was to be struck one raucous night at the Boem by the astonishing Dimitri Papas. Dangerous Dimitri, funny old bear, so sure of himself, but awkwardly gentle and considerate, and the more dangerous for all that. He seemed to be constantly in love, half the time with one new woman or another and half the time with his wife, to whom he would return more in love than he had ever been. Sylvia had known all that, but what woman could resist him? He was so full of life and so happy to be alive in the world. Not pretty, certainly, nor even handsome in any traditional sense, but powerfully attractive. She didn't quite know how that could be, but it was. And with him, all the masks had fallen and she had finally let herself go. He had called her his Snow Queen, and then he had shown her what it was to boil. They had boiled all over the place, in hotel rooms downtown, over a couple of weekends in Büyükada, in the back stairwell of a friend's house in Beykoz, in the stateroom of a sailing yacht in Bebek harbor, by moonlight stark naked on a blanket at Kilyos beach. She remembered it all, in every detail, and she would never forget. But it was like magic and it was crazy, and it couldn't last. She remembered beginning to cool and telling Dimitri that an adventure was something you went home after, and Dimitri had said,

That sounds like something young ladies learn at school.

Sylvia hadn't answered him. Dimitri had an unsettling gift for getting things exactly right. He had looked momentarily aggrieved, but he had smiled—always the forward-looking fellow that he was—and he had taken her up in his great arms and kissed her on both cheeks, as he would continue to do whenever they met, and he told her that he understood—she hadn't the least doubt of it—and that, for him, she would always be—delicious.

She hadn't at first caught the implications of his calling her the Snow Queen, but she realized in retrospect that she had failed Malone as much as he had failed her. Her love for him had never been—warm. And now she had failed Dimitri too, in a way. She had known, or supposed, from what she had heard of Dimitri's habitual behavior, that the affair couldn't last, that it would follow the predictable periodicity of things. But as Dimitri turned the heat up and she continued to respond, she had conceived the possibility that this time things could be different, that there was no telling where his wildness, and her own, might lead, and she had been afraid. Her fear had saved her, not from Dimitri, but from herself. But it had been a righteous fear, she decided, and though she had emerged from the experience feeling wrung, so did she finally feel indulgent towards herself. She no longer felt inadequate, nor did she feel she had gone too far the other way. She felt about herself, like Goldilocks in bed, "just right."

iii

Shortly after her breakup with Dimitri, Sylvia began taking Turkish lessons from Mimi Toledano. Though not a native speaker, Mimi could pass for one in most circumstances. She had early decided to come as near as possible to mastery of the language of her husband's country, where she fully intended to spend the rest of her life, and she had taken the full range of courses for foreigners offered at Istanbul University. She had continued on her own with a reading schedule in modern Turkish literature and conversational exchanges with the well-educated wife of the playwright Enver Yakut, who lived just down the street in Kuzguncuk.

In addition to acquiring an excellent command of Turkish, she had come away from her studies at Istanbul University with some sound approaches to language pedagogy. For example, she used to begin each lesson with a proverb, having Sylvia repeat it several times and then periodically throughout the lesson until she had it memorized. The proverbs of all countries are tersely worded and phrased in such a way as to make them easy to remember. In addition, they are a particularly rich repository of cultural information, as well as containing lessons in phonetics, grammar, and vocabulary. It was an excellent way to start a lesson, particularly in a language and culture where the natives quoted proverbs all the time, or coined variations for comic effect.

One of the more amusing and useful proverbs that Sylvia remembered learning from the earliest days of her course was *Deli için her gün bayramdır*, which meant, "For the mad, every day is a holiday." The meaning seemed clear enough, but Mimi had explained that, strictly speaking, a *bayram* was a religious feast, the only kind known to the Turks of Ottoman and Islamic times. The secular republic had given the word new meaning, but without eradicating the old. The Turkish language, like the city of Istanbul, was a cultural palimpsest.

Other culturally rich expressions, still widely in use, were: *Her ağaçtan yay olmaz*—"Not every tree will yield a bow"—which harkens back to the days of the mounted archers depicted in the early miniatures. The expression can now be heard used by teachers or mothers bemoaning the conduct of a recalcitrant child. Or there was the Turkish version of "The die is cast"—*Ok yaydan çıktı*—meaning, "The arrow has left the bow." Or the wonderfully useful *Kavuk büyük ama altında efendi yok*—"The turban is big, but there is no gentleman inside." You might, for example, use this in traffic on the careless and arrogant driver of a new Mercedes, as you might also ask him, at the stoplight, if for him, *her gün bayram mıdır?*

Other useful expressions were: *Dikensiz gül olmaz*—"There is no rose without thorns"—or the more comical *Kenesiz tavuk olmaz*—"There is no chicken without fleas"—or *Baz bazla, kaz kazla* (Falcon with falcon, goose with goose), *Yıkmak yapmak-*

tan kolaydır (It's easier to ruin than to build), *Tereciye tere satılmaz* (You can't sell watercress to the watercress man), or the apparently obscure *Atı alan Üsküdar'ı geçti*. This proverb recalls the latter days of the Ottoman Empire when effective power in many of the Anatolian provinces, and as near as a few kilometers beyond Üsküdar, was in the hands of petty princes who were often defiant of the central authority. The proverb means, literally, "The horseman has passed Üsküdar," indicating that he has got away, it's too late, and implying that, whatever the circumstance, there's no more to be done.

Sylvia and Mimi had a high old time over these lessons and they quickly became great friends. They even began giving each other cooking lessons from Turkish recipes each might select, and many lessons were built around the buying and preparing of food. Sylvia remembered a tripe soup (*işkembe çorbası*) that Malone had once obtained, already prepared, from a shop in Ortaköy, and that they had served in their back garden at midnight to the usual group of friends. Sylvia and Mimi went shopping together for the necessary ingredients, and Mimi came up with a couple of proverbs concerning soup. Soup had been for ages a staple of the Turkish diet, and the names of some of the most popular soups expressed their ancient tribal origins, for example *yayla çorbası*, soup of the high pasture. Soup had also provided the staple diet of the elite troops of the Ottoman army, the Janissary Corps, whose great soup cauldron became a symbol of their power and which, when overturned, served as a declaration of revolt. Senior colonels in the Corps proudly bore the title of *Çorbacı*, which Mimi translated as Souperman. Another pedagogical proverb, still frequently heard, was, *Tatsız çorbaya tuz neylesin, boş başa söz neylesin*, meaning, "Salt won't improve a tasteless soup; words won't improve an empty head." Often a Turk will simply say, "Salt won't improve a tasteless soup," and the rest will be understood. There was also an idiom meaning to make a contribution to something (a conversation, for example) by putting salt in the soup—*Çorbada tuzu olmak*—and a soup proverb praising, or perhaps lamenting, the infinite variety of the world: "Of a thousand soups, no two the same" (*Bin çorba, bir değil*).

Not long after the beginning of the Turkish lessons, Mimi learned from Yakup that the owners of the Grand Cafe de Pera, downtown, were going to open an outdoor cafe on the Bosphorus just upstream from the ferry landing in Bebek. Apparently there was an abandoned lot behind the local pastry shop, accessible from the street through a narrow alley that ran between the pastry shop and the Bebek Hotel. The owner of the Cafe de Pera, a longtime friend of Dimitri's, had leased the lot from the hotel and had removed the usual accumulation of debris by having it bagged and lowered over the seawall into a barge tied up below. Once cleaned up, the lot had been leveled, the concrete poured, and the site readied for use within a week. These fellows could move quickly when they wanted to.

The cafe was due to open on Friday night. It was to be a gala affair, and Dimitri had reserved a big table and asked Erden to spread the word. Sylvia had felt apprehensive about seeing Dimitri again and awkward at the idea of showing up all by herself, and she was thinking of giving Frank Corrigan a call when he called her. She already knew Frank, or thought she did, considering him a solid and even stolid sort, civilized and dependable, intelligent certainly, but perhaps lacking in flair. She remembered that once he and Erden had taken Malone and herself on a walking tour of Balat and the district around the Greek Patriarchate, then on to see the early-fourteenth-century Byzantine mosaics in the Kariye Museum (formerly the Kariye Mosque and before that the Byzantine Church of St. Savior in Chora), and finally to the Fethiye Camii, or Mosque of the Conquest, formerly the Church of the Theotokos Pammakaristos (the Joyous Mother of God) and seat of the Patriarchate from 1456 to 1568. More palimpsests. Frank had described the many architectural alterations that the church and mosque had undergone and had walked them into what had once been a side chapel in the southeast corner of the church. It was in this side chapel and on this very spot, from 1456 to 1459, that the Patriarch Gennadius and the Ottoman Sultan, Mehmet the Conqueror himself, met to discuss, in the warmth of a genuine friendship, the fine points of Christian and Islamic theology. Listening to Frank, Sylvia had felt as if the life of the vanished chapel had been given form again. It was an experience quite different from remembering, as it was mediated entirely by words, but haunting nevertheless, this knowledge that you were standing on the very stones where Gennadius and Mehmet had stood.

She had ever since been rather awed by Frank. She thought of him as a disembodied voice, like one of those charismatic bards of old, and she couldn't imagine holding his hand, for example, or kissing him. The impression changed little when he came to pick her up that night. As they walked by Hamlin Hall, he talked of how Cyrus Hamlin, the founder of the school, had analyzed the mortar used by Mehmet's engineers in the fortress at Rumeli Hisarı and had reproduced the formula for the construction of the hall later named for him. As they walked down the hill, he had talked of the nearby Aşiyan Museum, formerly the home of Tevfik Fikret, one of the leading poets of the "New Literature" at the end of the nineteenth century and for many years professor of Turkish Literature at the College. The museum now held his papers and memorabilia as it did those of the great lady poet and diarist of the day, Nigar Hanım, who had been Tevfik's friend. At the bottom of the hill, he talked of Mehmet's great castle of Rumeli Hisarı and the dervish cemetery that lay under its walls and, walking along the Bosphorus on the way into Bebek, of the beautiful wooden summer palaces that the Ottomans had built on both sides of the water and of those that had survived the building boom along the Asian shore, and of the families that had lived in them and their romantic histories. Sylvia had listened with genuine interest, but she was beginning to have difficulty concentrating, when Frank, who must have noticed something, suggested they have a preparatory drink at Nazmi's, a cafe at the water's edge.

Frank took them to a corner table by the seawall. They ordered *rakı*, which arrived in a carafe along with a pitcher of water and little tub of ice. Frank poured them each half a glass of *rakı* and added water until the mixture turned milky white.

A little ice to take the edge off, he said. It's going to be a long evening.

She smiled at him and nodded. He gave them each a cube, and they lifted their glasses and said, Cheers. They drank in silence, looking out over the water as the setting sun flashed in the windows of the palaces across the way. When the ice in their drinks had melted, Frank shared out what *rakı* was left in the carafe. The warm calm of the evening and the *rakı* were having their effect. The water flowed slowly by them in dark, sensual undulations, and Sylvia thought how lovely it would be to go for a swim. She felt wonderfully at ease, but it was time to go, and it seemed to her perfectly natural that as they walked out of the cafe together, Frank should take her by the hand.

They walked slowly through the village, thinking their own thoughts, and past two or three closed-up shops and through a shaft of light glaring from the entrance to the Bebek Hotel and back into the dark. At the corner, still holding her by the hand, Frank stopped and, drawing her towards him, lifted her face and kissed her, very gently, on the lips.

It had been so smoothly and sweetly done that she wondered how it had, and she felt a little stunned as they walked together down the alleyway between the hotel and the pastry shop and into the warm yellow glow of lamps. It seemed the workmen hadn't yet gotten the electricity installed. There were no electric lights, and the bartender had had to use an extension cord run through the back window of the pastry shop to power his refrigerators.

The cooking was being done over wood fires set in braziers (the ancestral *mangal*) and, with trellises and potted plants along the walls and the soft suffusion of lamplight, the cafe might have belonged to a time when Bebek was a country village and the city a thousand miles away.

The atmosphere was having its effect, and everybody seemed to be talking to everybody else. There wasn't a free table in the house, and the overflow of customers was drinking at the bar. It didn't seem to matter who was where. People who were seated at one moment were standing the next. They looked for Dimitri's table and there it was, in the far corner of the terrace, next to the seawall, and all the old pals were there.

Dimitri saw them coming. It was the first time he and Sylvia had seen each other since breaking up, but he greeted them in his usual expansive way with bear hugs and kisses and clappings on the back. There were general hellos and kisses all round, and Mimi waved Sylvia over next to her where she had saved two seats. Faruk and Verda Selvi were there, with two of Faruk's colleagues from the newspaper; Yakup, next to Mimi, was sitting next to Elena Papas, with Dimitri at the end of the table and, next to him, across from Elena, a young American Fulbright scholar who was nominally assigned to the Sociology Department, but who was really there to learn Turkish. Next was the young American's strikingly pretty young wife—Scholar beware, thought Sylvia—and Erden and Verda and the rest. There was no orchestra, but the cafe had hired a disk jockey, and the music, Turkish and Greek, was going like mad. The hot and cold *meze* were circulating right behind the *rakı*, and the dancing had begun, circles and serpentines—not a foxtrot in the house—and before you knew it there were more bottles and, between dances, you were eating grilled lamb and pilaf and, with the dancing and the general interchange of acquaintance on the dance floor and in the milling around the bar, you were never sure who might be sitting at your table next.

Dimitri and the scholar were feeling no pain, and Dimitri, as dance instructor, had taken the young man out to join a circle of a dozen men forming on the floor. As the music started, the dancers joined hands, circled to the right and stopped, kicked, circled to the left and stopped, kicked, converged on the center with linked hands raised and a tremendous shout, retreated to the perimeter and started the process over again. After half a dozen repetitions, the rhythm began to accelerate as the melody shifted to a higher key. By this time, several other circles had formed, both men and women, and the dance floor had become so crowded that the circles began to intersect. It looked as if chaos might ensue, when Dimitri broke from the dancer on his right and led his circle away in a single file. The other circles broke in turn to follow him. He led them, weaving among the tables, through a full circuit of the cafe, returning to the dance floor just in time to catch the last dancer in line. A new circle having been formed, Dimitri leapt into the center, and had begun to execute a series of violent leaps and spins around the floor, when he was joined by a very handsome young man who moved with the fluid grace of a professional. They made an amusing and astonishing pair, and when the dance was done, they laughed and clapped each other on the back, and Dimitri asked the young man to join them for a drink. The young man sat between Dimitri and the scholar, and, what with the heat of the evening and the alcohol and the violent exercise, the three of them were sweating like wrestlers.

Cheers, said Dimitri in English, and Cheers, said the scholar in English, and Şerefe, said the handsome young man, when there appeared from nowhere a visibly angry giant of a man, all muscles and chest hair, who began to abuse the handsome young dancer. He was evidently the dancer's lover. Dimitri decided that the wisest course was to stay clear, but the scholar, whose weak Turkish gave him no idea of what was going on beyond the fact that the giant was angry, put his arm around the dancer's shoulder, and presumably intending to diffuse the situation with an innocuous comment on the heat, tried to say *"çok sıcak"* (It's very hot); but what he said was *"çok sucuk,"* which means "much sausage." Dimitri exploded in laughter as the giant, furious, seized the scholar by the shirtfront with one hand and lifted him clear of his chair. He was about to slap him with the flat of his free hand, when Erden, who had anticipated trouble, stepped in and explained to the giant at top speed that the young man he was holding had made an innocent mistake because he was an American and, by definition, had no idea what was going on. The argument appealed to the giant, who smiled and set the scholar down and straightened his shirtfront and agreed to join them for a drink. They were to see him frequently in the future with his handsome young friend in various restaurants and watering holes downtown, and they never failed to recall the anecdote of the scholar's gaffe.

By two in the morning, the party had begun to break up. Faruk and Verda and the two colleagues had already left. They had contributed little to the festivities, but their departure was, for Dimitri, a bad sign. He hated to see an evening come to an end, and he knew that the moment had come for him to announce, with a general refilling and hoisting of glasses, that he had a surprise.

He left the table and crossed the dance floor and disappeared behind the bar. He reappeared moments later carrying a great steaming soup tureen, followed by a waiter carrying bowls and spoons.

Ladies and Gentlemen, he intoned, setting the tureen down in front of him, To continue the evening on a yet more festive plane, I present to you the noble and popular, the potent and inspirational soup of the ages and of all vitalities: Istanbul's very own, the miraculous *işkembe çorbası*!

The announcement met with a general cheer, punctuated by Mimi Toledano's rapping on an empty bottle with her knife.

Ladies and Gentlemen, she said, rising and facing Dimitri, We must drink in salutation and profoundest gratitude to our dear friend, Dimitri the He-Tree, who will henceforth also be known as—pause—Çorba the Greek!

There was another general cheer and laughter, and Erden said, How is it that nobody ever thought of that before?

That's my Mimi, said Yakup.

You Yakup, Mimi said, Me Mimi.

The soup was delicious and had a universally soothing effect. Soon Elena Papas was asleep, her head on Dimitri's shoulder. Dimitri was smiling happily to himself in a world of his own imagining. Erden was talking to an old friend at another table. Yakup and Mimi had left. The scholar had gone safely home with his pretty wife.

Let's have that swim, said Frank.

What swim? said Sylvia, startled, remembering her earlier thought at Nazmi's.

The swim I've been thinking about ever since Nazmi's, he said.

Well, she said, you certainly can surprise a girl.

Have I surprised you before?

A little, she said, this time thinking of the kiss. She wondered if he was serious about the swim, and she imagined them taking off their clothes in the empty and darkened cafe and climbing up onto the seawall and standing there, for a moment, naked in the moonlight—for there really was moonlight—and his holding her by the hand and saying, One, two three, before they jumped, and his holding her close against him with the silvery water slick on their skins and caressing her body as he entered her, and she thought, *Çok sucuk*, and laughed out loud.

What's the matter? said Frank.

Nothing, she said, I just feel a little punchy like Dimitri over there. Would you settle for a dance?

We'll swim another time.

It was the first time they had danced together, just the two of them, and they danced once slowly around the floor, and Frank held her very close and kissed her cheek and they slowly danced between the tables and into a dark corner of the cafe and they danced very slowly, his thigh between her thighs, and he kissed her, very slowly and seriously this time, and her whole body was coming alive as she felt his body coming alive, and she made a noise in her throat that wasn't like laughter at all.

Let's go home, he said. There's a taxi stand out front.

Sylvia ran on, remembering that night with Frank and the great adventure of the early days of their love as if it were yesterday; but it was time, now, to break the rhythm and go home again to the long day that lay ahead and all the long days that lay ahead, to a quick shower and preparing breakfast for Nicolette and a quick hello and goodbye to Frank and to meeting Mimi at the Aşiyan Museum in the afternoon to work on their translations of Nigar. It was true, of course, that you never knew what Mimi might do or say next or what surprises might be waiting for them in Nigar; and—Sylvia had begun to recover already—there was tonight at Boncuk, with everybody imaginable and Malone.

5
MALONE

i

The sun had set, and the evening call to prayer had sounded from the mosque of Sultan Ahmet on the Hippodrome to the mosques of Beyazıt and Süleyman, from the mosques of Beyoğlu and Beşiktaş to the mosques of Üsküdar and Kuzguncuk and Kandilli on the Asian shore, and from the graceful little Bebek Camii to the village mosque of Pertek Ali Bey below the fortress towers of Rumeli Hisarı. In Beyoğlu, the entire length of İstiklal Caddesi, from its midpoint at Galatasaray to Taksim Square, was a continuous blaze of light. Along its lower end, however, between Galatasaray and Tünel, there were no cinemas or commercial arcades, and its few scattered restaurants were tucked away in obscure, angular side streets. The bookstore at Tünel, with its sextant and its telescope and the logbook of the steamship *Vidar* and, further along the avenue, the traditional small shops, survivors from an earlier day—shops selling inexpensive children's toys, or uniforms for nurses, doormen, or domestic help, costume jewelry, wigs, and antique prints—had long since turned off their lights and closed their doors and rung down their iron mesh curtains for the night.

In a small side street off İstiklal, the beer hall where Malone had been drinking was dark. It's amazing how quickly these fellows can close down, he thought. You turn away and in an instant the place is dark and dead silent and you'd think it had never been there at all. He stood for a moment musing in front of the door. He had shaken the hand of an old toper with whom he had had some conversation, and watched him limp off to wherever it is that old topers go. Would somebody be waiting for him somewhere with a warm meal in a lighted room? His clothes had certainly seen better days. Had he also seen better days? There had been something courtly about the man that suggested a familiarity with … what? What might he not have been familiar with? And Malone's musings were interrupted by the wailing call, distant at first, then near at hand, and repeating, echoing across the city, of the evening call to prayer: Allaaaaahhhhhu Akbar. Malone looked up. The street where he stood was dark, and the night was clear and, with the privileged clarity usually found only in open countryside, he could see the stars. He walked down the street to where his friend of a few moments ago had disappeared and, turning into a narrow alley, soon found that the alley opened into a lovely old residential square, enclosed by wooden houses in the old Ottoman style, none more than three stories high, with an open garden in the center, planted with hedges and flowers, and in one corner of which towered a venerable sycamore. The city was full of unexpected wonders, he thought. You never knew what you might find next. The houses all looked inhabited and well maintained, but none had been restored. They were unashamedly, even defiantly old, and they had lost nothing of their self-respect. Most of the houses showed a light somewhere, with clean white curtains in the windows. Two or three were dark, but Malone supposed that the family would be saving on electricity and would be gathered in the kitchen at the back of the house.

Malone walked farther into the garden and stood for a moment under the great sycamore. The reiterated calls to prayer still echoed overhead. A light wind blew, and the filigree of new leaves in the sycamore rustled slightly, and their flutterings seemed to mix with the winking of the stars. The vast sky overhead seemed at once immeasurably distant and very near, achingly strange and achingly familiar. At a corner of the square stood a house very much like all the others, dark but for a single light showing on the third floor. It pleased Malone to imagine that this was where his toper might be, alone, with two or three cats, perhaps, a few good books, an album of photographs, and, he was sure, a gramophone. He was sure there must be a gramophone, because he was sure he could hear music coming from that room, though he couldn't have told you what was being played nor what the instruments, so faint it was and muffled within the rustling of the leaves. Malone stood very still a moment longer, watching and listening, when he began to have the eerie sensation of having been here before, of somehow having previously gained access to this very place, perhaps under very different circumstances, but essentially the same. Malone stood, and the sensation held. He listened. He was sure there was music coming from a gramophone playing somewhere, but, walking towards the corner house to verify its source, all he could hear momentarily was the crunching sound of gravel underfoot. He stopped. He looked around the square. Nothing had changed, but the wind had fallen and the silence was complete. The light still burned in the upstairs window, but it was as if he no longer knew why, and he wondered how much of his previous certainty had been imagined and how much had been real. It had all seemed perfectly real a moment before, the old man and his cats and the bowl of warm milk on the floor—was the image returning?—and the wistful, creaky music of the gramophone. Was that it again? Or was that the wind only, or a ringing in his ears?

    The experience had been so convincing that Malone tried to analyze its components. The square and the garden were indubitably real, and the sky and the stars and the leaves and branches overhead, and the corner building with the third-story light. The old man too was real enough, as the toper had been real, though putting him in the upstairs room with his books and cats was entirely the work of old Andy's fertile brain and Andy had been perfectly aware of it. The music, however, had been something else entirely. He hadn't imagined the music at all, or not in any willful sense. He had heard the music, and he had only subsequently imagined the gramophone to explain it. So the music had come entirely unbidden, entirely independent of his will, which meant that it had either been real, which was very doubtful, or that it had been drawn up from somewhere deep within himself by everything else in the experience that it was not. The experience had been so composed as to require and call up the music to complete itself and to become suffused with its life. And when I moved, he thought, I not only made a noise, but by changing my position, I also disturbed the precise configuration needed to call the music up.

The atmosphere of the square was wonderfully serene, and wonderfully suited to his mood. He looked around again, feeling no desire to be on his way. He saw that, upon entering the garden, he had crossed a patch of grass to the approximate point where he had first heard the music, but he was sure he could not repeat the experience through any conscious effort to do so, and he had no wish to try. He noticed that a gravel path led to the far corner of the garden and what looked to be a wrought iron bench. There was nothing irritating or disruptive in the sound of the gravel now as he walked along the path to the wrought iron bench. He sat down. The bench was remarkably comfortable for the material of which it was made, and Malone's feeling of tranquility was undisturbed. From where he sat, he could see again the lighted third-story window through the leaves of the sycamore.

I could sit here all night, he thought, and make up stories about my old toper up there. He has three cats, and they are just now having their supper of brown bread soaking in a bowl of warm water. The old man has very little money, but he doesn't worry about the cats. He leaves a window slightly open during the day, so they can go out and fend for themselves. He brings them some bread for their supper only if he happens to find some, as he did this evening crossing the square. The old man spends every morning writing his memoirs, or this is the story he tells. He was a career army officer, and he had fought in the battles of the Sakarya and Dumlupınar, and he was with Mustafa Kemal when the army rode into Izmir. He had been wounded six times and decorated for valor twice, but he had been passed over for promotion to full colonel "for political reasons" and had been forced to retire. His pension was small, and, as prices rose, it got smaller every year. He was writing his memoirs. They would be published some day, soon perhaps, and the officials and the public would learn something that they didn't know. At this point the old man would lower his voice and assume a conspiratorial tone—perhaps the very tone that had got him into trouble—and repeat that they would learn something that they didn't know, that they didn't want to know, that they were afraid of. So the moment would come and the old man would be fully vindicated and the light of truth would shine upon that somber moment in the history of the republic when the memoirs that he wrote in the mornings were published, and after lunch he would go out into the city, which he knew as he knew the palm of his own hand—he would show you the scar in the palm of his hand—to see if he could be useful to his friends—for he had many friends—or find something that might be useful to himself. Then, to end each day, he would drink one beer somewhere—the Çiçek Pasajı, the Pera Palace, sometimes even this small bar—and even a second beer, if there were someone kind enough to offer it. And assuming again the conspiratorial tone of some moments before, he would lean towards his interlocutor and say,

You haven't got a cigarette, have you?

Malone, taken somewhat by surprise, for these were the very

words the old toper had spoken to him, remembered answering, No, but wait a minute. Malone had then climbed down from his stool at the bar and walked up to the corner of the street where he had seen a newsstand and had bought a pack of Bafra cigarettes, for old time's sake. Mustafa offered me a cigarette at the bar under the bridge, he thought, and another when I was sitting outside at the table by the rail daydreaming, and both times I told him that I hadn't smoked in fifteen years, and Mustafa had said that in Turkey everybody smoked, which was true and obvious enough, adding that it also served to remind you to carry matches. Malone remembered being puzzled by that one, until he thought that Mustafa must be perpetuating the bomb joke, which meant that he, Malone, would be expected to respond in kind, but he could think of nothing witty and instead had asked Mustafa for the bill. So he had remembered to buy a box of matches with the Bafras and, back in the bar, he hitched himself up on his stool next to the old man and said, This is the first pack of Bafras I've bought in twenty years, adding,

It takes me back.

Where? said the old man.

Here, said Malone, wondering if he had used the idiom correctly.

But you are here, said the old man, looking slightly puzzled.

You're right about that, said Malone, and he smiled at the old man and offered him a cigarette, and the old man smiled and took one, and Malone struck a match and they lit up, and Malone, remembering, said "fire" to the old man and the old man gave him a startled look.

Yes, said Malone, The only thing that distinguishes men from the animals is the ability to produce fire. Nothing else matters. Not houses, not clothes, not language. The birds build houses and dogs wear sweaters and everybody knows these days that dolphins and whales can talk. But they can't produce fire, none of them. So the real reason why men smoke in Turkey is so that they will be reminded to carry matches and be always able to produce fire, like true men.

This is a very Turkish idea, said the old man, and a very true and original one.

It may be Turkish, said Malone, but it's not original, at least not with me. I heard it from a friend of mine earlier this afternoon—Malone, unable to resist, had asked Mustafa to explain about the matches when he brought the bill—but do you think he meant it as a joke?

No, no, no, no, no, said the old man. This is no joke. This is a very profound idea and a very original one. I know an original idea when I see one, and I shall use it in my memoirs.

Had the old man really said that? He had indeed. Malone reached into the inside breast pocket of his jacket for the cigarettes and tapped one out. He had split the contents with the old man, and they had smoked a few, so he would be needing some more. If the old soldier is smoking up there—for how could it be anybody else?—I hope he doesn't accidentally distinguish himself—ha, ha. Malone lit up. He inhaled deeply and lazily and stretched his legs out in front of him and his arms out along the back of the bench. Perhaps an old lady lived up there, somebody like Madame la Comtesse, as he called her, for they had always spoken to each other in French, or Madame Bishkek. More like Madame Bishkek, but a terrible old harridan, who kept no cats, but two canaries in a small cage, and the female tortured the male incessantly, tearing the feathers from his neck, and he would soon die, and the old lady looked on dreamily. She had lived her life for physical pleasure, and by it, but she had never fallen in love, and she was now old and bitter and bent. She wore tattered clothes and ate little and had only one lamp, which she moved from place to place as she needed it. But she was rich. She had money in the bank and gold hidden on her closet shelf. She had two secrets, her gold and her birds. Nobody would ever know the story of the birds, but one day, should the building burn, they would find the gold, scattered in droplets among the charred remains, and wonder how anyone so rich would choose to live as she had done.

Quite a little melodrama, thought Malone. Balzac might have made something out of it, but I don't see him around. He lifted the cigarette to his lips and took a drag, and as he did so the light in the window momentarily dimmed, as someone inside the room passed between the window and the lamp. There was somebody there, all right, but who it was really he would never know. What had called up the story of the old woman in his mind? Was it a companion story to that of the old man? Very likely. There were similarities. But it seemed to Malone that there was a bitterness in the story of the old woman, a cruelty, that was absent from the story of the old man. He wondered to himself what might be the source of that bitterness and cruelty, and having discovered the question, the answer was obvious. There was only one person he had ever felt truly bitter about, but she had been the most important person in his life for the five years of their marriage, and perhaps she still was. He couldn't even pronounce her name without protective irony. There were times when her name or image, or some remembered act of hers or something she had said, would take him by surprise, and the shock of it would stop him dead in his tracks.

He remembered one summer day on the beach on Plum Island north of Boston watching a little girl digging trenches at the edge of the water. She must have been about three, dark, very pretty, and very concentrated on her work. He had been watching her from a short distance, admiring her, her eager gestures, her straight little back, not wishing to intrude, when a young woman, probably her mother, called, "Sylvia, come here a minute, will you please?" But before turning towards her mother, the little girl had first looked up at him and said, "I have to go now." The little girl had known all along that he was there and had felt perfectly secure and that there was no reason for her mother to call her away, and Malone knew that such a child might have been his but would never be.

On another occasion, in a seminar room of the Humanities Building of Essex College where he taught, they were just waiting for the last few students to arrive. There were eight of them there already, seated at a long rectangular table, Malone with his back to a broad window looking east over the salt marshes to the ocean. There were eleven students enrolled in the seminar and two or three minutes to go before they should start, and Malone was making solicitous small talk with a young woman seated to his left who had sprained her ankle running in a cross-country meet the previous Saturday. It was fall. Malone took off his wristwatch and leaned forward to place it on the table in front of him so he could watch the time, when the young blond woman on his right stood up from her chair and, pointing over his shoulder and out the window, cried out excitedly, "Oh, look!" Startled, Malone looked up at her where she stood with her arm extended and, turning towards the window, perceived, in simultaneity, a great flock of Canadian geese flying from left to right across the marsh and the unmistakable odor of *rakı* and *meze* and grilled fish. He stood then and crossed the few steps to the window, glad to have his back to the class as his heart beat wildly in his chest. He leaned forward with his hands on the windowsill and his forehead against the glass. He could hardly breathe. He wondered for a moment if he weren't having a heart attack. The other students began to arrive at the window to have a look, and Malone managed to calm himself with a few deep breaths and returned to his chair, glad that the general disturbance would give him time to collect himself. He tried to smile at the young woman on his left, who hadn't moved. Their eyes met, and she winced, and Malone wondered if it was her ankle or something she could see in his face.

ii

During their time together in Istanbul, Malone and Sylvia had lived in a small frame house just below the south end of the College terrace behind Hamlin Hall. They had arrived in late June by ship. The voyage had been like a honeymoon, because they had been married when Malone was still in graduate school and he hadn't been able to take any time off. The voyage had lasted eighteen days, the first fifteen in the old *Vulcania*: six days to cross the Atlantic, followed by stops in Lisbon, Gibraltar, Barcelona, Cannes, Naples, Palermo, Bari, Patras, Dubrovnik, and Venice. At Venice, they had transferred to the *San Marco*, twin ship to the *San Giorgio* in the old Adriatica Line, with a dramatic trip through the Corinth Canal and a stop in the Pireas. Sylvia had been very happy to arrive. After the charm of novelty had exhausted itself, she had found life on a ship terribly confining.

During the Atlantic crossing, the weather had been fine, but there was no pool in Tourist Class, and they had spent a great deal of time sitting in deck chairs. Like Malone, she had brought some books along and had tried to read, but she could only read so much, and she began to regard Malone's capacity for reading with some resentment and even a touch of distrust.

Still sitting there?

What did you say? For he thought he had heard those words, but he wanted to hear her say them again.

How can you just sit there and read all day?

It's Conrad, he would say, or Balzac, or a biography of Atatürk, as if that were explanation enough, at least until he became fully aware of her standing there rather sternly in front of him and of the full import of what she had said, and he would realize that to tell her what he was reading was to miss the point entirely and be guilty of insensitivity or stupidity or both.

Where have you been? he would say, closing the book. We'll go for a walk and explore all the decks and climb over that little gate up to First Class. What do you think?

I think, she said.

Therefore you are, he said, and she had forced herself to smile at the old joke.

Sylvia had tried to run, once, but even though it had been early in the morning and there had been no passengers about, the motion of the ship, and the deck chairs and stanchions and other shipboard impedimenta, and the general lack of space, made running impossible. You could never let yourself go. So she had tried speed walking and, properly dressed, or overdressed, she managed to break a sweat and get something resembling a workout. By the time they had reached Lisbon, it had become her routine. She would be up and out by five-thirty or six and walk for an hour, jogging occasionally when the coast was clear, running the stairs between decks, and when Malone woke, she would be gone. In the evenings they went to the movie, after which Malone would go to the bar, sometimes with Sylvia, sometimes not. Alone, he sometimes stayed in the bar until it closed. When he returned to the cabin, Sylvia would be asleep, and when he woke in the morning, she would have already returned from her workout and showered and dressed and gone out again to get breakfast on her own.

The rhythms of their life shipboard might have given some hint of their life to come. Sylvia had been enchanted by the little frame house. There was a lovely terraced area out back about the size of a tennis court. It showed the unmistakable signs of once having been maintained as a formal garden, and Sylvia looked forward to restoring it. At the back corner of the terrace, there was a small kiosk, or belvedere, with a fine view of the Bosphorus below and the Asian shore. The house itself, however small, had great charm. Upstairs there were two bedrooms and a modern bath. The east wall of the master bedroom opened onto what the Turks call a *cumba*, a large bay window extending some five feet outwards and supported by cantilevered beams built into the floor. The *cumba* afforded a panoramic view over the garden and the Bosphorus and the Asian hills beyond. Sylvia had set up a small table in the *cumba*, with two chairs, and she would sometimes come here to sit and read or make plans or just to think. The first thing she did in the morning was to cross to the *cumba* for a long look out, and the impression of open expansiveness and, as it were, of possibilities, never failed to act upon her as a tonic.

Not all of the house was equally to her liking. The ground floor consisted of two large rooms, one a living room, the other combining the kitchen and dining into a single space. The kitchen area was clean and efficient and perfectly satisfactory, and the living room had a handsome little brickwork fireplace to get you through the dark winter months. Centered in the rear wall, beneath the *cumba*, was a set of double doors that opened onto a brick landing and two steps leading down to a gravel path and the garden. At the opposite end of the living room, however, Malone had installed himself. He had commandeered the dining room table—they had been able to get a second one—and moved it into the living room for use as a desk. It took up too much room, but Malone needed every inch of it and more. The table was strewn with books and papers, with more of the same underneath, and he had installed two sets of floor-to-ceiling bookcases, one of which completely obscured one of the front windows. Sylvia considered the whole arrangement an intrusion. She had tried to get him to take over the second bedroom, but he had insisted he could work better downstairs, where he wouldn't feel confined. She began to notice that there were some books and papers that never seemed to move, and she began to wonder if this tremendous show of industry were entirely sincere. She began, in fact, actively to dislike having to walk through the front end of the living room, and in the winter, when she loved to build a fire, she would sit with her back to Malone's "study" and pretend it wasn't there.

They had had good times together, of course, going to parties, or out on the town, or having people in, just as they had found release during their voyages on the *Vulcania* and *San Marco* in their various ports of call, from Lisbon to the Pireas. But even these moments of release began to acquire, for Malone, an ambiguous and sometimes bitter quality. He remembered an incident that had occurred during a walk along the shore outside Dubrovnik, their last stop before reaching Venice and leaving the *Vulcania*. Sylvia had been feeling particularly edgy after fourteen days on board, and she seemed almost giddy from the release. It was towards midafternoon and hot, but they were determined to enjoy themselves. They walked close to the water along a rocky beach. To their left were the broad harbor estuary and the open Adriatic beyond. To their right, the ground sloped upward to where it had been leveled to accommodate a railroad line running north along the shore. They noticed a road crew working on the line up ahead. They were apparently digging and swinging picks, and as they approached, Malone could see the sweat gleaming on the muscles of their arms and backs. As they came up opposite, one of the workers, perhaps needing a break, stopped digging to wave to them and shouted hello. Sylvia, who had been watching them, looked away, but Malone waved back and shouted back, "Bonjour," all of which commotion had roused a sleeping dog, perhaps a stray, but more likely belonging to a member of the road crew.

The dog dashed down the slope with his tail wagging in circles and a woof, woof, woof, and he was clearly happy to meet somebody who might play with him. He jumped up and down and turned circles on himself and grabbed his tail and was altogether comical and friendly. Malone patted him on the shoulder and then took his head between his hands and shook him from side to side. Understanding that he had made a conquest, the dog then ran and got a stick, not a piece of a broken branch, but a piece of milled pine about eighteen inches long and two square. He was obviously a well-trained dog, because he dropped the stick at Malone's feet and sat down, looking straight up, the very tip of his tail going back and forth in the pebbles. Malone picked up the stick and threw it down the beach.

    The dog dashed off, pebbles flying, pounced on the stick and brought it back. He had repeated his performance of dropping the stick at Malone's feet and sitting down, when Malone heard one of the workers call out. He looked up the slope and saw one of the crew gesturing to him to throw the stick out into the water. Malone picked up the stick and, under scrutiny, gave it a tremendous heave. The dog was gone in the instant Malone released the stick. He hit the water at full speed in a great shower of drops and swam steadily straight out to where the stick had fallen, his bushy tail spread out in his wake. The dog continued to swim for a minute, then grabbed the stick and made a graceful 180-degree turn to come back to the beach.

    Malone clapped his hand to his thigh and called, "good dog," by way of encouragement, but it seemed that the dog, in spite of his strength, was making no headway. He seemed to have got hold of something that wouldn't move. Malone then thought that he could perhaps distract the dog by throwing another stick. Perhaps he would release the anchored stick he had and bring the other one in. But the dog wasn't having it. Malone repeated the experiment three times. On the second and third, the sticks fell very near to where the dog was swimming, still powerfully, in place, and Malone could actually see his eyes shift when they hit the water. But he was not to be distracted, and Malone realized that there was nothing for it but to swim out to the dog and take him away from the anchored stick.

    Malone kicked out of his shoes and put them side by side and released his belt and stepped out of his jeans and folded them and put them on top of the shoes. Sylvia was watching with some amusement. Malone looked up the slope and saw that the workers on the railroad crew were also watching him, leaning nonchalantly on their picks, and the one who had previously prompted him with the throwing gesture repeated it and laughed. Malone was beginning to feel some annoyance, and he articulated to himself, "If you think it's go goddamned funny, asshole, why don't you come get him yourself?" Only Sylvia would have understood—and would she have thought he had dared to say it only because he wouldn't be understood?—so he kept quiet and pulled his tee shirt off and folded it over his jeans. He decided to keep his socks on, because the rocks and pebbles were very uncomfortable underfoot.

In spite of the socks, the stones were still very painful, and he thought he must have made an awkward figure going into the water. Once in, however, he began to enjoy himself. The water was fine, clear and cool without being cold, except in patches. It must have been spring-fed. Malone swam a crawl for about forty feet and then a breaststroke that brought him to the dog. He scratched the dog's back and said, "good dog," and he noticed that the stick he held in his jaws was tied to something, probably a makeshift lobster trap or a mooring, holding it in place. He looked around for one of the other sticks he had thrown and saw one about ten feet away. He swam over and brought it back and, having succeeded in persuading the dog to make a swap, they both set out for the beach.

Malone imagined that the effort must have tired the dog, but in fact it had tired Malone. As he swam breaststroke, breathing as easily as he could, the dog swam on ahead, and the water was still too deep for him to stand when the dog reached the shore. Sylvia had wandered a short distance up the beach, looking for interesting pebbles, having lost interest, apparently, in Malone's heroics. He looked at her with some resentment as he thought also of the painful and awkward struggle of going ashore, and his feet had just hit bottom when he saw the dog shaking himself violently right over his clothes. Malone gave a shout as he saw the dog then proceed to throw himself down on the tee shirt and jeans, rolling over on his back and squirming in pure delight and—who knows?—perhaps in doggy gratitude. But his clothes were soaked and he was going to have to put them on for the walk back to the ship. He was afterwards to think that everything would have been fine had it been just the two of them, himself and the dog, but as he struggled from the water he was furious with Sylvia for paying no attention until it was too late and then for laughing as she had done, right along with the workers, who were also laughing, and Malone thought then that there was apparently nothing he could do that Sylvia wouldn't find, in some way, foolish or contemptible.

By the fifth year of their marriage and the third year of their stay in Istanbul, there wasn't a word or act of Sylvia's that hadn't, for Malone, its coloring of ambiguity. He remembered again the night at the Boem, after their visit to the dervish *tekke* with Erden and Frank and Marco, and Sylvia's having been swept away to the other end of the table by Dimitri, and he remembered seeing, out of the corner of his eye, Sylvia lift her glass in his direction. She had not called or otherwise tried to get his attention, and Malone thought afterwards that her salutation had had the wistful quality of a farewell. He had then turned fully towards her and lifted his own glass in return, but she had turned away, and he had found himself saluting the back of her head. In subsequent weeks, it became clear to Malone from Sylvia's behavior that something was up. She would seem embarrassed telling him how she had spent her afternoon or she would put him off entirely, saying indignantly that he had no business checking up on her.

    Is that what I'm doing, Malone would say, checking up on you?

    Of course you are, and it's insulting.

Can't I ask you how you spent your day out of innocent curiosity? Can't I be really interested in what you do?

I'm sorry, she would say, realizing that her persistence could only make matters worse. It's just that I don't really have anything useful to do, and I hate having to pretend.

It was a perfect answer, because perfectly sincere, and Malone decided that, if a good portion of the problem might be attributable to Sylvia's feeling that she was wasting her life, then that was a terrible thing and, filled with optimism, he had decided that they must go home, where Sylvia could get a decent job or, better yet, go back to school and get an advanced degree of some kind, and—who knows?—they might end up teaching together. What a lark! He wrote to his graduate department in the States, and they discovered a few openings and sent his dossier out, and in late January, on the strength of his academic record and the recommendations of his professors and with only a telephone interview, a precious saving in time and money, he was offered a job at Essex College, north of Boston. It was the perfect job in the perfect place. It made everything possible, and it was in a mood very much like optimism that, on the point of telling Sylvia, he realized that he was surely kidding himself. He knew there was more to it than he had been pretending, and he couldn't claim that Sylvia's cool reception came as a surprise. In fact, she had decided to try to get a job at the Istanbul Community School—a job that was later to materialize—so he oughtn't worry about her and there was no need for doing anything so radical as going home. Malone had not yet accepted the job, but what he said was,

So, I'm to go home alone? He knew the question must have sounded pretty lame, but she replied,

If that's what you want, which also sounded pretty lame.

Malone knew right away that they were finished, but they were going to have to do better than that. It's not what I want that matters, he said. It's what you want. You can't blame me.

How could anyone blame you, Malone? Good old blameless Malone.

He was sorry he had given her the easy opening, but he went on, And if you don't get the job at the Community School what will you do?

I'll take a job at the College, she said. I've been promised a job....

At the College? You aren't even qualified....

I've been offered a job as a secretary.

Where? said Malone.

In the Sociology Department, she said.

Dimitri, said Malone.

Yes, Dimitri, she said.

She told him then quite openly that Dimitri was her lover. He had smarted under the blow, but the fact that it was Dimitri had made things somehow easier. You couldn't help liking Dimitri, even when he'd done something like this. He asked himself what "something like this" might be, and he realized that he felt towards Dimitri much as he had felt towards his shaggy swimming companion from Dubrovnik, and the idea had made him smile the curative smile.

iii

There was scarcely a half hour left before they were due to foregather at Boncuk, and Dimitri and Malone were sitting in the Çiçek Pasajı with a small bottle of *rakı* between them. It was the most delightful hour of the evening in this most lighthearted and light-headed assembly of cafes and restaurants in the city. The pause between work and play was past, and the *akşamcı*, the habitual evening drinkers, were on the town. The long day of labor and time clocks had been dispelled by the evening call to prayer, echoing from mosque to mosque and pious soul to soul. The cats had gone home to their bowls of milk, and the mice had come out, as the saying goes, to dance. Malone had finally torn himself away from his musings in the little square and made his way up the dark end of İstiklal towards Galatasaray. As he approached the square, he noticed that the ground floor of the Şimşek building was a blaze of light, in spite of the hour.

He had decided to cross to see what was going on when he became aware of a trembling in the cobblestones underfoot, as of an earthquake much like those they had experienced years ago, but accompanied now by a basso rumbling coming at him from behind. Malone turned and saw two ribbons of steel track form along the center of the avenue in the powerful glare of an oncoming light. The tracks had been there in his day, or the ancestors of these tracks, but they had served only as a reminder of the trolley service that had been abandoned years before. Malone had never seen a trolley on İstiklal, and he was as surprised as if a plane were landing there or as if he had been carried back to that earlier day. As the cars went by him approaching Galatasaray, the conductor hit his breaks too hard and Malone saw several passengers, who had stood up in the aisle to start for the exit door, pitch forward and out of sight. At the same time, the rear wheels let out a screech and a shower of sparks, and when the trolley had passed and Malone could see across the street again, he saw a man he thought he had seen looking in at the Şimşek window a few moments before, but who had evidently turned towards the trolley as it passed and who was now looking straight at Malone. God's holy trousers, he quoted to himself, that looks like Dimitri Papas or I ain't The Malone Eagle.

My dear fellow, said Dimitri, leaning forward now and patting Malone fraternally on the arm. May I pour you another drink?
    You may, said Malone. He was feeling decidedly better now.

His lengthy abstinence in the little park had taken the edge off, but he was better now. And what a lark, running into Dimitri like that. Just the man for a drink or two, or three, in the Çiçek Pasajı. His shaggy friend. Things were looking up. There was nothing to be worried about. Things would be fine.

My dear fellow.

It was Dimitri again, and Malone waited for the follow-up, but there was none, and he worried that Dimitri might be feeling somewhat maudlin about their reunion.

How does it sound? asked Dimitri.

What? said Malone, how does what sound?

How does it sound when I say "My dear fellow"? Does it sound all right?

It sounds fine, said Malone, though it was true that the expression sounded somewhat out of character, Dimitri having learned his English in American schools. Why do you ask?

It's a phrase I picked up from Erden. No, that's not exactly right. It's a phrase that Erden has been trying to get me to use. He says that native speakers of American have some excuse, but that foreigners learning the language should learn the best, and that means saying "My dear fellow" all the time. But I don't feel natural saying it.

My dear fellow, said Malone.

Yes, said Dimitri, but he looked unsure.

I'm only an American, but if I were to express my full meaning, it would be, "My dear fellow, I understand your position perfectly and agree that you are being put upon and you have my full sympathy," or words to that effect. It's a way of expressing full understanding and assent. If I were to say to you, for example, the drinks are on me, what would you say?

My dear fellow, said Dimitri, as he smiled his understanding and assent.

And we shall have another half-bottle, on me, said Malone, because we still have a little time and the gears mustn't be allowed to grind and you said you were going to tell me what was going on at the Şimşek building.

Malone had crossed İstiklal to where the man he thought might be Dimitri Papas was standing. He was peripherally aware that there seemed to be a great crowd of people inside the Şimşek building, with some overflow onto the avenue itself, but he was able to make out Dimitri's features with increasing clarity as he approached, and Dimitri, apparently, to make out his.

Malone, Dimitri bellowed, They tell me you come back to Istanbul for dinner and now I believe it. How are you, how are you, and he enveloped Malone in his massive embrace and clapped him on the back and deposited shaggy kisses on his cheeks.

I'm fine, I'm fine, and how are you, Dimitri? You look every inch your amiable self, and Malone meant every word.

I'm fine too, and the finer for seeing you before we go to meet that mob at Boncuk. Let's go and have a drink together in the Çiçek Pasajı and you will tell me everything.

No, you will tell me, said Malone. I'm the one who's been away.

And so you have, while we have stayed here and done nothing but grow weary and gray. But you—the Malone Ranger; I remember everything—you have been far away on mad adventures amid the most romantic scenes imaginable. Boston! Just think of it. The great Tea Party, and "one if by land and two if by sea," and the Widener Library and sailing on the Charles and the great Red Sox and all those bars. There is nowhere a town with more good bars. Boston has the stuff as dreams are made on.

That's *The Maltese Falcon*, said Malone, supposing that to be Dimitri's source, and you're dreaming about San Francisco.

No, said Dimitri, that's Shakespeare, and Shakespeare tells us that the scene is an uninhibited island.

An uninhibited island?

That's right.

And that's Boston?
That's my Boston.
And your Shakespeare.
My dear fellow, said Dimitri, you have found me out.

Dimitri had then hooked his arm under Malone's and turned him up the avenue, and it was then that Malone had asked him what was going on.

I pour and you pay, said Dimitri, the second half-bottle of *rakı* having been delivered to their table, and he poured out two half-glasses of *rakı* and added water, leaving just enough room in each glass for two small cubes of ice. I come down here myself to see what is going on, and what do I see but a great crowd of people standing outside in the street. They are supposed to be inside, of course, pretending to look at the paintings, but they are outside so I wonder what is going on. So I walk closer. With all the people outside, I am a little afraid I will be recognized if I come too close, but I get just close enough to smell this smell.

Dimitri paused and waved his hand in front of his nose. Whew, he said.

But what was going on?

And do you know what that smell was? How can I tell you this? It smelled like, you know, like the giant urban asshole itself had let one, boom, you know what I mean? And I think to myself, I hope nobody lights a match.

!

But I don't see anybody I know, so I go right over to the window and this guy standing there tells me that somebody just set off a stink bomb inside. Like we used to do at school, you know what I mean?

Şerefe, said Malone. It sounds as if you'd had a close call.

Oh, a near miss, I can tell you. Those people will have to send their clothes to the cleaners.

But you still haven't told me what all those people were doing there.

Dimitri told him, then, about Marco's twenty-five years in art and the fact that with all his genius and accomplishments, this was the first show he had ever had, and that Marco had been all but overwhelmed with gratitude until he found out that the show was really a scam put together by some collectors to make money selling at enormous prices paintings they had bought for nothing years ago, and he had been all but overwhelmed again, but by anger and humiliation and shame, and he had asked, no, he had ordered all his friends to stay away.

But we'll see him tonight at Boncuk, said Dimitri. We'll see everybody at Boncuk tonight.

6
NICOLETTE

i

Nicolette Corrigan and Esther Toledano were writing a play. Some weeks before, they had been invited with their families to the dress rehearsal of a new work by the celebrated playwright Enver Yakut. Enver Bey was a neighbor of the Toledanos in Kuzguncuk and, in spite of his celebrity, but perhaps because he was a playwright, he liked to spread the net of his social acquaintance wide. He was on friendly terms with all of his neighbors, some of whom called him by name in greeting several times a week, without having more than a vague notion of who he was. Enver was an immensely kindly man, in spite of his celebrity, and nothing pleased him more than being able, through this partial anonymity, to talk idly to neighbors on matters of no importance without being held in awe or expected to perform. He enjoyed telling the story of buying a fish down at the ferry landing one day and having the fisherman say to him pleasantly, but with no particular surprise, as he prepared to wrap the fish in newspaper, "Enver Bey, you're in the news," and, as if proffering the fish for his inspection and flipping it slightly to one side, the fisherman said, "Look," and sure enough there was the face of Enver Yakut staring up from the page, but an Enver Yakut who seemed older by several years, a premonitory modification brought about by the union of photograph and fish. The future lies all about us, Enver would say, no less than the past, but we must be able to step out of ourselves to see truly either one of them.

Such sallies often left his listeners perplexed and even worried lest their friend fall into superstition, but, as a playwright, Enver Yakut had cultivated the art of stepping out of himself. He enjoyed cultivating relatively innocent disguises even in the conduct of his daily life, pretending to believe something he didn't believe, for example, to see who did believe it, or might be brought to believe it, including himself. Or he would indulge in the sort of ironic mystification we have just seen illustrated in the anecdote of the prophetic fish. He didn't believe in fixed opinions and he didn't believe in fixed personalities. Consider the range of human experience one finds in Shakespeare, he would say, by which I mean the plays that are with us today, of course, but we must remember that the plays once came out of the man Shakespeare, and Juliet was Shakespeare no less nor more than Falstaff or Lady Macbeth or all the Kings Henry and Richard and Desdemona and Shylock and Hamlet. Think of it! All humanity is there! And think of Balzac, he would say, citing the example of his other god, twenty-five hundred fictional characters, each stamped by the mark of a powerful individuality, no two alike—with resemblances, of course, as there are among us—but with no repetitiveness, no two alike, and they were all imaginative extensions of Balzac. And Enver even believed in a sort of prophecy, for if the present may be better understood through an understanding of the past, may we not logically project that understanding of how the past became the present into some understanding of what is to come? Not as a relation of mechanical cause and effect, but as an organic relation, admitting chances and mutations and surprises, even, but carrying forward something enduring in the form.

Enver had cultivated the art of stepping out of himself in the composition of some thirty-five plays, depending on how many you counted of those he had written as an undergraduate at the American College in Istanbul or during his graduate years at UCLA. His most recent, in English translation, was entitled *Anatolia*. It was a play for a single actress who would embody, in a series of eighteen avatars, the changing forms and abiding spirit of Mother Anatolia, first represented by Cybele, the Earth Goddess herself. As Enver writes of Cybele in his outline of the cast of characters, "All the other characters are in a way her children or her various reincarnations in different ages and cultures." Other of her various reincarnations include Andromache, wife of Hector at the fall of Troy; Artemis of Ephesus, the virgin huntress who was later to become, for the Christians, their Virgin Mother of God; Theodora, the circus performer who became Empress of Byzantium as wife of Justinian the Great; Holophira, the Byzantine princess who, as Nilüfer Hatun, married Orhan, son of Osman, founder of the Osmanlı or Ottoman dynasty; Nigar Hanım, poet and chronicler of the last days of the old Ottoman world; and Halide Edip—soldier, politician, friend of Mustafa Kemal, professor, and novelist—witness to the birth of a new world out of the ashes of the old. In an epilogue, the actress who has played all these roles appears in her final role as actress, and we understand that another avatar has been achieved when she says, "I can best endure as myself the more I change."

This was a rich and heady spectacle to pass before the eyes of two highly intelligent young women whose intellectual and emotional horizons were expanding at an explosive rate. Nicolette and Esther were more like twin sisters than friends, and even more like two variations on a single theme. They had been together since their first day in kindergarten at the Community School, when they had gone off slightly apart from the others to play. Neither knew the other's name, nor did their names seem to matter much when they were introduced. For the second day of school, the teacher had prepared name tags for each child and had begun a game of introductions in which the children were paired off and asked to pay attention to the first letter of his or her new friend's name. When the teacher came to Esther and Nicolette and introduced them to each other, the girls said, "Yes, yes," as if impatient with the interruption, and it turned out that they both already knew how to read. The teacher was later to recall that she had then noticed that the girls had exchanged name tags and that she had been about to remonstrate with them when she realized that an unusual bond had been formed and that it would be obtuse to interfere. During the summer between their fifth and six grades, they read *Ivanhoe*, and when they returned to school in the fall they were calling each other Rebecca and Rowena, the names of the two heroines, for whom they had rewritten Scott's ending in such a way as to give them brothers for husbands and neighboring castles high on a romantic bluff overlooking the sea.

The dress rehearsal of Enver Yakut's *Anatolia* had left them in a state of shock. The basic idea was brilliant. The writing was brilliant. The staging and the actress were brilliant. As a sheer act of memory, the performance was a tour de force, as were the rapid changes of costume behind a screen and her clever manipulation of a limited number of props, one character's bow becoming the next character's cane, a peasant girl's bandana becoming, with a quick fold, an imperial crown. But to be convincing in eighteen different roles or nineteen, really, it took your breath away. It had certainly taken their collective breath away, and they walked in silence up the street in Kuzguncuk to Esther's house and in the front door and up two flights of stairs to Esther's special room in the attic—not her bedroom, which was on the floor below with everybody else's rooms, but her special room. The room had been İshak's until he had started at the American College two years ago, but now he had another special room near the upper campus in Etiler where he stayed during the week, and he had given the attic room to Esther. She loved her older brother and thought he was brilliant and handsome and kind, and Nicolette thought so too, and Esther was especially grateful that İshak loved her also because he was so brilliant and handsome and kind and she thought that maybe for the last six months or so İshak had begun to show an interest in Nicolette, but if that were the case, it would be a little different, wouldn't it? They were growing up and the world would change them if they let it, but they wouldn't let it, and she consoled herself remembering the line the actress had spoken in her last role as the actress, "I can best endure as myself the more I change." They sat in Esther's special room, and the train of Esther's thoughts had begun to make her feel a little sad when Nicolette leaned forward in her chair and asked, a little breathlessly,

"What did you like absolutely"—pause for emphasis—"the best?"

Coming from Nicolette, it was a real question, and Esther knew she couldn't just say "the whole thing" because they understood each other well enough to know that obviously "the whole thing" was what anybody with any sense liked best but that each expected the other to be already beyond the obvious, and Esther knew that by simply allowing the honest answer to find itself, as it were, it would.

"I liked Halide Edip," she said, "and I know why," for this was the next step in the game they played. First they would express a preference for one thing or another, as spontaneously as they could and with no consideration for which thing might be more fashionable or moral to prefer, and then they would try to see if they couldn't figure out why. It might be a preference among colors, for example, or something much more complicated like the contents of a whole museum, when otherwise extraneous considerations like inattention came into play, or a movie or a party, especially one of those really late dinners with their parents downtown, sneaking a smoke or a glass of *rakı* behind their backs. That was a gas!

I liked Halide Edip, said Esther, because I was reminded of my mum. It was perfectly true. Esther had sat in her third-row seat completely enthralled by the actress's portrayal of Halide Edip. The actress had long, dark hair, like her mother, like herself, which she wore for this part drawn into a knot at the back of her head, like her mother, like herself. She had come from a wealthy and aristocratic background, had received her early education in an American school, just like herself, but had thrown her comforts away to follow Mustafa Kemal and the cause of the new nation, the new liberties, a new life. Great was it in that dawn to be alive, she quoted wistfully to herself, knowing that she would never know such times, but that her mother had. Her mother too had thrown it all away and left the States and moved to Israel, where she had lived on a kibbutz and worked and dressed like a man, like Halide Edip in trousers and a tan shirt worn open at the throat, and worked for the birth of a new nation. Yes, she had liked Halide Edip the best and Nicolette understood her reasons perfectly, and Nicolette too liked Halide Edip, but she liked Nigar Hanım best.

Nigar Hanım had thrown nothing away, but time had taken it from her. In her youth she had been beautiful, but she had been married to a man who had poisoned her life, as she herself had written, and now she was old and her health was failing. Her life and that of the aristocratic Ottoman world she had known were a guttering candle flame, and she had little left but her memories and her diaries and her art. But that was her whole secret, said Nicolette, jumping from her seat and raising her arm dramatically.

What are you talking about? said Esther.

I've just had an idea.

I can tell.

The world grows dark all around her, but she has learned to see in the dark. It isn't the material world she sees, of course, because she never moves from her special room, but she has dedicated her whole life to her art and she sees in a world she has made up, but that world is true because it holds the form of her soul.

That's beautiful, sighed Esther, but there was nothing like that in the play. You're making it all up.

I know, said Nicolette. Now tell me what your very first reaction was when I asked you what you liked best. Your very first reaction, no matter how corny or obvious.

My first reaction was to say I liked the whole thing.

Me too, but I've just realized that in this play, there's a way of saying that you like the whole thing without being corny or obvious. You could say you liked the actress best, do you see what I mean?

I do, said Esther, I really do, because she is everybody all through the play and then at the end she is herself.

Let's write a play for ourselves, said Nicolette.

A play for two actresses, said Esther, and we'll play Nigar and Halide. Nigar will wear a beautiful late Empire robe, and Halide will wear trousers and a tan shirt open at the throat.

And in the first act each of them will occupy her own half of the stage, said Nicolette, each in her special room, and in the second act they will mix in a common space ...

And in the third act, interrupted Esther, we'll change roles! I'll play Nigar and you'll play Halide, which means that Nigar will become Halide and Halide will become Nigar.

It'll be a play about friends, said Nicolette. But will Halide die for Nigar or will Nigar die for Halide?

I hadn't thought of that, said Esther. We'll have to decide.

Rebecca and Rowena had become Halide and Nigar. Whenever they could, they lived their roles. Sitting in Nazmi's cafe after school in Bebek drinking tea, Nicolette would ask Esther what Halide was thinking now, and Esther would sit for a second and say, Halide is in her tent on a hill overlooking the battlefield of Dumlupınar. It is past midnight, and her shadow, cast by the flame of a small kerosene lamp, moves distortedly back and forth over the walls and sloping roof of the tent.

I like "distortedly," Nicolette would say, but you sound like a narrator. Maybe we'll have to add a narrator.

It is well past midnight, Esther continued—I like "well past," said Nicolette—and she has spent the last two hours struggling to put down in writing her impressions of the horrors of the battle she has seen today. The shadow lengthens along the roof as it crosses the tent, then shrinks and is gone. She too has learned to see in the dark.

And Nicolette, excitedly, interrupting: I like that. That's terrific. They can both see in the dark.

Yes, I too have learned to see in the dark, and my cot is narrow and cold, and I am alone. I stare into nothing and finally I close my eyes and I am warm and safe remembering my grandmother's house in Moda, a beautiful, stone building with an enclosed forecourt and a path for carriages to drop off all our beautiful and witty guests at the door, and a terrace running the length of the house in back overlooking the sea, and it is evening and I am alone in my room above the terrace and I can hear music rising from a gramophone ... You know, I used to think it was a grandmaphone.

A what?

A grandmaphone. It belonged to my grandmother and she was always the one who played it, so I thought it was a grandmaphone.

My God!

So I can hear music and the muffled sound of voices rising from the terrace below and far out over the water I can see the dark mass of Büyükada looking like a stylized volcano in the setting sun.

That's beautiful, said Nicolette, and I—by way of transition—I, Nigar, have received my husband's permission ...

His what?

Oh, yes, that's how things were in my day. I have received my husband's permission to open the house in Büyükada, where I arrived this very same afternoon on the steamer from Istanbul, with seventeen trunks—I can't live without my books—and my little dog Frisky, and it is evening now and I have settled in and I can hear the voices of children playing in the forecourt of the house next door. For me their voices carry a music both joyful and sad, for I am childless myself, and I think of my friends in Moda, and of their beautiful summer house, the lights of which I can see from where I stand, a beautiful house that I have been able to visit only once in my life, and I imagine the whole family gathered there, four generations—just think of it!—right down to snotty-nosed little whatshername, said Nicolette, becoming playful.

And who might that be? asked Halide, momentarily indignant.

If the shoe fits, said Nicolette, introducing the first line of one of those slightly complicated jokes they had between them, this one a spoonerism requiring that the listener know that the word "fou" means "madman" in French.

If the shoe fits, said Nicolette.

The fou shits, said Esther, and the two girls collapsed in laughter. There was something in this joke, when they had first thought of it, that reminded them of a Turkish toilet, and, used sparingly, it never failed to crack them up.

ii

They were sitting in Nazmi's this afternoon waiting for Esther's brother to show up. They had dropped off their schoolbags with their mothers at the Aşiyan Museum, where Sylvia and Mimi had met to work on their translations of Nigar Hanım's poetry. It had at first annoyed Nicolette that her mother had conceived an interest in Nigar. Her mother was a highly competitive person, and the only way for Nicolette to survive, short of disappearing or giving up—impossible solutions—was to compete back. Her mother never bragged about her own successes. She never even mentioned them, but she didn't have to. They were quietly known. Perhaps it was her father who allowed them to be quietly known, to encourage his daughter without talking about himself. He was a professor, after all. But her mother's academic successes, and her athletic ones too, for that matter, had become part of the household atmosphere, an atmosphere not always easy to breathe. But Nicolette was now almost a woman, and she had become conspicuously attractive to boys and, as she was perfectly aware, to men. She knew too that she had a capacity for work and a ready mind and her grades had placed her year after year, with Esther, at the top of her class, and she was at ease socially and her friendship with Esther was something that nobody else could possibly compete with. At least she thought this was true until she learned that her mother and Mimi Toledano were working together on the poems of Nigar Hanım, but she decided that that was different. She and Esther were spinning a web of their own fancy, an illustration of the breadth and complexity of their private world. Their mothers' work as translators was governed, on the contrary, by all sorts of objective constraints, and she knew that her mother's view of Nigar had been formed in large measure by her reading of history and criticism, whereas her own was her own. Her mother's view was that Nigar's poetry was the expression of her public life, that art and life shared the same content, documentable. Nicolette believed that the poems were not about the world at all and that whatever content they had was the perhaps necessary but no less contemptible medium through which to express the barely audible whisperings of her soul. For Nicolette, the relation of life to art was that of matter to spirit: antithetical.

The idea of Nigar Hanım had first appealed to Nicolette as a paradigm of failure. Nicolette loved history, and the more history she learned the more she learned to love Istanbul. Her father was a historian, and though he had been originally trained in modern European history, he had now been in Turkey for more than twenty years and he spoke the modern idiom and he had studied at Istanbul University during the summers for many years to learn the old Ottoman language, laden as it was with Arabic and Persian locutions and words, and the old Ottoman script. It was fun to hear him talk about old Ottoman days—he had a highly dramatic way of describing events—but it was even more fun to accompany him on one of his walks downtown, especially if Erden Bey was along. Erden was an expert in the town's geography and folklore, and he and her father would recall the past in the presence of some living reminder, each trying to enrich the other's version, weaving them together until the dramatic fabric of some far-off epoch was spread out before their eyes.

She remembered visiting Haghia Sophia. Her father spoke of the architects, of Anthemius of Tralles and of the assistant who was appointed to succeed him at his death in 532, Isidore of Miletus. He then spoke of the city of Miletus as the cradle of Greek and Western philosophy, of Thales the geometer, who first argued for the uniformity of nature, a principle that has guided or disturbed Western philosophy and science ever since, and then Isidore again and the fact that he too had been a geometer and had been the director of Plato's Academy in Athens until it was closed by Justinian in 529. And they spoke of the Nika riots of 532, during which an earlier church of Haghia Sophia had been burned by the mob, and of Justinian's panic and the fortitude of his wife, the Empress Theodora, who surely saved her husband's throne; and Erden commented on her probable origins as a circus acrobat or a prostitute, or both, and he recalled the description given of Theodora by Procopius in his *Secret History* of an adolescent Theodora dancing, naked, and performing all sorts of lascivious contortions, a passage that may have inspired

Flaubert in his description of the dance of Salomé in "Herodias." And standing in the east gallery before the tomb of the blind Venetian Doge, Enrico Dandolo, who had conquered the city and the church in 1204 only to be buried within its stones, Erden recalled the other, more definitive conquest of 1453, and the last mass ever celebrated in Haghia Sophia on the evening of the 28th of May, when, according to legend, the priest elevated the Eucharist and, retreating slowly backwards with two altar boys swinging censers, disappeared into the wall, leaving behind them only a cloud of aromatic smoke. There was perhaps a trace of comic irony in Erden's telling of the tale, but, as he said, there were Greeks who still believed that when the day of reconquest came, as it surely would, the priest and the Eucharist and the boys with their censers, still smoking, would reappear.

For Nicolette, the story of Istanbul became a story of longing and loss, of variations on a theme. Byzantine or Ottoman, the theme was there wherever you turned, death and ruin, ruin and death. Her father had said that one of the marvels of the city was that it preserved the memory of the past in all its imperfections, which served as a corrective to romantics. She could hardly believe he had said that. As a theory, it seemed in perfect contradiction with the emotions aroused by the stories he told, for it seemed to Nicolette that imperfection was at the heart of longing and loss, that imperfection was the most romantic thing there was. She wondered if she hadn't perhaps missed his point somewhere, but she was happier pursuing her own idea than his, and she took another long step in her own direction when one day, in French class, or English class, the teacher talked about Villiers de L'Isle-Adam. It must have been in English class, because they were talking about Yeats and his theory that the advancing phases of the moon mark out the alternate waxing and waning of the objective and subjective worlds and the fact that, as a young man, Yeats had considered Villiers' *Axel* to be one of the world's sacred books. The play traces an artist-hero's gradual retreat from the empirical world into the world of pure spirit—the teacher had quoted the famous line, "As for living, we'll let the servants do that for us"—but the retreat is never consummated for the simple reason that Villiers died before writing the last act. But the void of that unwritten act and the artist's having died, with his artist-hero, into that void meant that, for the symbolists, the artist had fused with his creation, and his necessary silence meant that the unwritten last act of *Axel* was an emblem of the absolute.

Nicolette had listened to all this, fascinated, and fascinated all the more because she knew something about another Villiers de L'Isle-Adam, Grand Master of the Knights of Saint John of Jerusalem, then resident in Rhodes, who had commanded the valiant defense of his island against the Turkish siege of 1522. Yet he too had been doomed, foreshadowing the doom of his descendant, the poet, childless and, as he knew himself to be, last of his illustrious line. Emperors and Sultans, princes and heirs, overthrown, blinded, beheaded, sewn into weighted sacks and hurled into the Marmara, or, more benevolently, exiled to an island prison on Büyükada. She was daily confronted by such tales of woe, heard or read about or epitomized in some still-proud ruin, the crumbling yet colossal land walls of the city, or the great castle of Rumeli Hisarı, which she walked under every day on her way to school.

But these events, in whatever form, left her untouched by anguish or rage, resolving themselves into emblems—the light of sunset flashing briefly from the window of the abandoned Ostrorog villa which, from Nazmi's, she could see right now across the way, or the Kız Kulesi at the lower entrance to the straits. But the resolution was more often imagined to occur in the mind of an emblematic survivor—Villiers, Nigar—exiles, she thought, "in faery lands forlorn," and she declaimed aloud,

> "Perhaps the self-same song that found a path
> Through the sad heart of Ruth, when, sick for home,
> She stood in tears amid the alien corn ..."

We've come a long way from shoe fits, said Esther, whose mind had been wandering too. They often fell into dreaminess after a spell of violent laughter, as after tears, and their meditative mood had been remarked no less than their hilarity by a group of young men seated across the path that ran down the middle of the cafe terrace. The young men looked like university students, and one of them, at least, was probably from Bebek or not far from home, because he was holding, on the end of a leash, an enormous blond dog, evidently a superior specimen of Kangal, the Anatolian sheepdog. The dog looked very young, not over a year, but he was already almost as big as a Saint Bernard, with a broad skull and chest and a long bushy tail that he wagged enthusiastically when anybody went by. The girls had made a point of not looking in the direction of the young men, though they couldn't help looking once or twice in the direction of the dog. The owner of the dog finally noticed this, and he decided to let the dog out on his leash. The dog too had noticed Esther look at him, and he lumbered across the path with his tail waving and his floppy paws flopping and put his great head down on her knee. Esther was not well accustomed to dogs, and she was feeling reassured only by the fact that the owner still held his end of the leash when the waiter came by, frowning at the idea of there being a dog in his cafe, and the owner dropped the leash to let the waiter pass. Esther's face then took on an expression of surprise and near-panic as the dog assumed a sitting position and offered her his broad toothy smile and one large floppy paw.

Esther looked across at Nicolette and was about to appeal to her to intervene when the afternoon call to prayer burst from the minaret of the Bebek Mosque next to the ferry landing up the street, and the dog, lifting his great muzzle straight into the air, howled his response. Allaaaaaaaaaaaoooouuuuuuuuuuuu, sang *müezzin* and dog, and their howling music filled the air and rose above cafe and village until heads turned to listen, surely, on the College hill and as far away as Etiler and Kandilli—who knows?—on the other side, and then the sound abruptly stopped, but the dog was quicker to catch his breath and it was the *müezzin* who then seemed to imitate the dog. It was too much for Esther, who retreated to Nicolette's side of the table, while the young men across the way nearly fell out of their chairs laughing. The amusement was general, and even the waiter had to smile, though nothing would change his opinion that dogs didn't belong in cafes. Dog and *müezzin* continued to howl until, quite incredibly, one moment of silence was broken by the arrival of the ferry from Kuzguncuk. Whoop, whoop, whoop, said the steam whistle and again, Whoop, whoop, sounding for all the world, in this context, like a soprano relative of the dog, and the dog then renewed the fervor of his howling, and Nicolette thought the young men across the way would kill themselves laughing, and a voice beside her said,

> And thus did Aucassin
> Find Nicolette
> In joyous company.

You just made that up, she said, for it was İshak and they had been waiting for him and it was true, as Esther said, that he was brilliant and handsome and kind, and that was very romantic, what he had just said, and she couldn't help blushing, but only a little, because the lighthearted mood produced by the crazy comedy around her was too strong.

You just made that up.

No I didn't, he said, or only a little. But wait till you hear what I've made up for tonight.

And İshak sat down and unzipped the top of his book bag and took out a pad of paper and a pencil and began to sketch out a map of the area around Galatasaray. Here's the plan, he said, because he had a plan.

iii

Some two hours later, İshak Toledano stood in a corner of the square at Galatasaray, directly across from the gallery on the ground floor of the Şimşek building. The reception had started only a half hour before, and İshak was pleased to see that so many people had arrived on time. This wasn't always the case, and he had been afraid that he might have to wait. As it was, it looked to him as if there were many more people in the gallery than anyone had expected. The organizers must be rubbing their hands together in expectation. The thought pleased İshak. The bigger the crowd the better, he thought. Marco Fontane might not agree, not yet, but that didn't mean that he and Marco were at cross-purposes. İshak stood a moment longer in his protected corner. What am I waiting for? he thought, and remembering with a smile the old "on your mark, get set, go," he stepped from his shadow and started across the street.

He and Esther and Nicolette had stayed on a while longer at Nazmi's cafe while he showed them his plan. The girls weren't really part of it, because he didn't want them to be implicated in any way if he got caught. If he got caught it would be bad enough, but his parents would never forgive him for dragging Esther into it, or Nicolette. He knew they wanted to be part of it, or think that they were part of it, and it was flattering to him and a little thrilling to be escorted into battle, as it were, by his two girls, who would wait expectantly for his return and throw their arms around him, and in her excitement, because she would have been terribly afraid, Nicolette would let him kiss her and she would kiss him back, and he had looked up from his sketchpad and she was looking at him as if she might have known what he was thinking, and he thought he must have been blushing a little so he tried to smile and was sure, only, that he looked like a moron.

ISTANBUL GATHERING

İshak had sketched a map of İstiklal Caddesi from Taksim to Galatasaray, with details locating the Çiçek Pasajı, the Cafe de Pera, the Şimşek building, and the doorway across the avenue that he had scouted earlier in the week and where he would wait for his opportunity. Now, first, how should they get to town? They had always liked to take the ferry, the leisurely trip down the Bosphorus to the far end of the Galata Bridge, the ride in the underground tram up to Tünel, the walk down the sleepy end of İstiklal or the ride in the new trolley car, to end with the always exciting arrival in the lights and hubbub of Galatasaray. But they all agreed that their usual trip would take too long. To arrive too late would be unthinkable. If they were too early, they could always walk up and down İstiklal looking at the stores. So the plan was that they would take a cab in from Bebek to Taksim and walk from there. They would walk all the way together to the Şimşek building to get the lay of the land, then return to the Çiçek Pasajı or the Cafe de Pera—the girls would judge on the spot which place they thought would be better—and İshak would then go back to his doorway to wait.

But you've never told us how you're going to set the thing off inside, said Esther.

İshak turned the page of his sketchpad and drew a large rectangle, with another small rectangle in the upper right-hand corner. Here's the main gallery room, he said, and these two sides are all windows, on the avenue, here, and the square, here.

So, if we wait across the square we'll be able to see everything that happens, said Esther.

If you wait across the square, there will be about a million guys trying to pick you up, said İshak. No. We'll all go see what's happening together after I come back and get you. He paused for a moment to see if anybody was going to say, "*If* you come back." Nobody did, but both girls looked sufficiently impressed, and he thought they might be thinking it.

Now, you see this small rectangle? There's a ladies' room

here and a men's room here and a broom closet inside the men's room, right here.

I've always wanted to know where that broom closet was, said Nicolette.

Wise guy, said İshak. But believe it or not, it all fits.

Who fits? said Esther, and she couldn't contain herself and Nicolette choked on her tea and İshak hadn't a clue what they were laughing at, but he was willing to wait until they stopped being children and became young women again, and he turned to Esther and said, I thought you wanted to know how I was going to set it off, and she said,

Have you got it with you?

Of course, he said, pointing to his book bag.

Show us what it looks like.

Not here, he said. I'll show you in the cab on the way to town.

Then tell us.

No, he said, with a touch of annoyance, I just said I'd show you in the cab. I thought you wanted to know how I was going to set it off.

We do, said Esther.

We do, said Nicolette.

So, he said, resuming his composure, I come in the door, as cool as you please, and bow in response to the admiration of the multitudes.

Come off it, said Esther.

But I think I will take a minute to look at Marco's work. I haven't seen much of it, have you? Nobody has ever seen so much of it gathered all in the same place at the same time.

He asked me to pose for him once, said Nicolette, her mind wandering.

I'll bet he did, said İshak.

Not like that, she said, knowing what he meant. She knew that her mother had posed for him years ago, before she had married her father, but only on the promise that the painting would never be shown. My God, she thought with a start, I hope he hasn't forgotten his promise.

Not that you'd be recognizable, said İshak. They say none of his portraits are, except for the fact that they all look vaguely like his wife.

That's the most horrible story I've ever heard, said Esther. And there was a little boy too, wasn't there, who died. How can you go on after a thing like that?

I don't know, said İshak, but Marco did, and we're going to strike a blow for Marco. That's what we're doing, in case you've forgotten.

Forgotten?

I didn't mean that, he said, and he really hadn't because it was Nicolette who had spoken and she seemed hurt. He could have kicked himself for being a patronizing fool.

I'm sorry, he said, I really am.

It's all right, said Nicolette. But now that you know you'll be wasting your time looking for recognizable portraits of the various women in your life, what will you do next?

I'll have to content myself with the ones I don't recognize, he said. There must be a few left.

Would you mind telling me what we're talking about? said Esther. I thought somebody was going to strike a blow for Marco, not stand around mooning about his imaginary love life.

Touché, said İshak. So, back to the plan. I come in the door, here, and all joking aside, I will have a look at the paintings. I don't want to just sprint for the toilet, do I? Nobody we know will be there, so presumably I won't be recognized, and if there is a traitor he'll probably pretend not to see me. So around the room I'll go, cool as you please, and into the men's toilet, cool as you please. The sink and the broom closet are on the right. The toilet, in an enclosed booth, is on the left. First, if there's anybody there, I wait for him to leave. Then I get myself a broom from the broom closet and prop it between the edge of the toilet booth and the door, because the lock is broken. I want to be sure I have the place to myself.

The lock is broken, said Nicolette. The crucial importance of the broom closet is now revealed. You have the place to yourself.

And now you're going to have to tell us what that thing looks like, said Esther.

It's easier for me to show you, said İshak, and it's time anyway, so let's get a cab.

They got up and left some money on the table, and Nicolette crossed over to say goodbye to the dog, who looked at her soulfully and wagged his tale, and the young owner held his breath and then Nicolette smiled at him too and he almost fell out of his chair, but not from laughing this time, and Nicolette followed Esther and İshak out of the cafe.

They walked up the street to the taxi stand in the square in Bebek and climbed into the first one in line, all three in the back seat. The taxi stand was on the Bosphorus side of the street, in front of the pastry shop, and the driver had to execute a rapid U-turn to get into the lane headed towards town.

Whew, said Esther. This man would do for a getaway.

Okay, said Nicolette, You have the place to yourself. Now what?

İshak leaned forward and unzipped his book bag and, pushing aside the sketchpad and a sweater, reached down between two books and produced his bomb.

He did so with evident satisfaction. He hadn't actually made the bomb, but the idea for the container had been his, a cardboard cylinder from the inside of a roll of toilet paper. It was just the thing and he felt aggrieved that the girls, having expressed such high interest, now seemed so highly amused.

That's it? said Esther.

It's just the thing, said İshak.

It certainly is, said Nicolette. It'll feel right at home.

And the stink, said Esther, beginning to lose control of herself. Do you think it's big enough?

The guy who made this said it was big enough to stink up the whole of Beyoğlu, said İshak, and I've got two of them. Can you imagine? We'll be lucky if the air clears in our lifetime.

Just inside the entrance to the gallery, a security guard was sitting behind a table checking invitations. Another security guard was standing behind him, smoking, and looking vaguely at the people who came in and, from time to time, vaguely around the room. İshak produced his father's invitation. Both guards looked at him, and the seated guard motioned for him to go in. İshak moved casually. His presence in the gallery should seem the most natural thing in the world. Marco's works were everywhere, sometimes in double rows along the walls, and several panels had been set up in the middle of the room in such a way that İshak could almost always keep a panel between himself and the guards. Not that it mattered now, but it might after he had come out of the toilet to set the second bomb. The bar had been set up in the right rear corner, and İshak noticed that at either end of the table was one of those tall, cylindrical waste bins, with openings around the top, whose covers double as ashtrays. Just the thing. Next to the bar were a couple of straight-backed chairs, and İshak took one of them, placed it near one of the waste bins at the end of the bar and sat down. He smoked only very little, but he had brought a pack for the occasion and he tapped one out and lit up. He dropped the match into the ashtray and estimated that the openings at the top of the cylinder were easily big enough to accommodate his second bomb. The bartender saw him then and asked him if he wanted a drink. He had noticed that, as he was lighting his cigarette, someone had asked for a beer and that the bartender had left the bar momentarily through a door to the kitchen in back.

May I have a beer, please? said İshak.

Sure, said the bartender, You can have as many as you like. As expected, the bartender turned and went out through the kitchen door, which swung closed behind him, while İshak stubbed out his cigarette, reached into his book bag for the pack and lit a second cigarette before the bartender returned. I'll have plenty of time, he thought. These guys are observant and they have good memories and he'll surely remember me if I come back. That is, if he's still behind the bar. And what does it matter if he does remember me? He remembers a lot of people. The main thing is that he not see me light the bomb. He took a drag on the cigarette and a taste of the beer and thought, Now or never.

He shouldered the book bag and took the beer with him away from the bar and, pausing a moment, put it down on the corner of a table spread with plates of olives and squares of white cheese with toothpicks in them and pistachio nuts and some raw vegetables arranged on a huge platter around a dip and, taking another drag on his cigarette, he headed for the toilets. There was a recessed hall that he had forgotten about, but so much the better. It would afford him added cover. He stopped for an instant in front of the men's toilet, glanced at the louvered transom over the door, and listened. Nothing. He knocked. Nothing. Now, he thought to himself, and went in.

He closed the door behind him and discovered that, since his previous visit, somebody had repaired the lock, but he would still have no way of locking it afterwards from the outside, so he took the broom from its closet, removed the brush from the handle, and braced the handle between the lower hinge of the door of the booth where the toilet was and the back of the door leading outside. He then unzipped the book bag, took out a ball of putty as big as the palm of his hand and packed it around the hinge and the lower end of the broom handle so it wouldn't fall. He then tied a short length of string around the upper end so he could hold it in place as he closed the door from the outside. The maneuver could be carried out quickly and need not attract any attention. He was ready. He took out the bomb and stood it in the sink. He took the cigarette from where he had been carrying it in the corner of his mouth and lit the fuse. It would take the fuse just thirty seconds to burn down and ignite the powder inside the bomb, which would go off silently, but with a considerable emission of smoke and a blimp's own volume of stink. As the fuse took, İshak turned and lifted the broom handle from where it rested on the transverse molding on the back of the door, opened the door, and slipped out using the string to guide the broom handle as it slid down the inside of the closing door until he felt it drop into place. There was nobody waiting to go in, but there would be, and that too was part of the plan. He walked over to the plate glass window looking out towards Galatasaray, took a last drag on the cigarette, and stubbed it out in one of those standing ashtrays.

İshak pretended to look at a painting, a nightmarish landscape which had the power to distract him momentarily from what he was doing, while watching to see telltale signs of smoke come through the transom over the men's room door. It couldn't have taken three minutes, though it felt like an eternity, until a few wisps of smoke began to appear. An instant later, a man went into the recessed hall and over to the men's room door and knocked. He listened and knocked again and tried the door, which seemed to be locked. He then must have got a whiff of something, because he made a face and waved his hand in front of his nose and gave up. In another minute or so the smoke was quite apparent and had begun to fill the upper space along the ceiling of the recessed hall. One or two curious people came over for a look and rebounded as if they had run into a wall. Then somebody went for one of the guards at the front door, and İshak began to make his way across the room to the bar. He walked slowly, giving the news time to spread. He saw the seated guard leave his post behind the table at the front door and go over to see what was happening and perhaps to help his colleague. They had evidently still not been able to open the door and, thinking that there was a fire inside, the first guard ran over towards the bar and sent the bartender into the kitchen for a fire extinguisher. By now, everybody was aware that something was going on, that some accident had occurred or that a fire had broken out, and they were beginning to pile up against one another to get into the street. İshak watched and lit another cigarette. It reminded him of people trying to disembark all in a lump from the ferry at the landing in Kuzguncuk. The bartender ran by him with the extinguisher. There was now nobody left in that corner of the room, so İshak stepped calmly behind the bar, put his second bomb right on the table behind a row of wine bottles and was about to light the fuse when he decided that this would be a foolhardy deviation from plan. Somebody might see the small jet of sparks from the fuse and just come over and douse the bomb in an ice bucket, or, thinking that it was an explosive device, panic, which would be worse. So he sat again in the straight-backed chair, which nobody had moved, lit a cigarette and then the fuse, dropped the bomb through one of the openings in the side of the cylindrical waste bin, and walked over to mix with the crowd at the door.

It seemed to take forever for the crowd to move forward. Whew, said somebody. The stink was overpowering and it seemed to follow them out into the street. İshak heard one man joke that he was probably going to have to burn the clothes he was wearing. Whew again. İshak walked around the corner to the Galatasaray side to where he could see how the guards were getting on. They had managed to get into the men's toilet, so they knew by now there was no fire nor anything more dangerous than a stink bomb. The second bomb had gone off, but had been only partially consumed when the bartender located the source of the smoke and emptied his ice bucket into the bin. But the damage had been done, a blow had been struck. The gallery was completely empty now except for the two guards. The bartender had disappeared, perhaps into the kitchen. İshak looked at the crowd gathered in front of the door. After the scare, a carnival atmosphere had set in. Everybody was chattering away excitedly, when who should appear through the smoke but the bartender making a comical show of holding his breath and then gasping as he reached the street with an enormous tray of drinks, which he began to circulate through the crowd. Ah, the irrepressible bourgeoisie, thought İshak, and am I not one of them? Alas.

While İshak had been carrying out his heroic escapade, Nicolette and Esther had found themselves a table on one of the cafe terraces in the Çiçek Pasajı. They had ordered beers and a plate of pistachios to keep busy. They would have run out into the square to sneak a look but for fear of losing their table, and neither would let the other go alone, not even if they flipped for it. So there they sat until Nicolette, facing the entrance to İstiklal Caddesi, said, Here he comes.

İshak came quickly towards them and sat down and told them a little breathlessly that everything had gone even better than he had hoped. He was only just becoming fully conscious of what he had managed to do, and he could hardly contain himself. He would have liked to pound the table or shout, but he put his arm around Esther, whom he was sitting next to, and gave her a resounding kiss and squeezed her hard, and she said, Hey, and he looked across at Nicolette and smiled and reached over and grabbed her beer and finished it off in a long swallow, and she said, Hey! You owe me one, and Esther said, Me too.

Waiter! said İshak, and when the waiter came, I want to order three more beers and another plate of pistachios and some olives, please, and can you save our places for two minutes? I want to show my friends something at Galatasaray. But we'll be right back. I can pay you in advance, if you like.

Don't worry about it, said the waiter. You go ahead.

The waiter watched them go. He had already heard that

something was going on out on the square, that there was a crowd gathered not far from the trolley stop, and he hoped that there hadn't been an accident. He had moved to Istanbul from his home on the Black Sea thirty years ago, and he still couldn't get used to the idea of planes and trains and automobiles, and now they had put a train to run right through the middle of town. He remembered hearing once about a little boy who had slipped under a trolley car and had his foot cut off, and he was sure it was going to happen again. What was all the convenience and technology in the world compared to the life of a little boy? Abstractedly the waiter tipped the backs of the chairs forward against the table to save it for those nice-looking young people. God help us, he thought, We're doomed.

Waiter! called somebody from several tables away, a heavyset bear of a man who had just sat down, and who turned around now in his chair and raised his arm and called, Waiter! a half-bottle of *rakı* and two glasses, please. Oh, and some olives and peppers and white cheese, if we may.

For no reason other than a nervous need for variety, perhaps, İshak had led the girls out by the other end of the Çiçek Pasajı, so that he hadn't seen the bear-like man come in, nor had the bear-like man seen him. He turned left then and crossed the fish market back to Galatasaray and led the way across the square to where they could see into the gallery and the recessed hallway where the men's toilet was and, by moving around to the front, they could just see between two panels to the back corner of the gallery and the bar. They watched the crowd of merrymakers, one of whose number made a comic performance of passing among them with a tray of drinks, and they saw the bartender himself—here comes my old friend the bartender, said İshak—reappear from the kitchen with a powerful-looking fan, which he set up on a chair in the doorway facing outwards and turned on. The crowd let out an audible moan and fell back quickly on either side from the blast of air. The girls and İshak caught the smell of rot from where they were standing, but supposed it couldn't have been too bad outside until the bartender turned on the fan.

Who's that? said İshak.

Where?

Standing back along the building on the other side of the crowd. I thought I saw Dimitri.

I always think I see Dimitri, said Nicolette, Sometimes I do.

And what's that supposed to mean?

I'm getting punchy, said Nicolette, and somebody owes me a beer.

There are a lot of Turkish men who look like Dimitri, said Esther.

Which is nice because he's Greek, said İshak.

He's only half Greek, said Esther.

They were now just turning into the İstiklal entrance to the Çiçek Pasajı to go back to their drinks, when Nicolette, who had turned the corner first, stopped dead in her tracks. This time it really is Dimitri, she said, reddening and turning quickly back towards İshak and Esther before Dimitri had had a chance to see her. I'm not kidding, she said. Look towards the table where we were before. He's sitting facing us, about three tables closer to where we are now. Do you see him?

Yes, said Esther.

Is he looking our way?

No, he hasn't seen us, said Esther, but what's the big problem?

We'll go around by the back way, said İshak, which they did, resuming their former seats, which meant that Nicolette was now looking at the back of Dimitri's head.

So what's the problem? said Esther.

He gives me the creeps, said Nicolette. He's always looking at me. I can actually feel him looking at me.

That's creepy, said Esther. And he's at least a million years old, isn't he?

At least, said İshak, smiling, but I can sympathize.

He gives me the creeps, said Nicolette, who wasn't listening, and her face suddenly hardened and she said, I don't believe it! Now the creep that's sitting across from him is doing the same thing. My god, she said, pausing, I think I know who that is. That has to be the guy they're all having dinner with tonight.

Malone, said Esther.

Yes, said Nicolette, my mother's first husband. Now that's really creepy. I'm not sure I want to go to that dinner anymore. Do we have to go?

We can go anywhere we like, said İshak, but I suggest that right now we get out of here so Nicolette won't have to contend with all these ancients drooling after her. Finish your brews and we'll sneak out the back door and go over to the Cafe de Pera and listen to the Countess play the piano and make another plan.

Have you got another bomb? said Esther.

7

MARCO

sin otra luz y guía
sino la que en el corazón ardía
                    Juan de la Cruz

i

A fine sand pours through the throat of the hourglass as the waters flow ceaselessly from sea to sea through the straits. The arc of energy bridges two poles, two continents, and the arc of energy is everything. Today transforms tomorrow into yesterday, and today is everything. The future narrows into now, and in the narrows, now is everything.

I ask myself each morning how it is possible that I am still alive. I awaken and open my eyes and, turning my head, I look at the bare and immaculately whitewashed ceiling and walls, and I ask myself how it is possible that I am still alive. I lie on my back and close my eyes again and stretch, arching the small of my back, flexing my legs and arms, my hands. I throw back the sheet and draw my feet towards me on the bed, my knees up, and I cross my hands one over the other on my chest, like a cadaver, and

I lift my chest and shoulders from the bed and hold and then lie back and repeat this movement twelve times and pause and repeat twelve times again. I then lift my knees and I wrap my arms around my shins and draw my knees into my chest until I assume the position of an embryo or a diver midair in the tuck position or the head of John the Baptist as it leapt from the block and paused momentarily at the top of its arc before it fell. That's how I feel, detached.

I believe that if I were in pain, my consciousness of pain would reassert my relation to the world. But I am not in pain. At sixty-five years of age I might reasonably expect to be failing somewhere, to be visited by some sign. I drink *rakı* and I've been smoking since I was sixteen, but I've never had a hangover that lasted past breakfast and I can still swim underwater and climb the hill to Rumeli Hisarı at a stiff pace without wanting to rest. I go for long periods without washing so that my body may become repugnant to me or fall sick, but it never does. There are times, of course, when I enjoy my state of health, which is very like being asleep, but my waking consciousness tells me that if my health does not deteriorate gradually, then I must fear a sudden, general collapse or die violently, under the wheels of a trolley, perhaps, or that I shall have to provoke the event myself. When I think these thoughts, my feeling of detachment momentarily abates.

The feeling of detachment is death in life. I am a dead man who continues to walk, in perfect health, among the living. In such a state I make no plans for the future, evoke no memories of the past. Beyond the walls of my studio, I float in a blank timelessness. It could not be otherwise. If I were to return to life in the company of others, they would die. As I walk in the world, I must walk in vigor and smiles and bantering small talk and I must do everything I can to avert my mind and gaze from certain images which, if I could not channel them into my work, would radiate from me directly into the souls of others and be their death as surely as they were mine.

I rise from my bed now and stand upon a beautiful *kilim* that Erden gave me years and years ago, Erden my friend, one of the few to whom I have ever told my story. This *kilim* has, for me, a talismanic power which I must use sparingly and which I fear each day I may be using for the last time. The *kilim* is very old and faded, but I can tell that it was once a rioting luxuriance of color, of forms that move and meld into each other, restrained only by the dictates of the weave. Erden says, and he is right, that in the *kilim* the weave is everything, source of dynamism and control. The geometry of warp and weft is inescapable, but their point of intersection is fecund. Where the axes cross, one thing becomes another, and deep within, before their differentiation, is the place of union where one thing is another, where mouth is womb, the five senses one, the arc of energy.

I stand upon the *kilim* now and prepare to cross into my studio. My friend Enver Yakut the playwright says, Imagine you are other to discover who you are. Yes. The self is a weave, and deep within, the self is everything. I stand upon the *kilim* and close my eyes and empty my mind of everything but a humming sound that I make or is made somewhere within me, and from within the humming, the images begin to flow. It is long ago, over thirty-five years, and it is late at night in the old house in Ortaköy. I am in a back room on the ground floor of the old house proofing my thesis on the French poet Arthur Rimbaud. It is a thousand pages long, but I have been rereading for two weeks and I am almost done. It is late at night, and my wife and my little boy are asleep upstairs. I have been smoking heavily, and I smell nothing unusual. In fact, I am not aware that the house is on fire until I quite suddenly feel the sting of the heat against my back. I am immediately in the grip of fear. I rise and turn. My chair goes over backwards and I sweep a sheaf of papers from the table onto the floor. I rush to the door and open it upon a sheet of flame. The house has been burning already for some minutes, for some time. I know that the stair is opposite. I put my hands in front of my face and run into the flames. I burn my hand when I touch the banister on the other side to steady myself for the climb and in that instant the stair collapses under me. I think I remember climbing out of the cellar, but I am not sure and then, without knowing how I got there, I am across the street and the whole house is a torch. The heat is stupendous, and the roar, and I know that within the roar is the silence of death, and I ask myself what I have done or what I could have done, and there is no answer, because within me also is the silence of death.

My soul was taken from me that night, and my body was left standing in the street, alone forever and detached. It was then that I began to paint and to draw. I drew for six hours in the morning and painted for six hours in the afternoon, learning my craft, seven days a week, for five years. What else was there to do? I drew and painted from nature, and I learned to see, and my hand acquired skill. I was training myself, though I couldn't know for what, and I became an accomplished illusionist. I still am. I painted portraits and nudes and landscapes, some of which survive, and I remember the first time Erden visited my studio, over twenty years ago, and, knowing how even sophisticated people can be about art, I hung a large figurative painting along one wall, representing the roofs of the village and the Bosphorus beyond, which I had painted from a neighbor's balcony, so that Erden would see that I had the skill to paint realistically if I wanted to. I could tell he didn't know what to think about my recent work, but he complimented me on the studio, its size and airiness and light, and its fine view. In fact, my studio has no view. Erden had mistaken my painting for a window.

Those were the years of continual detachment, and those early paintings were the work of a detached man. The end of my apprenticeship was marked by a discovery. I was working on a landscape. There was a forest on the hill behind my house, above the American College in the direction of Etiler, and in the forest was a clearing where I could work undisturbed. In those days I liked to work as much as possible with the scene in front of me, *sur le motif,* as Cézanne said. I had a portable French easel with an attached paint box, and I had cut and folded and taped a big plastic envelope that I could slip the canvas into for protection. In the early morning, I would tramp up the hill, thinking about the scene and the painting as I went, and I would arrive in the clearing with no clear recollection of having walked up the hill. My mind had been entirely taken up by my memory of the scene and the evolving painting and by the sense of wonderment I felt at having been attracted to this scene in the first place. There was nothing picturesque about it. Nor was it particularly complex or compositionally significant. From the point of view that I had chosen to reproduce—and reproduction is the word for what I did in those days—I could see a semicircular patch of clearing in the foreground, with a patch of sky above, separated from the forest in the body of the painting by the irregularities of the treetops. The season was late fall, and the trees and ground were bare and all but colorless.

My painting was progressing slowly. I knew that with the coming of the rains I would be unable to continue working outside, and I had already begun to paint in the afternoons and evenings in my studio, using a photograph to replace the actual scene. It was black-and-white, but the same could be said, almost, of the original motif. I had had the photograph enlarged and as the weather confined me increasingly to my studio, I had it enlarged again, and then again. I had been working in my usual meticulous manner, so that with every enlargement my task became more difficult. The lines in the photograph gradually lost definition, and the closer I looked the more they became a blur. As a consequence, my painting too began to suffer, or so I thought then, and I began to pay increasing attention to the painting and less and less to the photograph, until I realized that the only way to compensate for the painting's lack of defining contour was to reject the artificially mnemonic photograph entirely and to turn my work into a feast of color. But a full understanding of what was to happen to me that evening will depend upon some knowledge of my family background.

My friend Frank Corrigan once said jokingly of me, All Europe went into the making of Marco Fontane. There is a good deal of truth in that, and he might have added an equal dose of Asia, too. The name Fontane derives from a French Huguenot family that fled to Holland in 1685 at the revocation of the Edict of Nantes. The name was originally Fontaine or Lafontaine, and I can remember being told by a great-aunt, the sister of my paternal grandfather, that we are related—it would be more accurate, if less poetical, to say distantly related—to Jean de La Fontaine, author of the Fables. I can believe it. There is more wildness and even savagery in the humor of La Fontaine than he is usually given credit for. My great-aunt also claimed a relation to the German poet and novelist Theodor Fontane, adducing as proof the fact that my father's name was Theodore, which was true enough. But the story becomes interesting when we know that a younger son in the original line of Dutch Fontanes removed to Venice towards the end of the eighteenth century to set up a branch of the family business there. The young man had money and letters of introduction and good manners and good looks. He moved in the best of circles, met Lorenzo Da Ponte, Mozart's librettist; the sculptor Canova, who knew Voltaire; the dramatist Goldoni; and Casanova, who was one of the first to speak to him of Constantinople and the romantic East. He also met the merchant princes of the day, among whom were members of the Great Council and those whose names shone like jewels in the fabulous history of Venice in its greatest days. And it was in that society that he met and married Caterina Giustiniani, a direct descendent of that Giovanni Giustiniani who was killed in defense of Constantinople at the final overthrow of the Byzantine Empire in 1453. Caterina was also a descendent, on her mother's side, of a noble Venetian family that counted among its number Caterina

Cornaro, queen of Cyprus as the wife of James II, the last king of the house of Lusignan, which derived its name from the castle of Lusignan in the province of Poitou in France. The castle was said to derive its name, in turn, from the nymph Melusine, who created the castle to conceal her love for a mortal man, first in the Lusignan line.

The newly married couple moved into an elegant small villa on the Grand Canal, a gift of the Giustiniani-Cornaro clan. The villa figures in a panorama of the Grand Canal that was painted by Canaletto sometime around 1760, a painting which now hangs in the Museum of Fine Arts in Boston, but that is another story. My ancestor's affairs prospered in Venice, to the point where it became apparent to him that continued successful expansion could only be assured by another remove. By that time, he and Caterina both knew Constantinople well, and on their last visit they had acquired the villa into which they subsequently moved and which today stands empty on the Asian shore just above Kuzguncuk. Once established in Constantinople, Jan and Caterina Fontane began to frequent the society of Levantine merchants whose families traced their origins to Amalfi, Genoa, and Venice—Caterina found distant cousins—but who had also contracted marriages with Greeks, Armenians, Circassians, and Georgians. By the end of the nineteenth century, they were also marrying into established old families of Ottoman Turks, from whose number comes—to make a very long story short—my mother, wife of Theodore Fontane, great-great-grandson of Jan Fontane of Amsterdam and Venice who was the founder of the family fortune in this part of the world.

How is it possible that I should know all this? In the first place, I know that if it were not possible, I could not be who I am. My great-aunt is, naturally, my primary source, but it must be understood that in families like ours such detailed knowledge of genealogy is commonplace. Anecdotes are transmitted by the fireside and at family reunions, but there is also the record of marriage contracts, carefully preserved, and there are business records, going back sometimes several hundred years, to establish an armature of fact. But the living genealogy is a continuous flow, one generation overlapping another, the lines between families crossing and recrossing and blurring and finally disappearing until the aggregate of private histories and public history become inextricably entwined.

In families like ours, the past is very much alive, investing the present with its glorious or inglorious example. On this score, my great-aunt is not always to be trusted. As regards her contention that the German novelist Theodor Fontane is our ancestor, she refuses to admit, for example, that he was captured in the Franco-Prussian War. The suspicion that he may have been the only German to have been captured in that war would make him ridiculous, and this she refuses to allow. On the other hand, she revels in the family's apparent genius, occasionally revealed, for heroic calamity. She never tires of telling the story of another Venetian ancestor, Marco Antonio Bragadino, martyred by the Turks for his heroic role in the defense of Famagusta in Cyprus in 1571, the same year as the Battle of Lepanto, where the great Cervantes lost his hand, but that is another story. As commander of the last Venetian garrison in Cyprus, it fell to Bragadino to conduct the ceremony of surrender to the Turks. He was received with courtesy, but the courtesy was a ruse. He was taken from the place of surrender into the open air, where his body was stretched into immobility and he was flayed alive. My aunt used to gloss over these horrors, of course, saying only that he had suffered the death of a hero and martyr. She used to tell me, and she gave other reasons, that there was no greater name to bear than that of Marco.

I stood that evening before my canvas having been driven, by an apparently ordered set of circumstances, ever deeper within myself, ever further back upon my own resources. The work would not be found in the world or in an image of the world.

The source of the work was not out there somewhere, but within. Nor was the source of the work in an ideal to be remembered or aspired to, because it was in the concrete now. It was as if I were at a crossroads where all avenues had an equal claim, and I was utterly immobilized. The avenues seemed to beckon me, to stretch me out in all directions, centrifugally, and I could not move. Then I experienced a gradual release of tension and a brief moment of suspension, like the head of John the Baptist at the top of its arc—do you remember?—in which I seemed to float. Then the forces began to reassert themselves, but in the opposite direction, now pressing in upon me and, as they did so, very slowly, I began to turn. With increasing speed I turned until a new state of equilibrium was achieved between the centripetal forces generating the spinning motion from without and the resultant centrifugal forces generated by the spin. The distinction between inside and outside, between here and there, was abolished as, from the center, I began to spiral downwards into the vortex of a maelstrom or a stupendous fire storm. My whole body was wracked with pain, as from a rhythmical series of electrical charges released into me from electrodes planted all over my head, and it was then that I felt the incisions being drawn across my shoulders and down my chest and back and the burning grip of the iron tongs with which they seized my flesh and peeled it away, strip after strip, from my shoulders and down over my buttocks and crotch. And still I burned and whirled in an agony of flame, and still I did not die. And the agony of flame but grew by what it fed upon, and still I did not die, because I was myself become that flame and agony, through which must pass all that I was, all that I had ever been: summer days, skies, rivers and cities, mountains and fleets, landmarks, taverns, rain, the sound of a steam whistle, ambition and fear and the ones I have so dearly loved, grain sent to the great Doge in Venice, Venice itself and the great Doge, writers and artists, Leonardo, Rimbaud, wolves, elephants, wars, and men in caves, and fire within fire within fire, the whole cavalcade of time. And I knew then that my suffering was exemplary and that I suffered in expiation of some great flaw or fault of which my issue would be purified. I suffered and I did not die and the more I suffered the more my power grew. I whirled in an agony of flame I had become, which had become my power and my exultant joy, and my completeness was the completeness of a god.

No one should imagine that the detached man who speaks to you now labors under any delusions. When I returned to my senses, as they say, they told me that I had collapsed in my studio from a neurological disturbance which they had been able to control with the help of certain miracles of modern science, injections and electric shock. I have accepted this explanation for what it's worth, but it is superficial. They tell me that my health has been restored, but it wasn't their cure but the disturbance that brought it back to me, brought back to me the soul that I left in the fire in Ortaköy.

Let me tell you something interesting. When I was a little boy, I was left-handed. My parents tried to get me to use my right hand, but it was unnatural and I resisted and they gave up trying and I can remember my father telling my mother not to persist because I was incurable. Then came the calamity of school. The schoolmasters found a cure. Whack! with a ruler across the knuckles of the left hand, surprised in its foul delinquency, and then for good measure, palm up, WHACK! I soon learned to write properly with my right hand so that I could hold my arm and wrist straight and not smudge the ink. But in sports I used my left hand all the time, and nobody said a thing, so that after a while I became equally comfortable using either hand, and I remember a couple of years later one of my little group of friends proposing that we have a special way of writing to each other, like a secret code. I don't know where he got the idea, but it was that we should write everything backwards so that you could read it only by holding it up to a mirror. It didn't take long for somebody to figure out that this wasn't much of a code, but I accidentally discovered on my own that, with a little practice, I could write almost effortlessly backwards with my left hand. I practiced a little and all effort disappeared. I began to keep a private journal and I wrote everything with my left hand. I was to discover later, in college, that Leonardo da Vinci had kept a journal that was written backwards, and I knew exactly how he had done it and why. I kept the journal all through high school and my studies at the American College and my graduate studies in France, and it was with me that night when my life ended, or was suspended, in Ortaköy.

That night in the fire I lost my journal and the book I had written on Rimbaud, and my beloved wife and little boy. That night I lost my soul and, at a stroke, the use of my left hand. I could still do with it the things that most right-handed people could do, but I could no longer throw a stone or use a hammer properly or write. So when the doctors told me that my health had been restored through their kindly ministrations, they could have had no idea what they were talking about, because the restoration had occurred, not through their corrective measures, but within the "neurological disturbance" itself, whose onslaught had been signaled by my recovering the full use of my left hand. I remember now as clearly as if it were yesterday that as I began to throw color at that black-and-white and blurred design, my brush moved unbidden into my left hand, and in that instant I stepped through the mirror and into my mirror image and was again complete. That simple gesture was my release, or the sign of my release, and I was possessed by a sense of power and certainty within my task that had nothing to do with the intuition of a plan and everything to do with a perfect confidence in the fecundity of the moment itself and in whatever the union of my skill and the moment might bring. My soul had been returned to me. It sang in me with the whirling and celestial harmony of the spheres. It danced in me in robes of pentecostal flame and spoke in tongues of color the secret speech of the correspondences, the synesthesia by which I could convert all that I was, purified, into my work.

Heraclitus said it was impossible to put your foot twice into the same river. A modern physiologist might say that it wouldn't even be the same foot. For Heraclitus, reality was not a substance like water, as Thales had thought, or even the less substantial air proposed by Anaximenes. For Heraclitus, reality was fire, because fire was not a substance, but a process. It follows, then, that as we are all living the reality of process, we are also living in fire in one or another of its manifestations. It also follows, or so it seems to me, that the differentiated species could survive only if their relation to reality were greatly attenuated. They would otherwise burn up. Of the various species, man is the only one capable of making fire—or rather of summoning it—of living in its constant and close proximity and even, up to a point, exploiting and controlling it. But no man—not the artist, not the medium or mystic, but with the sole possible exception of the insane—can live wholly and continuously within that ecstatic and terrible arc of energy.

I speak to you now as a man detached and I live as a man detached except when I have my paintbrushes in my hand. I have reversed the order of my days of apprenticeship. Where I used to draw in the mornings and paint in the afternoons, now I paint in the mornings and draw in the afternoons. I take a break at midday and go out and wander around the village for a while and then sit under the great sycamore in the middle of the *meydan*, the village square, and smoke and try to think of nothing and greet the passersby. The children are not afraid of me anymore, but I can sometimes hear their mothers whisper to them sharply to stay away from that filthy man. What do I care? I don't go out to please anybody but myself. I then go back to my studio and drink some coffee and I spend the afternoon drawing with the controlled lucidity of my right hand. I restrict myself to the various black-and-white media—ink, graphite, fusain—and I work from nature or from photographs as in the early days. I remember some years ago asking Sylvia Malone, before she married Corrigan, to pose for me. She is still a very beautiful woman, but in those days—it must be twenty years ago—her face had an expression of playfulness that excited me. It was crazy of me to ask her, but I did, and she accepted, crazy or not.

Now, I am an experienced professional and a very cool customer, as you will surely agree, and I had told myself that drawing this woman would be no different from drawing anything else, but when she dropped her clothes and stepped out of her underwear I began to experience a certain male reaction that modesty forbids me to name. We had agreed that she would pose reclining with her back and head propped against some pillows, like Manet's *Olympia* and so many others, and I cooled down as soon as I began to draw. My interior model was not Manet, but Ingres, the perfect draftsman, and I was determined to produce a drawing of classical fidelity to the appearances. Our first two sessions went very well. Sylvia was able to hold the pose for about forty minutes without discomfort. We would then take a five-minute break and then work for another forty minutes and then quit for the day. At the third session, however, which I had imagined might be our last, Sylvia was wearing a red rose in her hair, and when she assumed her reclining position she very gracefully detached the rose from her hair and, holding the stem delicately between her thumb and index finger, allowed the blossom to rest upon that portion of her anatomy which modesty forbids me to name. It wasn't even of Manet that I was reminded then, but of Baudelaire's "Lola de Valence," a little poem that rewards careful reading, and she looked straight at me and she said, Maybe this is a little nicer? A little nicer? She knew. The pose and the gentle question were superbly calculated, and I succumbed. Not as you are imagining or as the lady might, but I was possessed then of an absolute need to render in my art the tones of her magnificent flesh and, through them, the burning heart of a sexual reality that communicated itself to me like a current flowing from within her body through that artful rose. It was no longer her appearance that excited me, but her erotic soul. I had already prepared a fresh canvas for the following day. I put the drawing board aside, clamped the new canvas on the easel, took up my brushes, and began to paint.

Sylvia never posed for me again. I gave her the unfinished drawing. She must still have it somewhere. When I finally stopped painting that day, it was already getting dark and Sylvia was gone. Some part of me must have registered her departure, because I associate it with a moment in the progress of the painting when, fortunately, I had already taken from the model all that I needed. The painting was still recognizable as a nude, but I had already begun to work through the appearances to their source and to the heart of the work's source within myself. And the more I worked through the pulsing flow of colors and forms and their mysterious harmonies, the more the soul of Sylvia lost, like her body, its defining contours, merging finally with the souls of all beautiful women in that essential something which we have learned to call *l'éternel féminin*. I continued to paint, and, as the darkness began to thicken around me, the act of painting became increasingly instinctive and gestural. Through my hand and wrist I could feel the painting take on a life of its own, form emerging from opening form in ever-renewed exfoliations like the tireless song of the nightingale, a shower of harmonies in red and gold. My studio was filled with the odor of roses, and I bathed in a long caress as in that moment I realized that she had come to me. She had stepped from the soul of the painting and come to me. She came to me the following night and the night after that and every night. I kept the painting in my bedroom under a protective curtain, and nobody knew she was there but me. At night, I would turn the curtain back and stretch myself out on my bed and wait. She always made me wait, sometimes until I could hardly stand the tension. There is a special artfulness in knowing precisely when the maximum pleasure is to be extracted from the maximum pain. She never spoke to me. I never dared speak to her, never even to say her name. She has come to me less frequently in recent months and years, but she is still there, tonight, watching and waiting for the moment when my whole soul will cry out for her and she will come to me for the last time.

ii

Marco Fontane's studio was in the upper village of Rumeli Hisarı on a narrow road, hardly more than a lane, that led from the *meydan* up through the hills to Etiler. It was a small, two-story, frame structure with a small yard and an outhouse in back. Most of the yard was given over to a vegetable garden, to which Marco devoted, in season, a portion of two or three afternoons a week. From the yard, Marco stepped into a kitchen simply furnished with a wooden table and two straight-backed chairs, a gas stove, and a sink with a hand-operated water pump whose pipe came straight up from the well beneath. This was the only plumbing in the house. There was no shower or bathtub, but this was no great inconvenience because Marco almost never washed. For the rest, he had the outhouse in back.

From the kitchen, a door opened onto his one front room, which was so cluttered with the various accouterments of his work—drawing boards, reams of new paper, crumpled piles of old, uncut lumber for making stretchers, rolls of canvas, empty paint tubes scattered everywhere—that it gave the appearance from the outside of being a warehouse of some kind, though you could hardly see through the windows anyway, for the grime.

Also from the kitchen, a steep open stair led to the bedroom, the only room in the house kept spotlessly clean, and to the studio, in the far corner of which Marco had cut a wide hole so he could pass supplies up from the storeroom below or into which he could toss or kick whatever qualified as junk.

 Marco's days and nights were spent in this little house, except for his noontime walks down to the *meydan* for a smoke or his occasional afternoon foray, in season, in search of a motif. Of a rare Friday or Saturday night, he would break his routine to join one friend or another for dinner at somebody's house or, more likely, downtown. Marco was not a popular guest among the wives. Although he always washed as best he could before going out, his clothes were never really clean, and there trailed after him or hung about him, if he were standing still, a slightly gangrenous aroma. In restaurants he would be seated always at the head of the table, a gesture which he may have misunderstood, with his pals Dimitri and Erden on either side to supply a buffer zone. In addition to this, Marco was a ferocious drinker, especially on nights out. He drank *rakı* every night of his life, starting at sundown when he climbed down to his kitchen to see what might be lying around to eat. He hated to cook, except for the occasional bit of fish, and his diet consisted principally of cheese and olives, fruit and raw vegetables, bread, oil and vinegar, and a bit of chocolate or baklava, most often consumed standing or pacing about the kitchen as he drank. He drank his *rakı* before, during, and after his evening meal, and when he went out, the convivial sights and sounds of other drinkers fairly swept him away, and he had been known to fall off his chair or miss it entirely when trying to sit down or "otherwise misbehave," as his friend Erden would say. Marco's friends had not seen him now in several weeks. But it wasn't unusual for him to shut himself up during foul weather, and the past winter had been particularly long and cold and wet. Everybody had been looking forward to the coming of spring, and it was to coincide this time with Marco's grand opening show at Şimşek Emlak, with its attendant scandal, and everybody wanted to hear what Marco would have to say at the anti-Şimşek dinner tonight at Boncuk.

Marco had heard the late afternoon call to prayer while drawing in his studio. He was working from several photographs, taken from different angles, of the former library of Ahmet Vefik Pasha, situated just down the hill from his studio on the far side of the *meydan*. Ahmet Vefik Pasha had been Grand Vezir in the reign of Abdülhamit II in the second half of the nineteenth century. He had been a man of learning, intelligence, and taste, and his library was a beautifully proportioned building, beautifully situated, with great windows opening upon a garden terrace with views of the Bosphorus and the Asian hills. When he had started the drawing, some three weeks ago, Marco had thought that he might transfer the result to an etching plate and print a limited edition for his friends. They had all of them been to parties in the building during the time that the American writer James Baldwin had been living there, and it would be a nice memento. But over the last several days, with the approach of the exhibit, he had found it increasingly difficult to concentrate. He had started and restarted both the collage of photographs and the drawing four or five times, each time becoming more dissatisfied with the result. He had reshuffled the photographs, trimmed some with scissors, and started again; but his heart wasn't in it and he had realized, late this afternoon, that he would never get it right.

With deliberate calm, he unpinned the latest version of the collage and scaled the irregularly cut papers, like playing cards, one by one, in the direction of the hole in the far corner of the room. As he did so, he became aware of the late afternoon call to prayer and thought of his friend Erden. The last bit of paper missed the mark. He reached in his shirt pocket and pulled out a box of matches and his cigarettes and tapped one out and lit up.

Yes, Erden would be making the same gestures right now. He liked Erden and admired his discipline, and he liked the reassuring orderliness of Erden's shop, the meticulously kept books, the meticulously kept Erden. That was perhaps unfair. Erden was in so many ways an admirable man, but he couldn't help thinking that Erden had imposed limits upon himself that would forever inhibit the enlargement of his experience and understanding. On the other hand, if he, Marco, could be forever and solely the expert draftsman, who could make rational plans, like Erden, for tomorrow and for the next day and the next and for all of his allotted time to come, would that not be wonderful?

No, it most emphatically would not. It would be just going through the motions, and there could be nothing wonderful in that. But what proportion of our lives is actually spent that way? How often do we simply repeat what we have done before, or repeat what others have said or done a million times before or are doing right now, as I light my cigarette knowing that Erden is doing the same thing at the same moment on the other side of town? These are not ourselves, but illusions of ourselves, and perhaps after tonight a perfect illusion of myself will continue to inhabit this house and draw his drawings, and eat and drink and walk about in the world, as if nothing had happened, and nobody will know that the real Marco is not there. Perhaps my image will appear tonight at the dinner at Boncuk, and explain what I have done and why, so that my friends will understand.

And what is there to understand? What will they understand?

That the real Marco saw his chance and took it.

Marco stepped close to his drawing again, squinted disapprovingly, and struck another match. The drawing was stapled to the board on all four sides, but he thought that it would burn, nevertheless, and without creating a danger. For all its shortcomings, the drawing did convey an illusion of depth, and Marco wondered, with a smile, if that would make it more combustible. Only if the fire were an illusion too, he thought. He put the match to the lower right-hand corner of the paper and as the flame took hold, ran it slowly along the lower edge. The little line of fire climbed irregularly along the paper, faster in the middle where the paper billowed slightly like a sail, giving it more air. Soon there was nothing left but the charred edges where the staples held the paper fast to the board.

iii

Marco didn't want to burn the village down, so he made sure the fire was out before going downstairs to the kitchen, where he stripped off his clothes and washed himself at the sink. He then went back up to his bedroom and put on a clean set of underwear and a clean turtleneck and climbed back into his jeans. He accomplished these acts, as he always did, with his back to the corner of the room where the curtained painting stood on its easel. He was ready now.

He carried the painting, with its cover, into the studio and slipped it into a plastic envelope that he had taped together years ago for a similar purpose. He then secured the painting to his portable French easel and wrapped easel and painting in a canvas tarp, letting the easel's shoulder straps hang free. He carried his bundle down to the kitchen and, remembering, sat down and took a nip from a bottle of *rakı* and pushed his chair back from the table and put on his shoes and socks. He got up and took his overcoat down from its hook on the back of the kitchen door and checked the contents of the half-bottle of *rakı* he kept in the inside breast pocket. It wouldn't do. He went back to the kitchen table and nipped again and poured from the big bottle into the small, his companion for the road. He picked up his bundle, then, and swung it onto his back and tightened the shoulder straps.

He was all set. No. He went over to the corner window by the gas canister that fed the stove and picked up an adjustable wrench from the sill and put it in his overcoat pocket. You never knew. He went out and closed the back door without locking it, which he never did, and around the house and out into the street. He was halfway down to the *meydan* when he stopped and turned around and looked back up the street and thought, Why did it never occur to me to draw my own crazy house?

Marco was on his way downtown. For a week now he had felt increasingly like a somnambulist or a dreamer evolving slowly within a dream. He had been visited by Faruk Selvi, the writer, who had pleaded with him once again, in the name of the Arts Foundation, to show up at the opening. If they could be assured of his presence, they knew they could count on a huge crowd. They had been advertising the show in the newspapers and building the legend of Marco the reclusive genius. It would cause a sensation if they could now announce that the painter would be there in person. And Marco could sell his own work, anything he might have lying around the studio, at prices he had never dreamed of. This was, after all, a celebration of the artist's twenty-five years in art and it should include the artist's most recent work and the presence of the artist himself.

Marco didn't know why he was even listening to Faruk, but he was. Faruk's obvious implication that he could be tempted by money was annoying in the extreme, but he had let it go by. There was something in this whole affair that he hadn't yet seen clearly or completely, but he thought that he might at least let Faruk have a few of his paintings. He knew that this would mean going back on his earlier decision to have nothing whatever to do with the show, but that didn't seem to matter. He told Faruk to come with a van the following day. He promised some paintings—he couldn't yet say how many—and a final decision on whether or not he would come. That evening he had worked until midnight sorting through the work of the last six months, choosing those paintings which he would give to Faruk and those which would go definitively "into the hole." He had distributed the paintings around the studio, propping some up, hanging others from the odd nail in the wall, and he had passed from one to the other, assessing, as in a trance, the power of each. As he made his selection, eliminating the weaker ones and casting them out, the potency of the remaining ones seemed to increase and concentrate, and he realized that he could never let them go without the promise of accompanying them. He had given paintings away before and sold a few, but never in such quantity all at once, and never at such a juncture in his work. He usually had several paintings in progress at the same time, but now he had none. The only work he had in progress was the collage-drawing, but it was a plaything. The entire expression of his spiritual being, these vessels and channels of his soul's relation to reality, his life itself, were now to be concentrated in a single room at Galatasaray.

Marco cut an unusually picturesque figure crossing the upper *meydan* of Rumeli Hisarı. His long, dark overcoat, collar turned up, billowed slightly behind him as it almost swept the ground. His carried his lanky frame pitched forward to balance the weight of the easel which, wrapped in its dark tarp, gave a grotesque outline to his silhouette. It was getting dark. The wind was freshening along the Bosphorus, and Marco was glad he would have it at his back. He decided not to go down directly to the quay but to cut across in back of the castle along a protected lane leading to the College road. The lane took him down through a wooded area and up a steep hill on the College side and came out just above the Aşiyan Museum and below the old Piombini house where now Frank and Sylvia Corrigan lived. Marco paused for a minute—not to rest, and he noted again with pleasure this smoker's undiminished lung capacity—thinking of all the years gone by, of an opportunity missed, perhaps, with Sylvia Malone. What opportunity? Had he not made of their encounter something infinitely more precious? He had to admit that some part of him wasn't always sure. Just the other day he had had a terrible shock. He was returning to his studio from an afternoon ramble along this very lane when he had run into Sylvia as he remembered her twenty or so years ago. The lane was narrow and they had both stopped dead in their tracks and she had been startled by his appearance until she recognized him and smiled and he had then recognized her as Sylvia's daughter Nicolette. She was coming home from school. They had spoken briefly of one thing or another, of his ramble, and he had shown her his sketchpad and asked her if she would pose for him one day. But what had he meant really? Was he crazy? If she told her mother, what would her mother think? He knew very well what her mother would think, and she would be right. What had he been thinking of? He was a miserable old fool. He was a lonely miserable old fool. Lonely? Surely not. Was he not the famous artist Marco Fontane and was he not going to a highly publicized celebration of his Twenty-five Years in Art?

Marco walked down the College road. He walked past the Aşiyan Museum where the papers of Nigar Hanım the poet were kept. His great-aunt, the genealogist, had been an intimate friend of Nigar's and she had told him things she said nobody else knew, things about her terrible relations with her husband, who had "poisoned her life." She had also talked of the days when the Piombini family had held spectacular balls in the house where the Corrigans now lived and how one of the Piombini girls had fallen in love and run away with one of the housemaids, a beautiful Circassian girl about thirteen years old, but that was another story.

Marco walked down the College road to the Bosphorus and along the quay into Bebek. He stopped at Nazmi's for a *rakı*, sitting sideways on his chair because he didn't want to unstrap the easel. He had taken a couple of celebratory nips from his own bottle—one for the beautiful Nicolette, one for the once beautiful and now almost forgotten Circassian girl—but he didn't want to exhaust his private supply before reaching town and so had decided to have a few drinks in cafes along the way. From Nazmi's, Marco walked by the Yeni Güneş on the Bosphorus side of the road, a restaurant famous for its *meze* and its calamari and grilled turbot, where years ago they had spent many a happy evening on the terrace talking and watching the lights come on along the Asian shore. He had come here often with his wife before the baby was born, and even afterwards, and he remembered that they had come the first time with Erden and—it hardly seemed possible—Erden's father before the old man died. But that had been only just after the war and they were all so very young and full of promise and hope, and Marco stopped dead in his tracks from the pain of a remembrance that had come to him more frequently in recent months and seemed now to come to him every day. They had been so full of love, he and his little family, and the hope and the promise had been so terribly cut off, and the pain rose in his chest and constricted his throat until he thought he might not be able to breathe.

Marco forced himself to resume his walk and he was breathing again normally by the time he passed through a shaft of light glaring from the entrance to the Bebek Hotel. He stopped for a moment to read a poster advertising an American jazz trio—"Wednesdays through Saturdays exclusively"—and he thought there must be something wrong with the wording and that he would never hear the trio play. They would have come to hear them in the old days. They did everything in the old days. I'll drink to that, he thought, and he did, briefly. He resumed his walk and passed in front of the Bebek Mosque, behind which was the ferry landing, and he turned into the little park with its cluster of flowering Judas trees and stopped in front of the statue of Orhan Veli, the people's poet, who seemed to be waiting for a ferry to land, and he lifted his bottle again and saluted the people's poet and said out loud, "Whoop, whoop," feeling better now, and an old lady dressed in black and invisible on her park bench wished she could be transported to the safety of her apartment up the street and out of the reach of this towering mad hunchback who was now coming straight at her, and Marco thought, They must have moved that statue from the other end of town, unless I'm seeing things, and a small shrill voice very close to him said enigmatically, No, no, no, as his foot caught the edge of something in the dark and he stumbled briefly and stopped and steadied the easel and resumed his walk.

Marco had by now gone through half of his small bottle and he decided to go easy for a while. He walked the kilometer between Bebek and Arnavutköy at a steady pace and decided to skirt the village by keeping to the newly constructed road and walkway on the Bosphorus side. Another kilometer and a half would bring him to Kuruçeşme, halfway between Arnavutköy and Ortaköy, where he would stop again. Would he stop at Kuruçeşme or Ortaköy? He wasn't sure. He stopped for a moment to think. And to rest? He wasn't sure. He was standing at the head of the promontory separating the sheltered harbor of Arnavutköy from the south end of the bay of Bebek. The current here is very swift, and with the north wind blowing as it was, the current rounds the point at a speed faster than a man can walk. The water rolled by with a dizzying motion, the slick black surface broken by dancing flames of light. For all the power of its rolling undulation, it couldn't carry off the flames of light. Marco watched the dancing flames, the dancing images, which spread across the water and along the Asian shore. He resumed his walk. He looked down, and the flames on the surface of the water below the walkway moved with him. He looked up, and they danced before him as he strode, now easily again, and he felt an opening, as of a valve, somewhere in his brain and he was filled with a feeling of promise and hope and he knew he was to be given a second chance.

Ahead of him was the long, dark passage through Kuruçeşme—the place of the dry fountain—where the ferries no longer stopped and where nobody now stopped and he strode on and wished he were at the end of the dark passage and had already reached Ortaköy, and the images danced before him and, as if by magic, there he was on the ferry landing in Ortaköy. A steamer was just now making its way up to the landing from Kuzguncuk. It would stop briefly here and proceed to Kandilli, where Erden lived. He and his wife used to visit Erden in Kandilli in the early days and afterwards with their little boy and he remembered crossing for dinner and waiting for the ferry at just about this time of night and he was all but overcome by the hallucination of seeing himself standing there with his wife, who was carrying their little boy on her arm. It was no hallucination. There was a young couple with a baby waiting to board, apparently the only new passengers. They stood well to one side to allow the unruly crowd of disembarking passengers to pass. When the way was clear, the young husband, having noticed Marco, gestured respectfully for him to board first. Marco, very moved, stepped towards them and looked at the baby who was fast asleep. He observed the custom of not looking at the young woman and, addressing only the husband, said, God bless you all. Marco's emotion was apparent and the husband, imagining he saw tears welling in the old man's eyes, took Marco's hand and, bending, raised it to his lips and touched it to his forehead to render homage, and he said, God bless you too, grandfather. The young people were from a small village near Adana in the south. They had both grown up on farms where they cultivated vegetables of all kinds and apricots and tended small flocks of sheep. They had run away together to Istanbul in search of money and a better life, but they had felt utterly alienated by the confinement and brutality of life in the city and in the factory where they worked. They were going home. They would be forgiven, because they would show respect and ask to be forgiven and because they were returning with a beautiful little boy. They knew now with perfect certainty that they would be forgiven, for had they not just now been blessed by an elder? The kind old man had known everything and understood. Had they met more people like him in Istanbul—guardians of the old ways—they might have stayed. But they had not, and they were going home.

As the steamer pulled away from the landing, Marco waved to the young couple and the husband waved back and then waved again. As the stern began to swing, Marco noticed on the upper deck a dapper figure leaning on the rail and looking down, apparently fascinated, as he had been, by that perfect little family. The dapper figure then turned towards the landing, perhaps to see if he could make out the husband's friend, the object of this emotional farewell, and he lifted his hand to his lips in a gesture which Marco could not at first identify, and then figure and gesture and face assumed those of good old Erden Sakarya having a smoke. Another hallucination? Was the *rakı* playing tricks? Marco raised his hand to wave, but the figure evidently hadn't seen him and had turned away.

Surely it must have been Erden going home to Kandilli after work. He will have bought his two newspapers and read them front to back on the ferry, and tonight at Boncuk he will be full of the day's news. I wonder what happened today, he thought. No I don't. I don't care a damn what happened today, but I do care about the lives of those young people and the real Erden of my youth who survives in the commuter in spite of himself, and Nicolette, who carries within her the life of her mother, and Sylvia herself, from the womb of whose being arose the forms of that wild beauty he had loved and lost and found again in his art, in the painting he carried on his back, and with whom he would now live forever and ever, amen.

Marco resumed his walk through Ortaköy. He wouldn't stop again until he had reached Beşiktaş. Some years ago he had walked up the hill in Ortaköy to Lausanne Street where they had lived. Not one of the old houses remained. They had either burned, like his own, or been knocked down to make room for high-rise apartments, an alien world he had no wish to see again.

In Beşiktaş Marco again took refuge on the ferry landing. Unless a steamer were about to land, these landings were peaceful waterside retreats where you could sit for a while, usually quite alone. Marco held his bottle up to the light. There were only about two real drinks left. He would save what he had and buy one in a cafe before leaving Beşiktaş and another in Kabataş, perhaps, and a last one behind Galatasaray. The show was scheduled to run from five until eight, when the others would be gathering at Boncuk. He had promised Faruk to appear, but he hadn't said when. One minute to eight would be time enough, but it would be calamitous to be shut out and he should therefore arrive in the area of Galatasaray with at least ten minutes to spare. Not that these people were terribly strict observers of the clock, but they were erratic and known to do things capriciously on time.

Marco took a last drag on his cigarette and flipped it into the water and resumed his walk. He walked under the statue of Barbarossa, which hadn't moved, and by the Maritime Museum and the Fine Arts Faculty, where no one had ever heard of him, and Dolmabahçe Palace, built by a maternal ancestor, Balyan, and where Mustafa Kemal, the great Atatürk, had died. He strode on. His thoughts were beginning to concentrate. He had left Beşiktaş without stopping for a drink, and he didn't stop in Kabataş. He strode on along the coast road past Cihangir on the right and Tophane on the left as far as the mosque of Kılıç Ali Pasha, who had befriended Cervantes, but that was another story. With the mosque just in sight ahead of him, he turned onto Boğazkesen Caddesi and began the long climb to Galatasaray. By the time he got there, he was in a lather, but he was glad to have pressed on. He would never have made it if he had stopped for a drink in a cafe. It was a quarter to eight.

To the left of where Marco stood, the side window of the Şimşek Gallery threw a broad beam of light across the square. To his right was a high grillwork fence behind which was the wooded front garden of the Galatasaray Lycée. The fence was seated in a concrete wall, the outer ledge of which served during the day as a convenient display shelf for itinerant merchants selling neckties, wristwatches, cigarette lighters and the like, or as a place of gathering and repose for the various old men and loafers who hung around the square. At night, however, there being no streetlamp on this side, the wall was deserted, and Marco had it to himself. He unhitched the easel from his back and set it down. It would be perfectly safe during the few minutes it would take him to have a look.

He walked out into the square and turned towards the gallery and stopped. He fished the packet of cigarettes from his inside breast pocket and tapped one out and lit up. There could be no more than half a dozen people left in the gallery and, as he approached the side window, he could see that the waiters had already cleaned up the *meze* table and the bar. One of them was just now going around the room emptying the wastebaskets and ashtrays into a big plastic bag. Faruk and the director of the gallery were by the front door saying goodbye to somebody, and there were what appeared to be two security guards standing outside in the street smoking. A second waiter then appeared from the kitchen with a pail which he put down next to the *meze* table. He swept some debris into the center of the paper tablecovering and crumpled it into a ball and lofted it at his colleague across the room. The first waiter was about to loft it back when he saw the director gesture to him to stop playing around and to hurry up with his work. It wouldn't be long now.

Marco was well acquainted with the layout of the gallery. When Faruk had arrived at the studio to pick up the last of the promised paintings, Marco said he would accompany them downtown. Faruk was afraid that Marco might object to the obvious overcrowding of the walls and their recourse to panels, but not only did Marco not object, saying, quite unexpectedly, the more the merrier, but he had also finally promised to show up on opening night. His very words. Faruk was pleased to explain everything, about the security guards at the front door, the *meze* table and the bar and what would be served, and even the extra cooks who would be brought down from the executive dining room upstairs. Marco had particularly wanted to see the kitchen and had looked into every cabinet and behind every closet door. Of particular interest to him was a large storage room just off the front of the kitchen. It was filled with the usual brooms and pails and paper supplies, but it was large enough also to contain several racks of chairs and tables of various sizes, at least four sofas and as many stuffed chairs. These could be used anywhere in the building, Faruk explained—there was a service elevator by the rear door—but their primary purpose was for converting the gallery to other uses when they were not having a show.

From his vantage point outside in the square, Marco continued to observe what the waiters were doing, occasionally glancing over to see that his easel was still where he had left it. The waiter with the pail had produced a sponge and wrung it out and wiped the tables down and dried them with a cloth he carried tucked under his belt. The last guest had left the gallery. The director stepped out into the street and had a word with the guards. He paid them and they shook hands and the director stepped back inside the gallery and closed and locked the door. He then turned to Faruk and offered him a cigarette, and the two men lit up. At the back of the gallery, the waiters had opened the kitchen door and the door to the storeroom. Both doors opened into the kitchen, but they were hung in such a way as to allow the furniture to be moved directly between storeroom and gallery without maneuvering. Clever. The waiters turned the bar table up and collapsed the legs and carried it out. They went through the same motions with the second table, turned out the storeroom light, and closed the door.

By this time, Marco had disappeared. At the moment the director had stepped into the street to pay the guards, Marco had turned away and tossed his cigarette, gathered up his easel, and walked quickly into the alley and over to the kitchen door. The waiters had been taking garbage out, and the door was ajar. If it hadn't been, Marco would simply have opened it. He didn't have long to wait. The instant the second table was in and the storeroom door closed, Marco was in the kitchen. He walked quickly to the other end. He couldn't now open the storeroom door without being seen from the gallery, so he slowly closed the gallery door, giving it an extra small push at the end, as the wind might have done. In the instant that the latch clicked, he was inside the storeroom with the door closed. He turned the light switch on and off, and in the momentary illumination, as of a flashbulb, he saw where he would hide. Four steps, the edge of a sofa against his knee, and he was crouched down behind. He heard one of the waiters open the kitchen door. They had just been paid and didn't notice a thing. He then heard Faruk's voice and the director's voice saying something about the lights. Faruk evidently didn't understand, so the director repeated that they didn't have to worry about turning off the various gallery lights, because it was easier to disengage the master fuse at the back door. In another instant the sliver of light under the storeroom door went out, and Marco heard the back door close and a key turn in the lock. He stood and walked over to the door. Silence. He flattened his ear against the door and held his breath. Silence. He opened the door and could see absolutely nothing. He opened the gallery door and could see again. There was plenty of light to work by coming in off the square.

 There were three panels in the center of the room, one facing İstiklal, the other two at right angles. By drawing them together to form a "U" against the kitchen wall, Marco would minimally alter the appearance of the gallery as seen from the outside and create for himself a completely enclosed and private space. He did so and brought the easel in from where he had left it behind the sofa in the storeroom. He unpacked the easel and set it up and clamped the painting in place. On the walls of the little room were hung the concentrated essence of his recent work and, on the easel, his life's masterpiece. He then shook out the tarp which, completely unfolded, was big enough to span the opening between the panels and form an enclosing canopy. With the tarp in place, the light from the street was partially cut off, but it was still possible to see. He returned to the storeroom and brought out a straight-backed wooden chair and a standing ashtray and placed them next to the easel. He went back into the storeroom and reappeared with a two-wheeled dolly which he rolled to the rear of the kitchen and stood next to the gas canister by the stove. The gas canister was of industrial size, almost two meters high, and it weighed a ton. He checked to see that the valve was closed and, with the adjustable wrench he carried in his pocket, he detached the nozzle from the copper tube that led to the stove. He then took the canister in a bear hug and, tipping it slightly towards him, rolled it onto the lip of the dolly and rolled dolly and canister backwards out of the kitchen and into his little room. He then closed the kitchen door and sat down on the straight-backed wooden chair, and he fished the packet of cigarettes from his inside breast pocket and tapped one out and lit up. He wouldn't be able to smoke in a minute. This one would be his last. He took a drag and watched the smoke rise in a spiral through a shaft of light. He took another drag, but his mind was elsewhere. He could feel his pulse quickening with excitement. He stubbed the cigarette out and made sure that the ember was completely dead and pushed the ashtray aside with his foot. He got up then and opened the valve on the top of the canister and returned to his chair.

    He had come a very long way in thirty-five years, in the last week, in the last ten minutes. He had moved through life like a somnambulist, but there had been a plan. Again and again he had acted with apparently random spontaneity towards ends and purposes that were later revealed. He had learned to make of himself a void and the void had been visited by manifestations of a power emanating from within himself to meet and meld with powers rushing in upon him from beyond. Tonight, when he slept, she would step from the painting one last time and she would summon her sleeping sisters from each of the works that enclosed him now like an embrace and they would dance about him as the shadows danced. For he did see shadows, crossing and recrossing the dimly visible space in front of him, as on a screen, and he dimly perceived that these must be the shadows of people walking by in the street, and he thought that these were the appearances by which people live. Nor was reality to be sought in the material objects from which these shadows fell, but in the fiery source of light behind them which alone was real. And as the sisters began to turn about him, the air would fill with the sound of flutes and drumming and a smell of roses and almonds and an enormous lassitude. Each sister would then begin to spin upon herself, and together they would dance the orbiting planets in their whirling rotations about the sun, and vistas would begin to open before him, as the orbiting colors of the spectrum mixed and spread through unheard-of harmonies and dopplering velocities of light through distances contained only by that circle whose center is everywhere; and from that center she would come to him for the last time and for eternity, his beloved girl, and her glorious and ardent presence would ignite the combustible atmosphere of the universe and he would live forever within the pain and power of her fiery embrace.

8

BONCUK

i

Malinda Walters, Minna to her friends, lived in a handsome high-rise apartment building on the slope of a hill overlooking the harbor of İstinye. Her living room, in the southeast corner of the fourteenth floor—"It's really the thirteenth, but they don't call it that"—commanded panoramic views of the harbor and both shores of the Bosphorus to the new bridge, named for the conqueror—Fatih Sultan Mehmet Köprüsü—the towers of Rumeli Hisarı, and as far as Kandilli on the Asian side, where her friend Erden Sakarya lived. To the east and north she could see across to Çubuklu and Beykoz and, farther up, to the famous steamer landing of Hünkar İskelesi and Selvi Burnu, or Cypress Point, which made her think of Erden's journalist friend, Faruk Selvi, whom they called jokingly Faruk Burnu, for his profession and his physiognomy, the word *burun* meaning, in Turkish, both promontory and nose. A broad balcony ran the length of the living room on the southern side, with three sets of roll-down bamboo blinds affixed to the underside of the balcony overhead. On summer days, with the blinds down and the sliding glass doors open, the balcony became an extension of the living room, and in the evenings, with the blinds rolled up, Minna could sit there for hours in perfect silence watching the lights of the harbor and the ships swinging at their anchors or moving up and down the straits.

She had bought the apartment ten years before and had never once regretted it, in spite of the price. She had thought at first that her mother would move in and live with her, but the experiment had failed and now she had the whole place to herself. Her mother had felt uprooted and out of place in this town and in this kind of building, and she had moved back to her own apartment in Bebek, which hadn't yet sold and where she had lived without interruption for thirty years. She still had many old friends in Bebek and Rumeli Hisarı and she knew all the tradesmen and shopkeepers and could continue to live something of her old life on her own. It wasn't as if she wouldn't see Minna again, just not every day.

Minna's father, an archeologist who had first come to the American College on a leave of absence from the University of Chicago, had died twenty years before from typhus contracted while he was out on a dig. Minna remembered him well, having been fifteen at the time, and she remembered her mother's initial disarray at having to contend not only with the loss of her husband but also with the loss of income and housing. She could have appealed to her family in the States, but she knew that she would have had to put up with endless arguments, from the pleading to the threatening, that she come home: We miss you so—Minna belongs here—Think of the child's education—Who will she marry?—What kind of society do you keep? She had rehearsed these arguments both in her own mind and with her daughter, who was almost a young woman after all, and the very anticipation of the anger she would feel had worked like a tonic and restored her courage at a stroke. She would get a job. She would go to the College and ask if there weren't something for her to do, as a secretary, perhaps—she could type—or teaching English in the prep program to incoming students who didn't yet know the language well enough. Or she could teach history in the Community School. She had a degree in history and many years of experience working with her husband, and she thought she was at least as well qualified as anyone else at the Community School to take the kids out on field trips. She was offered two jobs, one as a secretary at the College and one as a history teacher at the Community School. She took the history job. She and Minna had had to move out of their College housing, but they had found a perfectly suitable small apartment in Bebek. Minna continued her studies at the Community School and graduated, with high honors, two years later, winning a scholarship to the Parsons School in New York, from which she graduated four years later, again with high honors and a degree in fashion design. Minna had had to work to support herself during the summers, and she had been able to afford visits to her mother only twice during the four years.

The long separation had been hard on both of them, but they promised to make up for lost time. Minna's mother flew over for the graduation, after which they wept copious tears and spent a week together in New York and Philadelphia, where they indulged themselves in some showing off to relatives. They then flew to Europe to spend two weeks in each of the great fashion capitals: London, Paris, and Milan. The trip was underwritten by a travel grant from Parsons, the grant itself being funded largely by the very designers she wanted to see. Minna was well received everywhere she went, both because of her outstanding record at Parsons and because of her plan to work in Turkey, which represented an expanding market and the promise of relatively cheap, skilled labor for the clothing industry.

Minna saw immediately where her advantage lay, not in design, but with an import-export firm. She knew nothing whatever about that end of the business, but she knew it could do her no harm to learn. She went back with her mother to the old apartment in Bebek and began commuting on the ferry to Eminönü, from where she walked up the hill to her new employer's offices by the Covered Bazaar on Nuruosmaniye Caddesi. Minna had come into the firm with contacts that were immediately worth gold. She was intelligent and conscientious and, with her natural gifts and training, she had excellent taste. In time she became an accomplished buyer, especially of leather goods, and she talked at length to the manufacturers about the drawbacks and virtues of the various skins and to the workers themselves about cutting and sewing and what they liked to see, and work from, in a design. She saw no designers, because she had her own ideas on that score, ideas that were maturing as she learned about the materials and about the limits inherent in the processes of manufacture.

When she was ready, she went to her boss with a series of designs which she would be willing to let him have for a percentage of the sales. The boss liked and respected her, and if he looked long and hard at the designs it was not because he had any doubts, but because he was quite thoroughly amazed at the inventiveness of their simplicity. Though not himself a designer, he knew design and he had hoped that one day he might hook up with a great designer, and here she was. When the orders began pouring in from Paris and Milan, it was clear that the public had seen what he had seen, and he offered her a junior partnership in the firm. She refused, saying that she didn't want more business to attend to nor that kind of responsibility. What she really wanted was to get out of the business end of things and devote herself entirely to design. He said that that was fine with him but that he still wanted her as a partner. He said he didn't want her to get away. She would be the firm's only designer or the head designer, if she wanted to hire assistants to work under her—anything she liked, but he wasn't going to let her get away. She would have her percentage, but it would now be forty percent, not twenty-five, and it would be forty percent of everything.

This was an offer that Minna did not refuse. It had come

twelve years before and happened to coincide with the publication of a prospectus describing a new apartment building to be built on the slope of a hill overlooking the harbor at İstinye. Her office received such publications regularly, but the proposed location of this building appealed to her and she read on. There was to be a fitness center on the ground floor, with a two-lane lap pool, and a landscaped garden on the slope of the hill out back and an olympic pool and two tennis courts on top. She went to see the agent—it was Şimşek Emlak—where she was told that if she were willing to put twenty-five percent down now and another twenty-five percent before the end of the year, she would save ten percent on the total cost of an apartment. She asked to see the elevation and the floor plans. The building was to be of fourteen stories, numbered one through twelve, fourteen, and fifteen. She wanted to be high up, but not on the top, where noise from the machinery on the roof and water leakage were sure to cause problems. Three apartments were still available on the fourteenth floor, including the one on the southeast corner. She put a small refundable deposit down to hold the apartment for a week and took the contract and a photocopy of the floor plan home. Minna's mother thought the prospectus and the plans looked beautiful, but that her daughter would be buying a piece of paper only and that she should get some advice. Minna answered that she was going to, but that she had wanted an initial reaction from her mother at the idea of moving. Mrs. Walters' only reply, perhaps ambiguous, was that she would be happy with whatever her daughter thought best.

 The first person Minna had thought to ask was her boss. He was a businessman and she trusted him and he seemed the obvious choice. But she remembered asking him in the past about small matters that lay outside his immediate expertise, and it pained her to see him flounder in embarrassment, ashamed to say he didn't know. The next best thing then was to ask him if he knew somebody in the real estate business, but the only person he knew was with Şimşek Emlak. She could always go to a lawyer, but you never knew who you were dealing with. What she needed was a friend, and then an idea came to her. He wasn't a friend, exactly, but almost. She certainly knew him well enough to ask him for advice. She had met him first about a year ago at a conference organized by the Chamber of Commerce for some buyers from New York. They had had a drink together and talked about design and she remembered his having regaled her with some very abstract ideas which she realized would have precisely matched her own philosophy, if she had bothered to have one, and he had asked her to come visit him in his shop in the Bazaar. Busy as she was, she hadn't done so for a month or more, but he remembered her and seemed pleased to see her and he had shown her about a million beautiful *kilim*s and *sumak*s and he had taken her to lunch at Aslan and they had picked up their philosophical discussion as if they had never left off and, having had some time to think, she was able to contribute something of her own. So she needed some sound advice and she needed a friend and the more she thought about it, the more she realized that she really liked this man and that she should have realized that she wanted to see him even without the excuse of needing his advice. It was Erden Sakarya, of course, and she owed him a lunch.

Minna sat now on her balcony looking down at the lights in the harbor and the occasional ship moving in the straits. She was waiting for Erden to take her downtown to dinner at Boncuk where the gang was assembling to celebrate Marco's anniversary exhibition and the return to Istanbul of somebody named Malone, whom she had never met, the first husband of Sylvia Corrigan. She remembered that second lunch at Aslan with Erden and drinking *rakı*, which she didn't then really like, but which seemed to have made it easier to ask him to look at the real estate contract. Erden had said he would take the contract back to his shop and read it through and then pick her up at her office at four o'clock—it was already two—and they could walk down to Eminönü and talk about it on the ferry home. After that lunch, a short afternoon had seemed a very good idea. She had felt groggy for the next hour or so, but sitting on the upper deck of the ferry on the way home had finally cleared her head. It had been a lovely spring afternoon and evening, much like today, and there had been a lovely, easy breeze blowing down the Bosphorus, and Erden had said that he thought the contract looked perfectly honest and complete. He had had some experience in real estate, having sold some years ago a house left to him by his father, and he had just had a summer house built for himself on an island off the Aegean coast above Ayvalık. Erden had talked about mortgages and building permits and deeds, but he had spoken also of the village of Cunda and the situation of his new house and the beauty of the island and of how he had first come to know the place with his father when he was still not much more than a boy. When the ferry reached Kandilli, Minna realized that she had become completely engrossed in this man's talk, and it had seemed the most natural thing in the world to get off the ferry right there and continue listening as they walked together up the road to his apartment building where, waiting for the elevator, he had kissed her and said,

Do you still want to come up? I very much want you to.

He was giving her her chance, but he was asking her to decide now. The quintessential gentleman, Erden, with a liberal dash of the sly dog. She had been charmed completely, she remembered. She had said yes.

They had been together for almost twelve years. She couldn't imagine a smoother relationship, founded as it was on mutual respect. He and she continued to have their own lives—but not other lovers—and the amazing thing was that although his shop and her office were only a stone's throw apart, they almost never saw each other in that part of town, drawing a strict line between their professional and sentimental lives. Nor did they manage many weekends together. Erden's shop was open on Saturdays, and Minna loved spending lazy, solitary Sundays right here in her beautiful apartment listening to music and idly sketching, not for the market but according to her mood. The only real breaks in their regimen came when they agreed to take a long weekend together in Cunda or, as happened no more than once or twice a year, a whole week, by the end of which time each knew that the other was ready to return to Istanbul and work. Not that there was friction. It was more like an easy and amicable parting of the ways. The fire had flared up, briefly, and gone out—the end of an episode—after which would appear the words, "To be rekindled at a later date."

They always went to Cunda in Erden's car, a car which he had bought for that sole purpose in the year he had acquired the property and begun to build. Sylvia Corrigan had named it the Erdenmobile, and Minna thought too that it was the only possible car for Erden. Erden must surely have thought so, because he had gone all the way to London to buy it and had driven it back across Europe alone through a meandering itinerary that had taken him two weeks which were, so he had told her, one of the finest times he'd ever had. The car was a 1948 Jaguar, the classic, convertible coupe. Having been manufactured for the English market, the driver's seat was on the right-hand side, but awkward as that might sometimes make driving on Turkish roads, Erden would have had it no other way. It was quite another thing for his passenger, of course, and Minna had thought on more than one occasion, as she swung out and over the center of the road into oncoming traffic, that she was going to die. These were in fact the only times she had ever felt an extreme or annihilating emotion with Erden, and she didn't like it one bit. She had told him about it, and, dear man that he was, he had done his best to be careful. She could scare herself just remembering one particular near miss. Her fear had become panic and, in that instant, she thought she had gone mad. I don't need madness, she thought, in any form. To hell with any goddamned madness in any form.

Why was she working herself up this way? Was she working herself up? She hadn't had a scare in a couple of years, and the trip had never canceled out the pleasure of a stay in Cunda. In fact, without the scares, the trip could be very nice. These days, with the new highway, it was only three and a half hours to Çanakkale and another two and a half through the mountains and down into the olive groves between Edremit and Cunda. You could leave Istanbul in midafternoon and be in Cunda for dinner in the restaurant of Erden's old friend, and his father's friend, Günay. And if they were going to be late—they sometimes couldn't get away until four or five o'clock—Erden would phone ahead and Günay himself would prepare the dinner and wait on them, having sent the waiters home. It was lovely. Mina wondered when they would go again. She had finished a small *rakı*, which she had learned to like—*noblesse oblige*, Erden had said—and she decided to have a smoke. She never smoked at all during the week and only on those weekends when she spent time with Erden. She asked herself now if the anticipation of being with Erden was enough of an excuse, realizing that she wanted one. If I'm looking for an excuse to smoke, she thought, I must be falling into the famous trap that everybody talks about. Did I hear you say it can't happen to me? I did, and it can't. So have another *rakı*, very small. I thought you'd never ask. She knew why she was feeling this way. I'm going out with my best pal Erden, and we're going to a great place for dinner to celebrate a special occasion, or two, with old friends, and they say this man Malone can be amusing, and I can sit a mile away from Marco, and Dimitri should be in form, and will you have a bit of water in your *rakı*? Yes, please. And can I offer you a match?

Minna stood at the balcony rail. She flipped the match out into the air and watched it fall. Erden was due. No, he was late. She looked down at the parking lot and the blue awning which shielded the front door. He would be arriving in a taxi. The taxis were bright yellow, as in the States. She looked out over the harbor and along the coast road to where the taxi would be coming up from the bridge. It was a lovely, clear evening. The air was still. She took a drag on her cigarette and inhaled. Lovely. She blew the smoke out slowly in front of her. Blue. She looked down at the parking lot again and, by the magic of a moment's inattention, there he was. He hadn't come in a yellow taxi, though, but in the beautiful Jaguar, and Minna smiled. They had always agreed on their departures in advance, and it was a new feeling to be so pleased by a surprise, because the Jaguar could only mean Cunda. On her way through the living room she put the cigarette into an ashtray. In the bedroom she opened the closet and took an overnight bag down from the shelf. She went into the bathroom and grabbed her toilet kit and she was putting things into it when the doorbell rang. It was Erden and he stepped into the room and gave her a hug, and she said, Shall I pack?

We'll go first thing in the morning, if you like.

Or course, she said and smiled, but she was thinking, Am I mad? A few minutes ago I was looking forward to this dinner at Boncuk, and in the next minute I had forgotten it entirely. If you can't trust yourself, who can you trust?

ii

Erden avoided the crowded coast road on the way to town. He drove instead from İstinye through the hills up to Maslak and back to the highway coming up from the bridge he had just crossed. This was the same highway they would be taking in the morning and Minna imagined that, if they were to leave before sunrise tomorrow, the drive would feel very like this. They left the highway at the next exit, picked up Piyale Pasha

Boulevard at Okmeydanı, the archery ground of early Ottoman days, and drove into Tarlabaşı at the first set of lights below Taksim Square. Somewhere in the labyrinth of streets on the hill to the right was Boncuk. Erden slowed down and pulled over into an open space in front of the dilapidated old Hotel Venezia. He turned to Minna and said, Hold on one second, and he hopped out and went in the door. He reappeared with the night clerk, who gestured elaborately while explaining to Erden that he should pull into the alley beside the hotel. The clerk disappeared around the corner into the alley and, when Erden turned the Jaguar in, he was holding an iron gate open for them to pass. They parked and Erden tipped the clerk, who locked the gate and explained that Erden should come get him at the desk when he needed the car.

It's a great comfort to be with a man who knows his way around, said Minna.

That's the kind of a guy you're with tonight, he said.

They walked a few paces back down Tarlabaşı and turned left into a narrow street whose only illumination came from a smudge pot burning in a broken doorway. Homeless squatters. The street seemed to be leading them straight into a stone wall, but lights appeared suddenly on their right, bringing them into a narrow but busy commercial side street and up to the intersection with Nevizade Sokak, where the evening was in full swing.

Nevizade Sokak joins two parallel streets running down from İstiklal Caddesi and, at its far end, is not five minutes' walk from the Çiçek Pasajı. There are three restaurants on one side of the street and four on the other and in the spring and summer, when they move their tables outside, they seem to flow together in a riot of happy diners who pass the salt and pepper and the *meze* and the *rakı* from table to table and between restaurants until the crockery is all mixed up and the waiters no longer know who to charge for what. It got so bad, or good, one night that the waiters from all seven restaurants got together and announced that everybody on the street was to be charged 1/166th of the total, an idea which met with cheers and applause. From where Erden and Minna had entered the street, Boncuk was the last restaurant on the right and, having no other restaurant directly across, its identity was fluid, as it were, on only one side. Erden and Minna made their way down the narrow aisle in the middle of the street, interrupting several conversations along the way, on one occasion helping to pass a plate of sardines from one side to the other. Their progress was slow. Erden cracked jokes with people he'd never seen before and was constantly being hailed and stopped by acquaintances from all over and one of whom, from London, he had never before seen in Istanbul. Erden invited him and his party, whoever they were, to join them later at Boncuk.

What news on the Rialto? said a voice. It had to be Yakup. We got here not two minutes ahead of you, not one minute ahead of you. We were at the old Pera Palace, having a drink or two. Mimi loves the old Pera Palace, lovely nostalgic old girl that she is. I can't say as I mind it too much myself.

Lovely nostalgic old boy that you are, said Mimi.

It looks as if we have some catching up to do, said Erden.

Hi, Mimi, said Yakup. I mean Minna. One of you two should change your name. I keep mixing you up.

You don't mix me up, said Mimi. I'm not so easy to mix up.

What shall we call them? said Yakup.

Well, said Erden, instead of calling them Mimi and Minna, we could call them Minna and Mimi.

If you think you've got us mixed up now, said Mimi, you're wrong. Just ask Mimi over there.

What's that coming over the horizon? said Yakup.

They looked up the street in the direction of the Çiçek Pasajı.

It's the Malone Ranger come again.
The Malone Eagle, himself.
Malone alone on a wide, wide sea.
Malone alone but with Dimitri, said Yakup, It's a paradox.
No, said Mimi, it's a pair-a-docs.

Dimitri and Malone were coming from the Çiçek Pasajı, and Malone had still not fully recovered from a shock he'd received a while before. It had been almost seven, and he was beginning to feel nervous at the thought that he would soon be among a lot of people he hadn't seen in twenty years. His nervousness only increased as he thought of Sylvia, at ease among her friends, and resentful perhaps of his return, and he remembered exactly how she had looked the last time he had seen her when they had said goodbye in the garden behind their little house, looking beautiful, as always, but worn and resentful. Dimitri had been explaining something more about Marco's tattered life, but Malone was lost in his memories of Sylvia and trying to imagine how she would look tonight when he was seized by the apparent hallucination of seeing her come around the corner of the rear entrance to the Çiçek Pasajı, Sylvia herself but grown younger as he had grown old.
You are not listening, said Dimitri.
I'm sorry, said Malone, looking over Dimitri's shoulder. I've just had quite a shock.
What is it?
A young woman who looks exactly like Sylvia has just come into the cafe, and now she's sitting down only two tables away from us.
How old? said Dimitri.
Not twenty, I think.
Ah, said Dimitri, I will tell you who she is even without looking at her, but first you must tell me who she is with, because she is with somebody.

She's with two young people about her own age, a young man and another girl, but they're facing the other way.

Your powers of observation are amazing, said Dimitri, but I will now tell you anyway who these young people are. The two who have their backs to you, as I have my back to them—so you will never guess how the trick is done—are İshak and Esther Toledano, the children of Yakup and Mimi, and you may even have met them years ago at Boem—the older boy at least—because Yakup liked to take them there so they would know something of the old music. And now—are you listening?—the scandalously beautiful young blond woman facing you—my dear fellow, you are decomposing as I speak—this is Nicolette Corrigan, Sylvia's daughter. She is about seventeen, and you must not beg, borrow, steal, or otherwise acquire—what is the expression?—hot pants for her. It is not permitted. I have had to explain to Marco that it is not permitted. I have had to explain to myself, more than once, that it is not permitted. I have had to explain ...

I didn't even know she had a daughter, said Malone.

You didn't know she had a daughter. How is it possible? Didn't you ever write? Didn't she ever write to you?

Christmas cards.

And when her father died? Her father just died, didn't he?

Yes, only a little over three months ago. We spoke on the phone, but she didn't say much. There wasn't much to say. The old man left orders that there should be no ceremony of any kind. He had outlived most of his old friends, all of them, I think. I used to go down to New York to see him when I could, but his last years must have been lonely. He and Sylvia were never very close. He told me that he had never been very close to his wife.

Strange old man, said Dimitri.

Oh, he was full of life, said Malone. He just didn't have much luck with the life around him. He told me that Sylvia was exactly like her mother, morally and physically, to the point where she might have been a clone.

And now there's Nicolette, said Dimitri.

And now there's Nicolette. It's uncanny.

No, said Dimitri. It's parthenogenesis. But we mustn't tell Frank.

No, we mustn't tell Frank, said Malone, wondering if Dimitri imagined that he, Malone, was ignorant of the fact that he, Dimitri, had been Sylvia's lover. It was possible. There was that much innocence in him. But even if Dimitri knew that he knew, he would expect to have been forgiven long ago as he would have forgiven, as he had in fact forgiven, other men and dear Elena too when she came back to him.

My friend, said Dimitri. I know these things can be painful. There are perhaps few things more painful in life. That is why I make fun of them.

Me too, said Malone, wishing it were true.

You know what? said Dimitri.

No, what? said Malone on cue.

If you tell Frank about the grandmother, I'll tell him about the parthenogenesis.

There were greetings all around and laughter and kisses, and nobody had changed a bit in twenty years. Erden had ordered two bottles of *rakı* and a variety of *meze* and they had just managed to distribute themselves at the table when Frank appeared at the corner of the street with Sylvia and Faruk's wife Verda. Sylvia was suffering from mixed emotions at the prospect of seeing Malone. She was nervous, and she was angry at her nervousness. But as they crossed the open space at the end of the street and she saw the animated crowd of her friends, her eye was drawn to the figure of a man seated with his back to her and, for the moment at least, perfectly immobile and apparently looking down at the table in front of him, and it seemed to her that there was something in the slant of the shoulders and the downward tilt of the head that was expressive of something infinitely sad. She recognized Malone. Her nervousness and her anger vanished, and she felt only pity for his loneliness and the loneliness of her father, whose death Malone's presence had brought back to her, and her own loneliness, perhaps, and when the whole gang rose to greet them, she went straight over to Malone and put her arms around him and wept.

I'm sorry, she said. I didn't want to make a scene.

It's all right, said Malone. It's all right. She was weeping and he was holding her very tight and feeling as if he had fallen in love with her all over again. He knew she wasn't crying over him, exactly, but he didn't care.

Tell me about Lafitte, she said, using their private name.

Malone told her about playing pool along Third Avenue and how Lafitte had talked about his wife, and of losing her, and how he had said that his daughter resembled her mother as if she were a clone.

And now there's Nicolette, said Sylvia.

That's my line, said Malone.

What do you mean? said Sylvia.

Their conversation was interrupted by an arm that fell between them delivering a platter of freshly grilled sardines. *Çok sıcak*, said the waiter, producing another platter of lamb chops and sausage. *Çok sucuk*, said Mimi. There was a ripple of laughter, and the platters were passed with the use of napkins as hot pads. When the sardines reached Dimitri, he held the platter for Verda Selvi and asked her when Faruk was going to appear.

He told me that he and Marco would come over right after the show.

What did you say?

There were looks of incredulity around the table, and Verda Selvi found herself in the unenviable position of having to explain that her husband had persuaded Marco to change his mind. There was still some unwillingness to believe what she had said, but she assured them that, earlier in the week, Faruk had taken a Şimşek van to Rumeli Hisarı to pick up a dozen or so new works that Marco himself would be offering for sale.

How is it possible?

Just when you think you know somebody.

This leaves us rather in the lurch.

But a very festive lurch.

Here's to the lurch.

Good health to the festive lurch.

And here comes Faruk, but Marco isn't with him.

There's something fishy in all this.

It's the sardines.

Where's Marco? said Erden. Verda said you'd be bringing Marco along.

He never showed up, said Faruk. I can't understand it. He agreed to come.

Faruk and the director had left the gallery through the back door. They had said goodbye in the square, and the director had walked up İstiklal to get a cab at Taksim. Faruk had checked his watch and looked around the square, but there was no Marco in sight. He looked over at the gallery. With the display lights turned off inside, the gallery windows reflected the lights in the square and the mobile and distorted images of the passersby. The images evolved in a strange phantasmagoria of colors and forms, and Faruk thought that this was what the artist's soul does to the world. He had already written his review article, but he would find a way to work that in. But he was worried. Why hadn't Marco come? The director of the gallery had not been pleased. A last-minute twinge of conscience on Marco's part? You can never trust somebody with a goddamned conscience, he thought. You never know what they're going to do next. With this thought in mind, Faruk crossed the square and, remembering that he needed cigarettes, he decided to make a detour and have a drink, and he arrived at Boncuk about a half hour later than his wife.

I saw your daughter in the Çiçek Pasajı, said Malone. I didn't know who she was, of course. I thought she was you, but when I said that to Dimitri, he knew who she was without looking.

Trust Dimitri, said Sylvia.

Marco said he would never go to the show, said Yakup, and he told all of us not to go. Whatever he may have said to Faruk, he didn't go and he's been true to his word. That's all there is to it.

But if that's all there is to it, said Erden, where is he now? He should be right here.

It's the lurch. The festive lurch.

If that's all there is to it, said Faruk, how do you explain the additional paintings he let the gallery have?

You don't, said Dimitri. You don't explain paintings. Nobody can explain paintings.

You still haven't told me about Lafitte, said Sylvia.

Malone knew what she meant. He told her about Lafitte's last days in the hospital and his great cheerfulness. He had known perfectly well how serious his condition was, but he never let on. He told her that Lafitte had talked about her and about her mother and his love for them, and that he had wished only that he had been a more open person and able to let them know.

He said that? asked Sylvia. I'd like to believe he said that.

Believe it, said Malone. He told me that the day before he died, and when the lawyer called, I knew he must have known the end was very near and that he had wanted to tell me that one last thing.

You're breaking my heart, Malone, she said, and she put her hand on his shoulder and looked at him.

Malone went on, telling her what the lawyer had told him on the phone, that there would be no funeral ceremony of any kind, but cremation in the hospital and a simple notice in the paper and a headstone next to his wife in Dedham whenever they could get around to it. I think he just wanted to slip away, he said, without causing a fuss.

Sylvia was silent for a moment and then she said, He left me quite a lot of money. A pile, in fact.

He left me a lot of money too, said Malone.

Oh, I'm so glad, she said, smiling with surprise and delight. You were like a son to him. It's only right.

I hoped you wouldn't mind, he said.

Why didn't the lawyer tell me?

I don't know, said Malone.

Here's to Marco, somebody said.

Where? said somebody.

And here's to Malone.

Malone's right here.

So he is, said Dimitri. Welcome back to the Malone Ranger.

They all raised their glasses and Malone said thanks and raised his back when Yakup, looking towards Malone, thought he saw a second Dimitri turn the corner into their street. This figure was followed by a small boy and a woman carrying an infant in a shawl wrapped around her back. Yakup realized that this was the figure whom he had seen earlier on İstiklal Caddesi and who had seemed to vanish when the trolley went by. He also realized, now, that this was the celebrated Yoldaş, or Çınar Baba, to whom Erden had delivered Faruk's new book this afternoon. He would have proposed a toast to Faruk, in spite of the awkwardness of Faruk's connection with the gallery, but he was saved the trouble by Yoldaş's noisy intrusion on their company. Yoldaş was obviously drunk. His eyes were wet and there was snot in his mustache and spittle in his beard, and he staggered slightly as he unslung a heavy backpack and dropped it to the ground and leaned backwards to straighten his back again. The sack was full of books which he began to hawk around the table. He pushed a book in front of Minna and leaned against her to steady himself. Erden rose quickly and took Yoldaş firmly by the arm and turned him from the table and said, My dear fellow, we meet twice in the same day.

The reminder was too subtle for Yoldaş, in his condition. He seemed to study it, and there came and went in his mind's eye an image of this man who was now standing in front of him and holding him, rather too firmly, by the arm, and another image of the same man standing in front of him under his sycamore and handing him a book at some unspecifiable moment in the past. But, whoever he was, he had no business holding him, rather too firmly, by the arm. Who did he think he was? And Yoldaş snatched his arm away and was preparing to take a swing at Erden when Faruk stepped right between them and, pronouncing the syllables of his name with the sharpness of a military command, said, Yoldaş! What are you up to, you old pirate? Faruk's quickness and determination came as a surprise, not least of all to the old pirate. Faruk led him away.

Where did you come from? asked Yoldaş.

I was sitting just a few seats away, said Faruk. You're pretty drunk. What are you doing in this part of town?

Selling books. I've come to sell my books, our books, and Yoldaş pointed to the open backpack, which was apparently filled with their bilingual editions of his work.

Why don't you just go into Boncuk now and wash your face? You'll feel better and you'll look better and you'll sell more books.

I am a poet of the streets. I sing of the streets and of the people of the streets and I will sell my poems in the streets.

Go along now, said Faruk. You write beautiful things, but you've got snot in your beard. Go wash your face.

Faruk came back to the table and sat down. He felt suddenly very tired. Another bad moment in a long and trying day. He looked down the table at Erden. Erden raised his glass to him by way of thanks and Minna raised her glass and said,

Let's have a toast to Faruk.

To the man of the hour, our fend an defriender, said Dimitri, Faruk Burnu, and amid the general acclamation, Yakup decided that the moment had come to propose a toast to the success of Faruk's new book. He was just raising his glass from the table when he froze. A pall of silence had fallen over the whole length of the street, as if time itself had stopped, and he thought, What in the name of God was that?

iii

Not many minutes before, the night watchman had come to check the Şimşek building. It was easy, routine work, and there was plenty of time and no danger in this part of town, and the watchman stopped for a minute on the corner across from the gallery to have a word with one of the regulars on the square, a blind accordionist who also sold cigarettes, one or two at a time, to pay for his own habit. The accordionist was a Russian. He was very old and was said to have lost his eyesight in the Russian Civil War. Almost every evening, the pianist from the Cafe de Pera would stop for a brief chat with him on her way down İstiklal to her apartment in the old Russian Embassy. She was one of the few people in Istanbul, or in the world, for that matter, to know the old accordionist's history quite exactly, to know that he had formerly been a member of an orchestra that played at the celebrated taverna of Boem, that he had been an officer of the Imperial Guard before the Revolution and had numbered among the finest swordsmen of his generation. He, on the other hand, was one of the few to know that her name was really Krinsky and that she ought to have relinquished her title as the Countess Drubetskaya with her divorce. But he wouldn't have breathed a word.

Now who was this? Ah, he could tell from a certain clearing of the throat that it was the night watchman about to check on the Şimşek building across the way. He offered the cigarettes and the watchman took two and paid him and he said to the watchman, I'll smoke to that, and they both lit up. Yes, it was a lovely evening, very mild. And was the sky clear? With the lights in the square, you couldn't be sure, but he thought it was. See you later, said the watchman. That's easy for you to say, he said, and they both laughed. He sat quietly smoking for another few minutes and then leaned over and pressed the cigarette out under his foot and hoisted the accordion back onto his lap. One or two more songs, he thought, and we'll call it a night.

    The night watchman crossed the avenue and peered in at the gallery window, cupping his hands against the glass. He couldn't imagine why they had left the panels in a cluster around the kitchen door, but that was their business. He then noticed the tarpaulin draped over the panels, and his curiosity was aroused. He didn't usually bother looking into the gallery. You could tell at a glance from the street that everything was all right. But they had told him there would be a show that evening and that he should check on the gallery too. The usual routine consisted of letting himself in by the back door and checking the kitchen. He would then take the service elevator up to the top floor, put it on hold, and have a quick look at each of the offices. He would then repeat the operation on the floor below and so on until he reached the kitchen again, turn out the lights, and lock the back door again when he left. He decided tonight that he would check the gallery last.

    When he turned into the alley, he noticed a pile of plastic garbage bags at the bottom of the three steps just outside the kitchen door, and he pushed one of them back from the step with his foot. Junk from the show, he thought. The light in the alley was dim, but he climbed the steps as he had done a thousand times, put his hand on the knob and fitted the key to the lock, as he had done a thousand times, and opened the door. He stepped into the dark kitchen, turned to his right, put his hand up to the wall and opened the panel to the fuse box. Fuses to the left, main switch to the right. He reached up and grasped the handle and pulled it sharply down into the contact clamps. And in that instant, a flash of burning air exploded towards him out of the gallery with a roar and a rush that picked him up and propelled him out the door and down the steps on his back among the garbage bags. The garbage bags had broken his fall, and the three steps of elevation had saved his life, for there was, in the next instant, a second explosion, of greater power than the first, that shot a fireball just over him into the alley wall. The length of the kitchen and the gallery were a mass of flame. He wasn't hurt, except for a headache and a terrible pounding in his ears. He got to his feet and walked out of the alley and into the light. It was late and there had not been many people in the square, but the unlucky few who had been anywhere near the gallery were strewn over the cobblestones, many of them burned and cut up by flying glass. The watchman put his hands to his ears. His palms were bloody. He could see the fire raging in the gallery and some of the wounded calling for help, but he couldn't hear a thing. I'm deaf, he thought, and his second thought was, I'll never hear the accordion again.

The explosion had been clearly audible all over Beyoğlu, and in the nearby Nevizade Sokak the concussion shook the crockery and rattled the window glass. Where he sat, Erden had felt it in his feet and thighs and had seen the *rakı* vibrate in his glass.

That sounded like a bomb to me, said Malone, a big one.

It sounded like the Çiçek Pasajı or Galatasaray.

It could have been a gas explosion, said Mimi, in one of the kitchens in the Çiçek Pasajı.

My God, said Dimitri, that's a harrowing thought. There are probably still a lot of people there.

Let's settle the bill, said Dimitri. The waiters will hold the table for us if we want to go see what's happening.

With the general agitation following the explosion and the number of tables calling for their checks, it was a few minutes before someone was able to catch the waiter's eye, and Faruk, finally unable to contain his impatience, said, I'll see you up there. Verda has the cash.

Faruk walked quickly across the open space at the end of Nevizade Sokak, rounded the corner, and broke into a run. He was able to maintain his pace through the fish market, now closed for the night, and as he came up the hill he could see in the distance, where the street gave onto the square at Galatasaray, the pulsing red glare of a fire, and he knew that the explosion had not occurred in the Çiçek Pasajı. Once on the square he stopped to catch his breath. The fire brigade was already there, and they were pumping water into the gallery through one hose in the front and two on the side. If the fire doesn't get the paintings, thought Faruk, the water will. A fourth hose ran into the alley in back, where they were trying to control the fire through the kitchen. The wounded were being gathered up and put into ambulances. Faruk watched two ambulances pull away. A third was waiting for the last two wounded, lying on stretchers, to be loaded on. They seemed to be not seriously hurt, as they were propped up on their elbows talking.

Faruk was stopped at the cordon, but he showed his press pass and the policeman let him through. They wouldn't let him inside the building yet, but he located the brigade commander, who had talked to the night watchman. It was already clear that the explosion had been caused when the watchman turned on the lights, igniting a considerable amount of escaped propane gas. There were two puzzling aspects, however. First was the sheer force of the blast and second was the watchman's claim that the explosion came from the gallery and not the kitchen. It added up to the possibility that this was not an ordinary leak, but that somebody had moved the gas canister from the kitchen into the gallery and then opened the valve. But that created another problem. The outside door to the kitchen had been locked, so how did the arsonist get away? Unless, of course, the arsonist had a key. In any event, the story was not complete, but the insurance people were on the spot and very interested in the possibility of arson, which would apparently let them off the hook.

The fire was now out and the smoke had begun to clear. A fireman climbed out through the side window and walked over to the commander. There's a body inside, he said. The fireman walked back to the gallery and the commander followed him. Faruk now began to experience the ripening of a sensation that had first declared itself when he heard the blast at the table at Boncuk, half awe and half fear. He followed the commander over the windowsill and into the gallery. There was nothing left but rubble and a few empty frames hanging at crazy angles on the wall. Faruk saw a piece of wood that might have been part of a panel stand. By the kitchen door was the gas canister with a gaping hole up its middle where its belly had blown out. And there was poor Marco, or what was left of him. Faruk knew. Marco had said he would put in an appearance on opening night. His very words. Well, it was still opening night and here he was. Yakup was right. He had been exactly true to his words. Faruk had half suspected and now he was sure. Poor crazy Marco. What a man! These people with a conscience, he thought, trying to control his emotion, you never know what they're going to do.

Malone had left Boncuk with Dimitri and Elena, and they had asked Verda Selvi to come along. Dimitri had made a detour through the Çiçek Pasajı and was immensely pleased to find it intact. They would come back and drink to the long life of the Çiçek Pasajı after they'd had a look at the square.

My God, said Dimitri, Somebody's blown up Marco's show.

They walked over to the gallery as far as they could, but were stopped at the cordon. They could just see Faruk inside, and Dimitri gave him a shout, and he came over and told them everything he knew.

How can you be sure it's Marco? asked his wife.

I can tell, he said. There's not much left of him, but I know it's Marco. If they go looking for Marco Fontane in Rumeli Hisarı, they are not going to find him there.

Faruk said that he had a couple of details to check. He wanted to get the watchman's name and check with the hospital to see if any of the wounded had died. There had been only one other fatality so far, a street musician whom he also wanted to identify. And then he would have to go to his office at the paper to write all this up for tomorrow's edition. He asked Dimitri if he would please see Verda home, as they lived within only a few blocks of each other in Cihangir. Verda started to cry, and Elena too, and Dimitri put his arms around them, and his own grief choked him suddenly. He had known Marco for twenty-five years, almost since the creation, and he felt that he had never known a braver human being, going on alone as he had done. He and Elena had never had children and they had not been conspicuously faithful to each other, but he realized how lucky they were and he wanted nothing so much as for the two of them to go home together now.

Do you think the Çiçek Pasajı will understand? said Elena.

I do, said Dimitri, but will Malone? Do you mind terribly our running out on you like this, Malone?

My dear fellow! said Malone.

We'll be in the Passage at five o'clock tomorrow evening, said Dimitri. Meet us there, and we can practice some more.

Malone stood in the square for another few minutes thinking about Marco, a man he hadn't seen in twenty years and whom he had hoped to see tonight and would never see. He was also wondering what to do next. He didn't believe in the evening anymore. The firemen were reeling in their hoses and a gang of street sweepers had been called out to clean up the glass. One of them asked Malone to move. He stepped over to the edge of the square and in another minute he was asked to move again. He smiled to himself at the notion of being swept up with the trash. He had been slowly moving towards the gallery, and he saw that all the store windows directly across had been blown in. He also noticed a strangely twisted black object lying against the wall and, as he came up to it, saw that it was a smashed accordion. Some of the keys were missing. Others had been fused together by the intense heat of the blast. He knew that the accordion must have belonged to the street musician mentioned by Faruk, but its presence in this setting, so grotesquely smashed, seemed to express the menace of something inexplicable.

 To regain his composure, Malone gave the accordion a push with his foot. He needn't have bothered. One of the sweepers came over and unceremoniously threw it into a wagon where it landed on a heap of broken glass. Malone tapped out a cigarette and lit up and wondered what he would do next. He didn't believe in the evening anymore. Frank had said, If we don't see you again this evening, come see us at the College any time. The stock phrase. Frank had obviously decided that the party was over, and it sounded to him now, in retrospect, that he and Sylvia weren't interested in finding out what had happened at Galatasaray. Dimitri and Elena had gone home. He would have liked to talk some more to Minna, whom he had met for the first time. She was a great swimmer, it seemed, and they had talked about swimming, and Malone had talked about the Atlantic beaches north of Boston and his recollections of great swims off Agia Galini and Rethymnon in Crete and off the coast of Turkey at Alanya and Bodrum and Ayvalık. She had jumped at the mention of Ayvalık, and it appeared that they had swum off many of the same beaches there and off Cunda where, she explained, Erden had built a house. She had become visibly excited talking about that house and their projected trip to Cunda in the morning, and Malone wondered, now, if they would still go. It had been great seeing Erden again—Erden's Merry Men, he remembered—and Yakup and Mimi, but he thought he remembered having had much more in common with them in the past. Was there anything more natural? Their lives had gone their separate ways, theirs from his and his from theirs. So it was only with Minna, a new friend, that he had hit it off, and Dimitri—his soul brother still in spite of everything and all the years—and Sylvia, with whom he was still in love and would never see again.

Malone took a long drag on his cigarette and kicked at a piece of broken glass between two cobblestones, and he looked across the square at the ironwork fence in front of the Lycée and an old man sitting on the ledge of the concrete supporting wall. Perhaps the old man had been there all evening and had seen everything, seen Marco sneak in at the back door, as he must have done, and had never said a word. Perhaps he had been questioned and threatened by the police, and still he had not said a word, because he was a very old man, without a friend in the world, and he was not afraid of anything, least of all of death. Malone imagined that he might even have seen Marco arrive and had watched him standing in the square, watching the gallery, as he must have done, biding his time. Marco had perhaps then seen the old man sitting in the shadows where he was sitting now and had come over to him and offered him a cigarette. While the two had smoked together, Marco, watching the gallery all the while, had told the old man his story and what he was about to do and, as the last guests were about to leave, Marco had said, It's time, and he had walked into the alley. The old man had waited, then, and waited as time slowly passed, and he had finally seen the watchman appear around the corner of the gallery from İstiklal and walk towards him, as he must have done, and then turn into the alley, and he hadn't said a word.

From the square at Galatasaray and north to Taksim, İstiklal Caddesi was still a blaze of light, but the cinemas had all let out long ago and the crowds had disappeared, leaving only the occasional late stroller and a few groups of young men wondering what to do next. The south end of the avenue towards Tünel and Galip Dede and the old Boem was dark. Malone wondered if he shouldn't go up to Taksim and get a cab. He hesitated for a moment and then turned towards Tünel. He would walk back the same way he had come.

9

MALONE

It was past midnight when Malone stepped from the lighted square at Galatasaray and into the long, dark corridor of lower İstiklal. The avenue stretched out before him into invisibility, but he knew that at the far end, beyond the old Russian Embassy, his path, curving slowly right, would bring him back to the top of Galip Dede Caddesi and the underground tram station at Tünel. It was a great comfort to know that the mind could take over where the eye failed. He stopped for a moment, fished a pack of Bafras from the inside breast pocket of his jacket, tapped one out, and lit up. His face emerged from the darkness, then disappeared.

A light mist had begun to settle over the city. This section of Istanbul, called Beyoğlu by the Turks and Pera by the Greeks since Byzantine and Ottoman days, commands one of the highest elevations in the city and is often subject, especially during a change of season, to sudden drops in temperature and visibility, while the weather might remain calm and unchanged along the Bosphorus and the valley of the Golden Horn. Malone wondered if he shouldn't have gone back by way of the brightly-lit north end of İstiklal and found a taxi in front of the Marmara Hotel. His way would then have taken him along the curving slope past

ISTANBUL GATHERING

İnönü Stadium and down to the Bosphorus road at Kabataş, the lights of Asia suddenly visible on the opposite shore, and along the coast road through Tophane and Karaköy and over the Galata Bridge to the old city, and left at the Yeni Cami and past the ferry landing at Eminönü and Sepetçiler, the Basketweavers, now housing the International Press Club, and around the long curve of Saray Point under the first hill of New Rome, past Topkapı Palace and Haghia Sophia, invisible on the hill, to the switchback turn under the railroad tracks at Mustafa Pasha and up the steep climb to the Hippodrome, now also dimming in the mist, and so to his hotel. The ride would have been swift and easy and he wished he were already there, tipping the driver and drawing the curtains in his comfortable little room. He could see it all as if it were real, but he had made his choice. He was going back the same way he had come.

The temperature had fallen perceptibly, and Malone began to feel a chill. He fumbled for an instant trying to engage the zipper on his leather jacket, but the clasp was unfamiliar and he couldn't, at first, engage it by touch. He tried again, this time holding the cigarette between his teeth, and was successful. He had bought the jacket this morning—no, it was already yesterday—to replace the one he had bought twenty years ago and which was now hanging, a worn-out relic, in the bedroom closet of his condo in Newburyport, north of Boston. Leaving his hotel shortly after breakfast—enough to last him through the day: white cheese, olives, a sliced tomato, a soft-boiled egg, salami, toasted Turkish country bread, butter and honey, glasses of tea—Malone had decided he needed a good walk. He had thought before eating that he would walk straight over to the Grand Bazaar, but he decided now to prolong the trip and he turned downhill to the Hippodrome, where he made a complete circuit past Sultan Ahmet Mosque and around the far turn by the ruins of the Milion, the marker from which distances from the capital were measured under the Byzantines, and returned in front of the Sultan Sofrası Cafe and the palace of İbrahim Pasha, the glorious and ill-fated first Grand Vizier of the great Süleyman, where he stopped. He had been thinking about the various histories of the city he had read over the years, and he realized that he didn't know in which direction the old chariot races had been run, counterclockwise, as horses are run in the U. S., or clockwise, as in the UK and Ireland and France. Hollywood had always shown their chariots running counterclockwise—he remembered *Ben Hur*—but that was probably because Hollywood couldn't imagine horses running any other way. Malone decided he would walk around again, but clockwise this time, for balance and—who knows?—for accuracy, which he did, closing the loop again at Ibrahim Pasha, and cutting across the terrace of the Sultan Sofrası and through the ruins of the early-fifth-century palace of Antiochus and up Divan Yolu to the Grand Bazaar.

He walked in at the southeast gate, having crossed the open courtyard of the Nuruosmaniye Mosque, and was immediately assailed by the powerful smell of leather. He had come with the intention of buying a new jacket, which he would need in the still-uncertain April weather, and which he had planned to wear right out of the shop. But he had forgotten the layout and atmosphere of the leather goods section, just off to his left, remembering it now as a confusing labyrinth of narrow, airless passages and airless shops, and it was still too early in the day to plunge into that smell. Feeling slightly nauseous, in fact—he shouldn't have eaten the salami—he turned and walked back into the open air, recrossed the courtyard, and started down Nuruosmaniye Caddesi, at the far end of which there was, or had been, during his earlier time in Istanbul, a newsstand where you could buy cigarettes and foreign newspapers and periodicals and the local English-language *Turkish Daily News*. Yes, cigarettes, he thought. He used to buy cigarettes at that stand in the old days if he ran low in the Bazaar or before going to lunch at Aslan, that wonderfully congenial restaurant where they used to go on

Saturdays, and where you always ran into somebody you knew, not including the waiters and the *patron*, who welcomed you as if you were a member of their special club, and Malone took a deep breath as the rush of nostalgia took on the unaccustomed but recognizable form of the desire to smoke. Now where did that come from? He hadn't smoked in fifteen years, and here he was wishing he had a cigarette as if he had never quit. Perhaps it was because he had come back, because he was remembering a former life, remembering Sylvia, now remarried, whom he hadn't seen in twenty years and whom he would see at dinner tonight, because he had been a smoker then.

But it was more than just Sylvia. It was remembering the whole configuration of their lives together and the people they knew and the house they lived in, and outings on the Bosphorus in the commuter ferries or, once a year, in the Embassy launch, as they called it—though the real embassy was now in Ankara—and trips to the Princes' Islands and Haghia Yorgi, and driving down to the Aegean coast—Çanakkale, Troy, Assos, Ayvalık, Cunda—and garden parties in the spring and summer, with those funny, lumbering land turtles that would appear out of the bushes and start wandering around underfoot, and the nightingales, the nightingales!—and the purple-flowering Judas trees! It was the complex weave of an emotional atmosphere, remembered now and here, at the top of this broad avenue lined at either side by early-blossoming linden trees, a diffusion of morning light through their fluttering leaves, and along the still-moist cobblestones and shop-front displays of gleaming Kütahya faience, knickknacks and table settings and jewelry in silver and gold, polished bronze and copper samovars and trays flashing like cymbals on parade, the multicolored carpets and *kilim*s, the passersby, the gestures and horseplay of the lounging men.

Standing in the dark, Malone took a long drag on his cigarette. Continuing along İstiklal, he had been drawn back into the present by the sight of the old Russian Embassy, where Yakup Toledano had his shop and where the two old ladies lived, Madame Bishkek and the Countess Drubetskaya. On the fourth floor, to his right, Madame Bishkek's rooms were dark, but on the same floor, at the far end of the building, the Countess was still awake. Malone remembered that, old as she was, she still played the piano for a living, but they didn't ask her to stay very late. He remembered Yakup saying at dinner last night that she was playing at the Grand Cafe de Pera, and that she played from four in the afternoon until about nine or ten, at the latest. Malone came abreast of her apartment and, as he looked up, her light went out. I'll probably never see either one of them again, he thought, but he smiled at the memory of a wild housewarming party they'd all gone to over twenty years ago in those very rooms.

He had bought a new jacket yesterday, and yesterday he had started smoking again. Was there a connection? He remembered walking down Nuruosmaniye Caddesi, between the rows of linden trees, feeling very pleased to be alive, but at the same time somewhat apprehensive at the notion that his joy was accompanied and perhaps in some measure caused by this forceful reassertion of his smoking self. He felt, in fact, that if he were to smoke again, the world would be as it had been in that far-off time. Accountably, he was struck by the unreasonableness of this idea, but he also supposed that it wasn't, strictly speaking, an idea at all, but an emotional complex, and therefore not accountable to reason. Whatever it was, it was fading away, and he was again able to direct his attention to the task of finding a leather jacket, when he noticed, at the corner of Mengene Sokak, just to his left, a leather goods store displaying handbags and briefcases and jackets for women and men. To the left of the door, two men were seated on short-legged wicker stools with a low table between them, playing backgammon. They were observed by a couple of friendly loafers drinking tea and smoking and permitting themselves the occasional comment that the players impatiently waved off. Malone hesitated for a moment before going in the door and, addressing one of the loafers, said, *Kolay gelsin,* a salutation normally reserved for people hard at work and meaning, "May it come easy." The loafer looked startled, but the other three turned to look at Malone and laughed and said "thanks" and *"sana da,"* meaning, "to you too." And Malone thought, What's all this about the sullen Turk?

He had half expected one of the men, acknowledging the arrival of a customer, to follow him into the store, but in their jeans and ratty shoes they didn't really look like salesmen. On the other hand, he thought, reviewing his memory of ratty-looking Turkish salesmen, even in chic stores—but his thoughts were interrupted by a well-dressed young woman who appeared behind the glass-topped counter and said, *Hoş geldiniz* (welcome) and, can I help you? What a pleasant surprise. A very pretty young woman, who looks like a young Elena Papas, whom he would be seeing at dinner tonight. No, he thought, she's more than just pretty. Malone took a deep breath. And why have I come into this store anyway? Leather jacket, thought Malone. Concentrate. The young woman brought out several jackets which he tried on without success. He knew what he wanted, something very like his old one, short and sporty, zippered, elastic at the hips, two side pockets and a breast pocket inside, with a stand-up collar and raglan sleeves, no pads, black.

He kept trying, but either the shoulders were wrong or the sleeves too short or there were too many useless pockets or fringes across the back, when the young woman came back from the rear of the shop with what looked like just the thing. She explained that it was the work of a local designer of women's jackets who had just launched a new line for men. It was of a perfectly classic design, no frills, in excellent leather, solidly sewn and lined throughout, and it fit. But it's gray, said the young woman, looking suitably downcast. They were speaking English now. Not at all, said Malone. That's the best black I've ever seen.

The young woman showed the trace of a smile. It's not just black black, it's living black, dynamic black, it's black in metamorphosis. The young woman showed another trace. Polite incomprehension? Disbelief? Reserve? I'll take it, said Malone, if it's not too expensive. Malone showed the trace of a smile. The sum she quoted in Turkish lira sounded astronomical, but in translation it came to just over a hundred dollars. I'll take it, he said, now smiling broadly, and he asked her if she would accept a Visa card. She went over to the door and stepped outside and said something to one of the loafing men. She came back in and explained that she had lent their charge card machine to the jeweler across the way, but that she had sent someone to get it. Malone wondered who the borrower might really be, not that it mattered. Perhaps the two stores kept common accounts.

Let me show you, said the young woman.

What? said Malone.

The young woman stepped close to him. He held his breath. She put her left hand on his chest and with her right hand drew the zipper down. You see? she said, When you put the jacket on, you must hold this flap back from the zipper to engage the clasp. I hope this won't cause you any inconvenience.

She looked at him.

Yes, said Malone, I mean, No, no inconvenience at all.

But I wanted to show you something else, said the young woman, stepping close to him again, and she reopened the jacket and showed him the label sewn on the inside breast pocket. This is the name of our new line of menswear. If everybody likes his jacket as much as you do, maybe it will be famous.

The label read, SAKARYA.

It's already famous, said Malone, I mean it reminds you of the great Battle of the Sakarya, doesn't it?

Malone paused again in his progress down İstiklal. The beer hall where he had met his friend the old soldier was off to the right, somewhere, on a side street running parallel to İstiklal and off Asmalımescit Sokak. He was pretty sure he could find it in daylight. Maybe he'd go back some time.

The old soldier was certainly a phenomenon. He had said he was writing his memoirs of the War of Independence. It all seemed quite plausible. He was old enough, and he certainly knew a lot about the war, citing names and troop movements and describing battles with which Malone was himself familiar from reading. Of course, the old man too might have read about these things and probably had, but there was no discounting his memory of small horrors that only a man who had been there could know. Late in the Battle of Dumlupınar, he had come upon a terribly wounded Greek officer who was being eaten alive by dogs. He had shot the officer. It would have been useless to shoot the dogs. He had ridden with the army into Izmir, where he had been shot from his horse by a sniper, his sixth wound, and where, recovering in the hospital, he had received his promotion to the rank of lieutenant colonel at the age of twenty-three. But he had received his first four wounds during the greatest battle of the war. They had saved the Republic at the Battle of the Sakarya, twenty-two days and nights of slaughter on both sides.

Eskişehir had fallen, he told Malone, but the army was intact and by forced marches had withdrawn in good order to the right bank of the Sakarya, where they made their stand.

We were defending the heights and the river was another obstacle, but the Greeks came right at us. They crossed the river and we mowed them down and still they came. The story went around that King Constantine imagined he was Alexander the Great and that he could think of nothing but his chance to cut another Gordian knot. The ruins of old Gordion were very exposed, in a hollow backed by a semicircle of hills where we were dug in, and within artillery range of the mountain of Karadağ. But King Constantine wanted Gordion, so they attacked us right there, infantry with fixed bayonets. Think of it. We hit them with artillery fire and mowed them down from our positions in the hills, and still they came right at us. Don't let anybody ever tell you they couldn't fight. They drove us off several hills which we took back, only to be driven off again. We fought back and forth over the same ground until we lost track of time, until a kind of stupor seemed to take hold of both armies, and there was a lull in the fighting all along the line. We had a chance to rest a bit and to move our troops around and my unit was taken out of the line and moved back to a place called Çal Dağı, overlooking Haymana. I confess I had a sort of premonition. We had thought before the battle that the Greeks might try to turn our left flank and attack Haymana from the south and get between the army and the capital at Ankara. And that's what they had finally decided to do. My bad luck on Çal Dağı. In the next few days I was hit three times. I'd already been wounded once, but the bullet had gone right through the palm of my left hand without breaking a bone—look!—and I was all right. We fought for twenty-two days and nights at the Sakarya, and during the last hours on Çal Dağı alone we lost eighty-two officers and over nine hundred men. By the end of the battle, lieutenants were commanding battalions. I was one of them. I was promoted twice before the battle was done. The commander was watching us. Mustafa Kemal Pasha. He saw everything. He was like a god. I think he knew if a private turned over in his sleep.

The old man stopped talking and leaned conspiratorially towards Malone, putting a hand on his arm. Malone, imagining that he was about to learn something that nobody knew, leaned towards the old man, who said, You haven't got a cigarette, have you?

And there it was. But what was it, exactly? The element of surprise?

I'm sorry, I don't, Malone said to the old man, but I'm going to get some up the street and I'll be right back.

There had been no apotheosis. Malone hadn't felt the least resistance nor the least twinge of guilt. He was simply going to start smoking again. He had slipped some money under his half-finished beer to reassure the bartender and gone up the street and bought a pack of Bafras, which is what he had always smoked, and a box of matches, and he had offered one to the old man and they had lit up.

Sağol, said the old man, Thanks.

Hayırlı olsun, replied Malone, May it be propitious to you.

The two men fell silent for a moment, meditating, perhaps, on the ineffable effects of nicotine.

This is my first in fifteen years, said Malone.

First what? said the old man.

My first cigarette.

And how does it feel?

I'm a little dizzy, said Malone.

That's the way I always feel, said the old man, abstractedly, and Malone concluded that the remark had not been intended as a joke.

The bartender came down the bar asking everybody to pay up. It was time to close. Malone decided to share his cigarettes with the old man, who was very grateful. He had slipped the package back into the inside breast pocket of his jacket, when he remembered. He opened the jacket and, pointing to the label, said to the old man, Look.

The old man squinted, and Malone turned towards the light, and the old man looked again.

Sakarya! said the old man, and again, Sakarya! God be praised! I thought you were going to show me your medals.

Medals? repeated Malone. I don't have any medals, wondering if he hadn't become the brunt of a joke.

You do now, said the old man, who opened his coat and unpinned a medal from his chest and gave it to Malone. Sakarya, he repeated, God be praised.

You can't do that, said Malone.

Sure I can, said the old man. You can buy them in the shops.

He had bought a new jacket yesterday, and yesterday he had started to smoke again, and there was indeed a connection: the Battle of the Sakarya. An absurd connection perhaps, but a connection nevertheless. The dizzying effect. That's the way I always feel, said the old man. Me too, thought Malone. It had been that kind of day, and night. He had lived the whole day in anticipation of the dinner last night and of seeing Sylvia again, and he would never forget what she had said when he told her of his last visits to her dying father in New York and of the old man's love for her. Malone, she had said, You're breaking my heart, and they had held onto each other very tight, and she had wept. No, he would never forget her words and broken voice. But not ten minutes later, she had seen him light a cigarette and said,

Still smoking, Malone? She had never been a smoker, and she had been particularly derisive towards the end of their marriage of his two or three failed attempts to quit.

I quit for fifteen years, said Malone. I started again this afternoon.

Sure, she said, giving him the same old look.

What did he care if she didn't believe him? He was through with her, wasn't he? Then why was she still able to make him feel so angry and ridiculous? Why couldn't he have waited until tomorrow—today—to start smoking again? Because he had finally needed the crutch. And it was because he had needed the crutch that her attack had hurt, even if he hadn't lied.

All that may be true, thought Malone, but it's too late to agonize, and he turned his thoughts again to the young woman of the leather shop, who was very pretty and who had indeed heard of the Battle of the Sakarya. She was a *lycée* graduate and had taken the requisite courses in Revolutionary History, and she remembered that, after the battle, the Grand National Assembly had awarded Mustafa Kemal Pasha the rank of marshall and the title of Gazi, the Conqueror. She had even visited Gordion some years ago with her parents, and they had seen the tomb of King Midas, if that's what it really was, and the guide had told them that the remains of the King had been taken to the Museum of Anatolian Antiquities in Ankara, but that they had been told by one of the curators in Ankara that the body had disappeared! Can you imagine that! said the young woman. The curator said that it was an unusually little body and that they couldn't find it anywhere. The young woman said she hadn't been able to control herself and had burst out laughing. She had burst out laughing again, telling the story to Malone, who had laughed with her. Malone laughed now, out loud, standing alone on the Galata Bridge in the middle of the night, looking out to sea and remembering.

Come back and see us, the young woman had said, almost the same phrase as Sylvia had used when the dinner had broken up last night, but spoken with more sincerity. Sylvia might have been momentarily glad to see him, but she didn't want to see him again. He was an irritant. The dinner hadn't really been to welcome him back. It had been primarily for Marco, as he had learned, and then for Faruk Selvi, who had just published a new book. Perhaps his return had been an irritant for everybody. I am a stone in the corporate shoe, he thought, an *emmerdeur*, as the French say. I should go back to France where they understand me. Malone smiled, looking out to sea and thinking, I should have told the story of the little body to Dimitri, my one true pal. I'll tell him tomorrow if he shows up in the Çiçek Pasajı. Why shouldn't he show up? Maybe I won't show up myself.

The scene spread out before Malone was a miracle of calm. From where he stood, in the approximate middle of the Galata Bridge, he could follow the line of lights strung out along the Asian shore south from Beylerbeyi through Kuzguncuk and around the point at Üsküdar as far as the ferryboat landing at

Harem, partially hidden behind Saray Point in the foreground; he could clearly make out, on the rising ground beyond Harem, the lights of the mosque and barracks of the Selimiye, where Florence Nightingale had labored, the Lady of the Lamp, whom he imagined he might almost see, over the distance in space and time, passing from darkened room to room. He remembered reading that in the early days of the Crimean War, the wounded brought to the Selimiye Barracks had suffered greatly from the lack of a night watch. Left completely on their own, the wounded were forced to struggle from their beds in the dark to get a drink or to help comrades more seriously wounded than themselves. Thousands had died from the lack of care, until the arrival of Miss Nightingale. He remembered reading about her in the memoirs of Cyrus Hamlin, the Protestant missionary and founder of the American College in Bebek. To support his early missionary work, Hamlin had established a bakery, and with the advent of war, he was asked by the British command to supply bread to the troops who put in at Bebek on their way to the front and, more importantly, to the new hospital across the Bosphorus at the Selimiye. As a man of high principle and broad humanity, Hamlin had had several run-ins with the arrogant and corrupt administrators at the hospital, and he was fully able to appreciate the value to the wounded men of the arrival there of the thirty-eight nurses led by Florence Nightingale. Many of her reforms were immediate, among them the institution of continuous night rounds. The Lady of the Lamp, indeed. Cyrus Hamlin had met her only once, but it pleased Malone to imagine the scene, the more moving for its brevity, two great spirits passing with a nod. Maybe that's what I was born to do, he thought, keep the night watch. Or pass with a nod.

The mist that had descended on the city had begun to lift, and the lights on the hills above Üsküdar and Kuzguncuk were coming into view. Malone looked back again towards the Selimiye and had the momentary hallucination of seeing the mosque and barracks begin to move. The formerly hidden portion of the ferry landing at Harem, as if carrying the Selimiye, mosque and barracks, began to slide with deliberate majesty from behind Saray Point. It was a great cargo ship, laden high with containers and brightly illuminated for the night passage through the straits. Malone could hear the deep throbbing of the engines and fancied he could feel the vibrations running through the bridge, as of traffic rumbling over the expansion joints, and he remembered the early afternoon of yesterday, drinking in the beer stall of Mustafa Terzioğlu under the far end of the bridge. One of those old GMC taxis had backfired—was that it?—or a gas canister gone off, and they had joked about a bomb. There had been no bomb, but there had certainly been an explosion last night at Galatasaray. The ground floor gallery in the Şimşek Building had filled up with escaping propane gas, according to Faruk Selvi, and the whole place had gone off with a flash and a roar, and Marco Fontane had never made it to dinner with them at Boncuk, nor would he ever make it to dinner anywhere. Marco was dead, and Malone now realized that, for him, it was precisely as if Marco had died twenty years ago, as if he had been dead all along without anybody's noticing, and that the time of life to which he had belonged had died with him. Remembering last night's dinner, Malone could see the restaurant tables crowded along Nevizade Sokak, the festive garlands strung across the street, the waiters passing and the faces and the hands and eyes and lifted glasses and the smiles and lights, and they seemed to him, now, as he stood on the bridge, like the components of a scene read about in a book.

I need a drink, thought Malone. I should have stopped in Galata. There are bars in Galata that stay open all night, or there used to be. Or down by the docks in Karaköy. A nice place to get mugged. Maybe I don't need a drink after all. I'll settle for a smoke.

He had bought a new pack of Bafras at Boncuk and was well

supplied. It was a great comfort. If he was mugged on the way home, he'd offer the guy a cigarette. They'd get along. He remembered a colleague who had been stopped at knifepoint on a back street in Beyoğlu. The thief had asked him where he lived. When he heard that the colleague lived up the Bosphorus in Bebek, he had given him back enough money for cab fare. But that was a long time ago. Maybe it's not so easy to get along these days, or nights. I'll be careful. I'll try and look big.

Malone lit up and tossed the match over the rail. He crossed the bridge and turned left at the Yeni Cami, trying to look big, and right at the Sirkeci railroad station and up Ankara Caddesi and past the darkened bulk of the Boys' Lycée to the foot of Nuruosmaniye Caddesi where he had been only yesterday in what seemed now like another life.

The avenue was very quiet, the whole city immobilized in sleep. Malone would join them as soon as he could. He walked straight on and across Divan Yolu to his hotel. He rang the bell, and the night porter let him in. You don't have to be afraid of the dark, he thought, not in Istanbul.

From the window of his room, he could look out over the Hippodrome and the mosque of Sultan Ahmet, and across the mouth of the Bosphorus to Haydarpaşa and Harem. More cargo ships were lined up awaiting their turn to begin the slow passage up the straits, and many more were waiting, a scattering of navigation lights, far out to sea. The more distant lights among them seemed to wink, like stars, and beyond those there was nothing at all.

tamam

GUIDE TO PRONUNCIATION

For proper names and some other words in this book, original Turkish spelling has been used. The following is a short guide to pronouncing these words.

Vowels in Turkish are pronounced as in French or German:
   a - as in father
   e - as in met
   i - as in big
   o - between the o in role and the au in author
   u - as in rule

In addition, there are three other vowels that do not occur in English:
   ı - undotted i, pronounced like the unstressed vowel sound in the second syllables of words such as herbal or function
   ö - as in German
   ü - as in German

Consonants are pronounced as in English, except for the following:
   c - as j in jam, e.g. cami (mosque) = jahmy
   ç - as ch in chat, e.g. çorba (soup) = chorba
   g - as in get, never as in gem
   ğ - is almost sılent and tends to lengthen the preceding vowel
   ş - as in sugar, e.g. çeşme (fountain) = cheshme